THE
DEAD
MAKE
NO MARK

MARK ATLEY

THE DEAD MAKE NO MARK

TULSA UNDERWORLD BOOK 4

4 Horsemen
Publications, Inc.

4 Horsemen
Publications, Inc.

Published By: 4 Horsemen Publications, Inc.

4 Horsemen Publications, Inc.
PO Box 417
Sylva, NC 28779
4horsemenpublications.com
info@4horsemenpublications.com

Cover by J. Kotick
Typesetting by Autumn Skye
Edited by Laura Mita

Library of Congress Control Number: 2023941334

Paperback ISBN-13: 979-8-8232-0276-3
Hardcover ISBN-13: 979-8-8232-0278-7
Audiobook ISBN-13: 979-8-8232-0275-6
Ebook ISBN-13: 979-8-8232-0277-0

DEDICATION:

To the real Valdez and Charlotte
To the real Jamison and Barbara

ACKNOWLEDGMENT:

M.E. PROCTOR REALLY HELPED ME SHAPE THIS book into something special. I wanted to say thank you for all the hard work and words of encouragement.

To my coworkers and family who have put up with me during many story breakdown sessions and to my friends who were the creative inspiration for some of these characters. I hope you enjoy the good bits and ignore the dramatic bad ones.

Always, thank you to each and every one of you who reads this novel. Without you, this would not be possible.

And a very special thanks to my wife.

TABLE OF CONTENTS

CHAPTER 1:

KADE

KADE WATCHES EDDIE DRIVE THE CAR. EDDIE ISN'T among friends. Kade is with him, angry, confused, and hurt.

They're on the highway, called a turnpike because nothing in life is free, and Eddie is behind the wheel of the black BMW, if it matters. But it doesn't because it will be left behind. The BMW is still new, new smell, built for luxury, but Kade didn't steal it for comfort, he stole it to fulfill a role, this role.

Kade is in the passenger seat with the gun pressed against his spine, hoping Eddie doesn't crash; he doesn't want the gun to break his back. He once heard that was a thing. Significant trauma to the back could paralyze a person. Must be why cops keep their handcuffs to the side. He's seen the television shows. Seen how the TV cops put them in the small of the back. But Kade's been around enough cops to know that ain't how it's done.

Kade notices things like that, small details, and sometimes he ferrets out the bigger picture too. Like how this never gets easier. It shouldn't, not like it's hard for him either, because it's not. If it were, he wouldn't be doing it.

Kade presses his back against the passenger door with his knees crammed against the dashboard because he's taller than the seat allows; he scrutinizes Eddie, who acts like he doesn't know where they are going and doesn't ask. That's for the best because Eddie doesn't need to know where they're going. Kade knows and won't be going where Eddie's going—everyone ends up there anyway, some quicker than others. Eddie fucked up, and that's why he has to go.

1

Dropkick Murphys plays on the radio, a live version of the song *Johnny, I Hardly Knew Ya*. Kade put the song on because it was their anthem, it's appropriate, and he needs to be in the mood for what happens next.

Killing Eddie won't be like before; it will cause problems. His sister Kirsten won't understand, but he can handle her. It's the others who will want to know who did this and ask questions; they will bring the fallout.

Not that it matters to Kade; his job's simple, kill Eddie.

The driver's seat creaks as Eddie shifts forward, his fingers fumbling with the dial on the radio, to turn the music down. Eddie straightens. "You going to tell me where we are going?"

Kade nods. "We need to make a run home." Eddie accepts the answer because home is their old neighborhood, and they've made this drive several times. There's no reason Eddie shouldn't accept the answer. But Kade doesn't miss Eddie's hands tightening on the wheel. So, he tenses as Eddie drives on, asking himself: does he know?

There's no way.

But the silence poses questions. Questions Kade's anticipated and cannot answer.

They are going where this started, where they met, fitting and poetic. They go where they came from. Everyone went to school here. Raised hell here. Ran from the police here. Sold dope here, stole here, fought here. It used to be being from here counted for something, and in Kade's view, it should've counted for more for Eddie. It should've bred loyalty, but it didn't.

Eddie fucked up.

Gilliam told Kade what had to happen. "Green on Green." And when Kade argued against killing Eddie, Gilliam told him, "Eddie's not Green, not like you're Green. Eddie's a half-breed, a mongrel, half Mexican half Irish—nothing." Gilliam never liked Eddie's skin tone; he'd say he's too brown, but Eddie was one of those kids that was always around, who everyone eventually accepted off the premise of his very continued existence, and Eddie's been soft on Kade's twin for just as long, just like Aaron, but Eddie's not like Aaron. The kid has enough balls and is willing enough to make a move, which is something Kade respects but means complications.

Gilliam said, "So fuck him, Eddie's not Green like you. He might be from here, where it started for us, might even think he bleeds Green like you do, but he fucked up—he has to go."

And that's how they both got to this point, where the country meets the city, their home, and the place where Eddie will die.

The turnpike makes a lazy, looping, left bend. The exit is a few miles away. This is the place.

Kade says, "Pull over."

"You sure? It's the highway," Eddie says. "I don't want OHP stopping us."

"Exit here cuz I think I'm going to be sick." Kade grabs at his stomach with one hand, concealing his right hand reaching to his back. "There's a road just off the highway." Kade withdraws the gun from under his long green and white striped shirt. There's a certain weight to the gun in his hand, and he keeps the gun low between the seat and the door so Eddie won't see it, and he won't show his hand. Not yet, but he will—that time will come.

"You just got this car," Eddie tells him. "Don't throw up all over it. Last time I couldn't get the door clean until I washed it like ten times."

"Don't worry about it." Kade feigns sickness overtaking his body. "It won't happen if you fucking pull over and let me out."

Eddie exits the highway, taking the loop to the country road. He pulls left onto the long dark road, which extends into nothingness, blackness, and farmland, nothing around for a long way, except one house off in the distance, a light in the cloudy night. Theirs is the only car on the road. No one's around, and that's the point. The car slows, kicking up rocks and dirt, as Eddie pulls to the side of the road. Kade bounces in his seat as the car rattles to a stop in a long slow roll. Right now, in these few moments, it seems to Kade like Eddie might know what's coming, and he doesn't want the ride to end, as the jostling and slowing continues. But this is the place, and this is the time. The car finally stops on the gravel shoulder with dust and leaves swirling in its wake, and the taillights illuminate the dust, lighting it up, giving the side of the road a red hellish glow and the whole scene an ominous feel.

Now's the time—Kade shoulders open the passenger door, letting the cool night air into the cabin. A cow moos in the distance. Kade keeps the gun back, adjusting his grip, hand sweaty against the handle, chamber loaded. He's worked this out in his head. Don't show the gun until the moment's right. He has to get this right because if he doesn't, he'll be like Eddie—fucked. He might already be.

Everything that's happened has led to this moment.

Kade acts like he's getting out of the car. He places his hand on the roof of the vehicle and lifts his rear from the seat but then doesn't, and quickly, before he loses his nerve, he twists in the seat, contorting his body, and sees Eddie there with his hands on the wheel, face blank, not looking Kade's way, staring straight ahead and sitting as if he's just waiting for this to happen.

And maybe he is; if Kade were in Eddie's position, he'd be waiting for it too. But he's not in Eddie's position. He's here holding the gun, and being here means he has to do this. Briefly, Kade ponders how their roles could be reversed. He could be the one in the driver's seat. Should he say something? Should he cough to get Eddie to look this way? Would that make it easier? No, just harder for him.

But Kade's done this too many times for it to be a concern anymore. He doesn't care what is hard or easy. Killing isn't either of those things and exists as something in the in-between. So let Eddie take it like a man, face to face; that's how Kade should do it, as a man, not a pussy. Don't shoot the guy when he isn't looking, like when he watched Billy Vaughn do Frankie Green. Eddie deserves that much, right?

But Frankie didn't deserve it, and Frankie and Eddie have the same sins. When Billy did Frankie, Billy didn't wait; he didn't make a noise. He just put the gun to Frankie's temple and fired the bullet through Frankie's head, making Frankie's blood spatter on the interior of the car and the back of Gilliam's head, who was driving. Frankie fell against Kade, his eyes dark and blank. Billy sat silent, pointing to Frankie's limp body, indicating that Kade needed to search his back pocket. When Kade found the phone, still recording, Billy said, "We're lucky it's not a live feed." He told Kade to burn it, destroy it—erase it from existence—scorched earth.

That's what Kade did, but here, now, he's not Billy. He won't kill the kid he accepted as a brother while not looking at him. No, it will be face-to-face. That's how Kade would want it done to him, face-to-face, so that's what he decides to do.

Kade coughs, clears his throat, coughs again, holding his hand to his mouth to sell the act. It causes Eddie to rotate his head toward Kade as Kade raises the semi-automatic pistol. Kade stays silent—because what's there to say—sees something on the kid's face, surprise, shock, acceptance, something burning across his face as he processes what's about to happen.

Kade pulls the trigger, launching the bullet into Eddie's forehead, rocking Eddie in the seat. The bullet travels through Eddie's head and exits through the driver's window, leaving a nice, neat, round hole staring back at Kade. It replaces whatever Eddie was thinking with nothing.

Whatever Kade sees on Eddie's face drifts away as Eddie's life fades and his eyes lose focus, clouding, and his body lets go, slackens, relaxing. The lifeless body tilts forward and slumps against the steering wheel.

Eddie dies alone but not alone at the same time.

Then time catches up with Kade, synchronizing with the world around him. He realizes he didn't hear the gun go off, but he hears a dull ring, and he sees the bloodstains on his shirt, feels it on his face, the wet goop beginning to cool and congeal, the heat fleeing rapidly, free of the body and exposed to the night air. The tang of blood hangs in the air. The radio still plays in the background, a soundtrack laid under the main action with the song wrapping up as Kade sings along, changing the words to "Guns and Drugs." He glances over at Eddie. "Eddie, I hardly knew ya."

Kade chastises himself for allowing the moment of killing to last so long. He experienced more than he cared for, making the act that should have been quick, longer than it need be.

All three of Eddie's blank eyes, the third open to a bloody void, stare back at Kade.

There's a cost for doing these things ... Kade knows. Like when he tries to go to sleep. Eddie will be there, with the others, with Frankie Green, in the theater of Kade's subconscious. They'll all come onto the stage, Frankie Green acting as an usher, like the guy with the boat on the river Styx. Frankie will wait patiently staring down at Kade sitting alone in the audience, then he'll greet and welcome Eddie. When Eddie ascends the steps, he'll pass through the crowd of others and join Frankie. Then the others, as they've done countless times before, will slap Eddie on the back and welcome him too, leaving Kade silent in the audience.

They're there because that's where Kade put them. He's handled the dreams so far. And when he can't, there's always whiskey to build the wall, keep the dreams away.

During Eddie's final ride, there were things Kade wanted to say to him, but nothing sounded right. Kade wanted to ask him why and wanted to find out if it was true, but he knew better. Gilliam said it happened, so it happened. And he knows in moments like this, you don't say shit. You don't wait. You don't talk. You don't think. You act. That's what he's learned. That's what this life has taught him.

It's a bitch, but it is what it is.

Kade exits the vehicle, falling out of the door and on the ground. He wants to throw up and can't. Every time he works his way to his knees, nausea forces him down. He pounds his hand against the concrete as he dry heaves. His stomach tightens, crawling up his throat. The rancid acid washes over his tongue. His mind screams to let it happen. Let it out, let it go.

But he can't. Then just as suddenly, it's over.

Kneeling on the gravel, Kade swallows the bile and spits what's left. Under the car, the glint of the spent shell casing catches his eye. He reaches for it, wrapping his whole hand around it, letting the warm casing sear his flesh.

Kade gets to his feet and drops the shell in his pocket—the gun goes back into his waistband. A car appears from the darkness without headlights and stops feet from the stolen BMW, kicking up the same dirt and dust. This one is a Lexus, white, if it matters. But it doesn't because it will be gone by morning.

Kade finishes the rest of the job, the sweet spot, the personal touch. He pulls the cop's business card from his pocket, lifts the passenger windshield wiper, and places the card underneath. Message sent.

With that done, he walks to the passenger side of the Lexus. The window rolls down. The driver, with his right arm stretched over the passenger headrest, peers over the passenger seat at Kade, who tells him, "It's done."

The driver asks, "Did he say anything?"

Kade shakes his head. "What's there to say?" He opens the door, enters the vehicle, and shuts the door. "He's dead."

CHAPTER 2

AARON

ARON DRIVES THE WHITE LEXUS ON THE TURN-pike because Kade asked him to drive. Which means Aaron knew what was supposed to happen to Eddie. Which also means—as far as the law's concerned—he's an accessory after the fact. Aaron's okay with this; it's not the first time.

Problems have to be dealt with, and sometimes, that means this, even if this means burning down everything he's ever known. Everyone has a job. A role. A part to play in life. And tonight, Aaron's was to drive, pick up Kade, and bring him back to Gilliam's, but that's only part of the plan because Gilliam doesn't want Kade back breathing; he wants him dead, as dead as Kade is supposed to make Eddie—that's the part of the plan Aaron doesn't like.

But that doesn't matter in this life, not that it would matter if he likes it or not. Gilliam said it's time for Aaron to cross that line from driver to killer, regardless of what Aaron wants or that Kade is his best friend.

Aaron pushes the Lexus around a looping turn and exits the highway, pulling left to the road where it's supposed to happen. He slows the Lexus, catches the flash of light through the BMW's back window, and understands it's done. He brings the Lexus to a stop on the side of the road directly behind the BMW and watches Kade do the bit with the business card. Then Kade walks toward the Lexus, gets in, and they're gone, leaving the BMW on the shoulder, abandoned and dark, with the dead "half-breed" in the driver's seat.

Turning the Lexus around on the dark two-lane road, Gilliam's words echo in Aaron's mind. Gilliam said, "Kill the half-breed and kill the fucker that brought him to us. It's like cutting off an arm that's rotted." Aaron asked about Kirsten. Gilliam responded, "Eddie is nothing now. What's she going to care?"

So, Aaron does the easy part right because there's nothing to it, driving, but Kade, Kirsten, the cops, they will be the hard parts. They are a family; the Green Mafia is all he's ever known, and it's as good as any family, but the unraveling started when Gilliam handed Kade the gun and told him to kill Eddie. And once they were gone, Gilliam turned to Aaron and told him he'd been a good tax collector. "You're a good fucking driver, responsible, and you get my girls whatever they need." Gilliam has several apartments, each with its stable of girls, all Aaron's responsibility. Gilliam said, "Each place has a taste of everything, blonde, brunette, red, whatever; this means lots of different needs, and you've done good making sure no one's breaking the rules. But tonight, you're going to pop your proverbial fucking cherry, and fucking shoot that rabid dog you call a friend for introducing that bean-fucking, tortilla-eating, cop-dick-sucking-retard, or I'll kill you both."

Now on the turnpike, Aaron plans to exit at Memorial, and then head back toward Gilliam's, working Gilliam's plan through his head and what Gilliam told him last night.

"After he's done and good and liquored up, take him to the river. There, you know what you need to do."

And what Aaron needs to do is kill his best friend, the only friend he's ever really known. He isn't sure he can do that, doesn't know if he physically can or has the heart to cross that line.

"Where you want to go?"

Kade, voice quiet and low, says, "I don't care."

Aaron grips the wheel tightly. "We could try Billy's place or Harjo's."

Kade is quiet for a long time, leaving Aaron to drive in silence.

"What's it feel like to kill another person?"

Kade stays quiet, leaning his head against the passenger's window.

"I've not done that and don't know if I could do that," Aaron says. "That's always been your job."

"It's my job," Kade says.

But tonight it's Aaron's job.

"How do you feel?" Aaron steers the car through the looping turn, going the other way now. "Like how does it feel? Do you feel bad? Do you think about it... later, I mean?"

"What are you asking? Are you asking if I get off on it or something?" Kade says, staring at Aaron. "How do you think I feel? He was like a little brother." Then Kade goes quiet for a moment. "Fuck!" He pounds his fist against the dashboard. "What am I going to tell Kirsten?"

"You can't tell her the truth," Aaron says, glancing at his friend.

Kade hits the dashboard again. "Then, what do I tell her?" He rubs the back of his head, fingers brushing the hairline. The aftermath of what he's done seems to be settling on him now, hanging on him, and changing his mood.

"Tell her you don't know what happened to him," Aaron says.

"She'll ask questions. I'll have to tell her something. Tell her how her..."

"I'll explain it to her," Aaron offers.

He has already started thinking of things he could say because Gilliam had told him, "You tell her, you sniveling fuck," and Gilliam said he'd fuck her after, called it consoling her sadness.

Kade says, "She knows something was happening. She knows Eddie's been weird, even if she doesn't know what was going to happen to him ... even if she didn't know I was going to shoot him. She can't know that part, I won't tell her that, but she'll know something happened, so I'll make up a lie, like one of those others. I'll tell her something; it's not like she's going to go to the cops to get the truth."

"Who will come sniffing around? She knows what this life's like. Live and let live."

"Or die," Kade says. "She'll know when he's found. She doesn't have to know what happened. Not for sure. And she doesn't have to know I was the one that did it. He was a kid, a fling. We've known Eddie our whole life. Grew up with him. Like you, he's always been around, but his mom didn't like me, didn't like Kirsten, so he kept his distance, sort of, but you know, marijuana is fun and so too is the guy that sells it. And if he's got a hot sister, then maybe the kid hangs around, hoping to get some. And since he was hanging around all the time, I figured, why not put him to work. His place was down the street from ours. You can't grow up in a neighborhood and not know a guy like him; I mean his mom... my mom still lives near his."

"This will bring some heat down on you."

Kade nods. "I'm afraid of what Gilliam might've done if I didn't do it." Dark demonic-looking eyes peer at Aaron from the passenger seat as Aaron fights to keep his eyes on the road. "I didn't have a choice. Choices

can be like that. Either you do them or you don't. Either there's heat or there's not. There will be heat. But the stupid shit brought this on himself, talking to cops like that, like what the fuck was he thinking?"

"Gilliam's not happy about it," Aaron says, but he doesn't say he wants to kill you too. "That bit with the business card... that your idea? I'm sure Billy's not happy about this either. Gilliam might be just as fucked as Eddie."

"Gilliam's not happy about not knowing what the fuck the little shit told or said," Kade says. "It took everything I had to talk Gilliam out of taking Eddie's mom and sister out. They're family. We aren't like that. Gilliam said he didn't need this with Billy. Said Billy didn't need this either. I'll be surprised if Billy even knows. Billy telling everyone the City's up for the taking and Billy's planning to seize the day, quoting Caesar or some shit. Gilliam said if Billy knew what happened, he'd want Eddie's family dead. Maybe Gilliam wants that. Gilliam made it clear he wants to clear the whole plate. Show people you don't fuck with the Green like Eddie's done. Show it to the cops and let them try to come after him. Wants to make it personal. So much so they lose the fight."

"He really wants to go scorched earth over this?" Aaron asks, trying to warn him.

"He was that angry," Kade says, nodding. "Fuck, I'm that angry."

"But that thing with the business card, whose idea was it?" Aaron asks. "That's going to make some noise. If heat comes, it comes because of that."

"That was my idea," Kade says, almost happy about it. "Gilliam had me standing there, with my dick in my hand, hearing about how my sister's boy toy screwed us. Handing me that damn thing, telling me my new little brother had fucked us all in the ass. Telling me, he wanted me to handle it like I'm not going to fucking handle this. How am I *not* going to handle this? I brought the fucker in on things, and the last year has been great—productive—but Gilliam says he noticed something going on the last couple of weeks. Said Billy's noticed it too so maybe he knows, maybe he doesn't. He brought it to Gilliam's attention at the last meeting they had. I was there. I didn't see it, or know it, but fuck them. Gilliam said it had to have been going on all year, since the beginning. Since the little shit got arrested. Gilliam told me that him fucking my sister wasn't beneficial to matters either, saying she might be corrupted. Not saying what he means by that, but I know what he means. He's threatening her, threatening me, my sister. Putting it out there in his tone, if not word, that he's worried about what she's said or going to say or might say. And I stood there taking everything in. Told him not to worry about her. I can handle her. But there he was, looking at me, doubting me. So I tell him, I'll take care of my fucking sister. He says, 'No you're going to take care of our little fucking problem.' Told me to do it like I did Casey. Said he'd take care of my sister. I told him if he does, I'll take care of him like how I took care of Casey."

"Casey wasn't the same," Aaron says.

"No shit," Kade says. "He fucking pulled a gun on me, pointed it right at me like he thought he was going to grow some balls and shoot me. Gilliam would be like that. Us, mano a mano. Fuck Eddie, he's rubbing off on me, speaking Spanish and shit. I told Gilliam he could fuck himself. He told me I needed to clean up my mess, or it'd be my ass riding in the seat, and it would be him behind me with the fucking gun. That's when he handed me the gun, spinning it like a fucking cowboy. Told me that the City and Billy can't know anything about this, because otherwise, it'd be his ass. Said that's what Billy said if anything happened or if Gilliam found out one of his guys was talking to the cops again. Said he's not fucking going down for no one..." and then Kade stops talking.

The sudden silence leaves Aaron alone with his thoughts. His mind mulling over what Gilliam told him to do to Kade, handing him the gun. Gilliam told Aaron to kill Kade or Gilliam kills him, which is pretty fucking motivating to someone who just likes to drive.

Red and blue lights flash in the rearview mirror, catching his attention and causing him to jerk the wheel to the left in response, startled. "Shit," Aaron says.

"What?" Kade glances back through the rear window. Then he withdraws the gun from his waistband and shoves it deep under the seat.

They're being pulled over.

CHAPTER 3:

BARBARA

B ARBARA RUNS THE TAG OF THE WHITE LEXUS IN front of her by typing the letters of the license plate into a large field on her state-issued laptop. She doesn't know why she does it, but she does. The laptop blares an alarm—the vehicle's stolen.

Oklahoma Highway Patrol Trooper Barbara Jones flips a switch—on the center console to her right—to activate her emergency lights; the roadside takes a red and blue tint as her overhead lights strobe against the darkness. She decides against using the siren. The lights should be enough for anyone.

In front of her, the Lexus's brake lights flash once, and the vehicle jerks to the left, crossing the double yellow line. She observes the silhouette of the passenger glance through the back windshield. The brake lights flash a second time, like hellish eyes in the black, blinking and peeping back at her, before the vehicle starts to slow, but doesn't stop.

Slow rolling is bad because it means the driver is thinking. Drivers shouldn't be thinking. State law says the driver must yield to the right and stop, and that's what should happen—the driver should know that.

This Lexus doesn't stop; it only slowly yields.

The nerves in Barbara's back clinch into a tense ball between her shoulder blades. She leans forward attempting to peer into the inky night, beyond the darkness off the roadway, to identify the mile marker posted just off the shoulder.

Barbara seizes the mic for the car radio and announces the stop over the radio. Her words echo in her shoulder mic clipped to her left shoulder

13

that is connected to her belt radio. She asks for a backing trooper because she knows it may be some time before someone can make it to her.

The Oklahoma Highway Patrol owns the turnpike, jurisdiction state-wide, and it handles what it owns, but Barbara doesn't fit their mold because the Highway Patrol used to be what Barbara is not: white, male, and over six feet tall. Everyone else need not apply, and at times, wishes it was still so.

Barbara's husband Stanley told her to look the other way when it became an apparent problem. Barbara accused him of plagiarizing from the Bible, and Stanley told her, "Of course, I am. I'm a man of God; His words are mine, but try to not let it affect you."

She said, "But how can it not? I'm black, south of five feet five, and a woman—the only one."

Stanley told her to try. So try she did, and after following his and God's advice, turning the other cheek, Barbara figured a change would be good. Now she is at her second Troop. She didn't get along with the one before, and this one puts her in the Tulsa area. She likes Tulsa; her two grown kids live and work in the city. But her husband, the preacher and her rock, got sick, real sick—cancer sick—and faded away.

Now she's alone—just as she is alone here on this highway.

The stolen vehicle notification could be a mistake. It happens more than Barbara would like; she'll have to verify.

The Lexus finally begins to stop. The two people in the vehicle, both male, both white, rock back and forth in their seats, which in her mind means they are reaching for this and that—this and that can get you killed. The vehicle comes to rest on the shoulder. Barbara pops her driver's side door open before her vehicle comes to a stop, and is out of the car, high-shined black boots on the pavement before the vehicle is in park.

That's how a traffic stop is done—one fluid motion.

In the dark, lights are her protection against death. Barbara's take-down lights illuminate the back end of the Lexus, throwing up a curtain of light, which awards her a safety barrier. She flips her spotlight on and directs it at the driver's side mirror to blind the driver, and she blasts the back of the Lexus with every safeguarding bulb at her disposal like it's Friday Night Football. The driver lurches to the side, then rights himself. Hand in front of the mirror, he adjusts his side mirror before the rearview, trying to help with the blinding lights or find her.

It doesn't help. He won't be able to do either.

On her feet and curving away from her driver's side door, Barbara, trooper-tan uniform, adjusts her hat with its leather strap nuzzling her chin and tilts the brim forward. The hat gives her a few more inches of intimidation. With her right hand, she tugs at her gun belt, flipping the holster cover down. With her left hand, she withdraws her flashlight from the belt and directs it toward the vehicle without switching it on. Then, silently, she steps between the two vehicles, crossing the area between them—a dangerous area to stand, a no man's land—keeping her focus on the silhouettes of the two in the vehicle. Both tilt back and forth, trying to find her. Not good. Movement is bad, and these two can't sit still. Barbara approaches on the passenger side. She doesn't want some drunk driver sideswiping her—drunk drivers are like moths to a flame. The driver's side window is where these two expect her.

Through the Lexus's windows, Barbara sees a flame flick to life in the driver's hand, a lighter, close to a mouth, then the flame vanishes. There's a stretch of darkness before the flame jumps to life in the passenger's hand now, meaning both are lighting cigarettes, smoking. Smoke covers up smells. Now the two are rolling the windows down to let the smoke into the cool night, the tendrils of the fresh smoke twisting and swirling in the bright lights of her vehicle.

Barbara approaches the vehicle cautiously, methodically, checking through the back window to make sure no one is waiting to surprise her—no one is. She uses her shoulder mic to tell dispatch or anyone else listening to hurry up as she nears the rear passenger window. She sees the passenger fiddling with something down on the floorboard between the door and his seat. Not good.

Barbara, one hand on the butt of her pistol, is ready to draw. If the passenger points a gun at her, those extra few seconds could save her life. Seconds are hours, and action always beats reaction.

Cigarette smoke drifts into the night through the thin slit in the passenger window. Barbara depresses the button on her flashlight, snapping the beam on, and aims the light directly at the passenger. He jolts with surprise, twisting in his seat to look at her with red, wild, bloodshot eyes— evidently guilty of something, guilt pasted all over his face, reminiscent of a boy caught behind the bleachers with a girl half-dressed, mouth open, jaw slack, whole body tense, taut, and ready to pounce. He is a predator, natural-born, and prison-honed. Tattoos show his gang affiliation, the clover, the numbers, the green—Green Mafia.

Beyond the cone of her light, Barbara makes out the driver in his seat. He swivels her way, pivoting from his window to her, and his complexion drains. Sweat drips down his face with the same wild furious bewildered look as his companion, like he too is caught doing something he shouldn't be doing. He clutches the wheel, fingers gripping and tightening, loosening, tightening, loosening as if he's trying to rev the engine. Teeth gnash and gnaw at his bottom lip.

Barbara motions for the driver to roll down the passenger window the rest of the way. The glass drops, and the sweet smell of fresh tobacco, mixed with the rancid smell of stale smoke, B.O., sweat, fear, and anticipation assaults her senses. The car might have smelled of something else before she stopped them, maybe marijuana, but now the cigarette smoke blankets everything.

Barbara shifts her weight and places her flashlight in the crook of her armpit. "Keys," she says loudly while drawing her pistol, hoping the road noise of a passing car obscures the obvious sound of metal grating against plastic.

The gun feels right in her hand.

The passenger glances at her from the corner of his eye and then over at the driver, who lets out a nervous laugh. The passenger is reptilian in his movements. He stays silent, facing forward. He plucks the cigarette out of his mouth, snorts smoke lazily through his nostrils, and holds the cigarette out the opened window. The driver offers her a sly smile and sucks restlessly on his cigarette, jaw and lips trembling. He leans forward to look around the passenger, red ember glowing in the dark cabin inches from his face, and through the smoky haze he tries too hard to sound normal. "What's the problem, officer?"

"Keys," Barbara commands. "Now."

She watches the internal debate flash across the driver's face, the squinting eyes and pressing lips as he runs through his options. If he's going to run, this is the time. She's had them do it before. Walked up to the car, said something like what she said, and then the driver would give her some of the same looks, debating with himself about what his options were. That's how her last pursuit started.

This could go bad. She hopes it doesn't.

The driver flicks his cigarette out his window as he says, "Okay," and kills the engine. He eases the keys out of the ignition and hands them to the passenger, who presents them to Barbara in the same hand as his cigarette, dangling the keys from his ring finger with the cigarette resting between his middle and index. "Here you go."

With her off-hand, Barbara snatches the keys from the passenger, shifting her body, and casts her flashlight right in the passenger's face. He squints and shields his eyes with his hand. "Can you point that someplace else?"

"No."

"Come on, officer. Look, I'll be honest with you, I told my friend here, Aaron... That's Aaron over there," he says, pointing at the driver who waves at her. "I'm Kade by the way. Kade with the letter K—I said Aaron don't pull over, and he said he had to it's the law..." Kade's voice fizzles for a moment and then he's back, "...and well, the reason for that is ... see ... I have a warrant. I'll be honest with you. I got a warrant."

"Kade what?" Barbara asks.

"Carradine," Kade says. "I don't want to go to jail. Aaron... he said he wasn't going to run from a cop, so he stopped. If it were me, I would have kept going. You know how it is. But it isn't me driving, so here we are. I mean the warrant's nothing. It's nothing. Not a big deal. A failure to pay some old fines."

Barbara steps back. "Can you step out of the vehicle?"

The passenger—Kade—debates with himself if he's going to do what she asked; his reptilian brain processes how this could go. He finishes his cigarette, opens the passenger door, and places both feet on the ground. He exits the vehicle. He's tall. Taller than she is, her face is level with his shoulder. He's taller than he looked in the car, lanky, but built of muscle, wearing jeans and a white shirt with a design on it. No, not a design... paint? Red...

Barbara brings her gun up, shoving it in his face. "FACE THE CAR!" she yells.

Kade slowly complies but makes a show of it, his hands up, body relaxed. Once turned, he assumes a position he's familiar with, hands behind his back.

Barbara tells the driver, "Put your hands out the window, so I can see both of them."

The driver does as he is told.

Barbara holsters the firearm and retrieves her hinge-style handcuffs from behind her back, snapping the cuffs on both of his wrists. Once

secured on both wrists, she traces her index finger between the cuffs and Kade's wrist. "Comfortable?"

"Not really," Kade says. "The cuffs are too tight."

Barbara double-checks the cuffs and swipes her hand across Kade's waist for weapons, swatting at his pockets and checking the ankles. She tells the driver not to move.

"I told you about my warrants." Kade wiggles his arms, testing the cuffs. "That should count for something."

"You did, and I appreciate it," she says. "But here's what we are going to do: I'm going to sit you in my passenger seat and run your information. If you don't have anything more than warrants for fines, I'll see what we can do about it."

"Gotcha," Kade says.

Carefully and without turning her back on the Lexus, Barbara marches Kade to the passenger side of her vehicle, stuffs him in the seat, and closes the door, locking it. She radios dispatch that she has one in custody. Dispatch confirms. She turns toward the Lexus. The driver still has his hands out the window. She tells him to exit the vehicle. "Use the outside handle to open the door."

The driver gets out and stands with his hands high in the air.

"You got ID?"

"In the car." He throws his head back toward the car. "Wallet's in the center console."

"Come back here." She directs him to the back of the Lexus. "Put your hands on the trunk. If you move, I'll assume you're aiming to do me harm, and I'll shoot you dead. Do I make myself clear?"

The driver nods.

Barbara backpedals, her eyes on the driver and her vehicle, and positions herself at the open driver's door so she can kneel to read the vehicle information plate on the panel. She adjusts the flashlight under her arm and uses her free hand to key up the mic, asking Dispatch if they're ready for the VIN to confirm the stolen car. Dispatch says ready. She starts to give the VIN to dispatch when her horn honks, and her attention flickers back to her patrol car. She spies movement in the front seat, Kade crawling over the center console, settling into the driver's seat, hands on the wheel, staring at her through the glass. She stares back. Her mind screams a warning about what's happening.

Barbara holsters her gun and sprints toward her vehicle, a mistake because she brings the key fob within range of the car. As she grabs at the door handle, yanking the door open, Kade kicks his left foot out at her. The blow connects with her midsection driving her back. He slips the car in gear and yells, "Thanks," out the open driver's side door as he punches the gas pedal. The charger kicks up dirt and grit as the engine roars, leaving Barbara grasping at nothing. The sudden motion slams the driver's side door closed. Kade drives away.

Barbara rushes back to the stolen Lexus, passing the driver, who still has his hands on the trunk of the car glowering at her as she passes. She jumps in the driver's seat while digging the keys out of her pocket and jamming them into the ignition as the taillights of her patrol vehicle dim in the distance.

With a harsh twist of the key, she brings the Lexus to life. The passenger door opens, and the driver starts to get in the passenger side, saying, "Let's get the fucker." Barbara glares at him, withdraws her pistol from the holster, sticks the gun in his face, and tells him to get out; he does. Without waiting, Barbara mashes the gas pedal, and the Lexus peels out, kicking up the same dirt and grit. She yells into the darkness at how stupid she is, knowing she'll never live this down.

CHAPTER 4:
VALDEZ

THE OFFICE BUILDING AT FIFTH AND DENVER IS home to the Major Crimes Task Force unit, put together to combat corruption, serial crimes, and major crimes—Valdez Jones's current assignment. The building used to be the YMCA, but now, refurbished, it is a historic landmark. It retains the white brick and red tiles, evidence of its past.

In a conference room, a room with gray walls, Valdez sits on one side of a large dark wooden table, with his hands clasped together, body erect, and staring at two people on the other side of the table, Jamison Sterling in a charcoal suit and Meredith Hudson in a powder blue suit. The room smells of fresh paint, white and gray, which is supposed to be soothing. It's not, and a lot has happened over the last few hours.

Jamison Sterling was once a friend. Now he works for the corruption side of Major Crimes as opposed to Valdez, who actually works crimes. He is the golden child with the mocha hue—his words, not Valdez's—who comes from a mixed family. His white father was Tulsa Police, and his black mother was a teacher from the North Side. None of that matters to Valdez, but it does matter to Jamison. He likes people to know where he came from.

Valdez doesn't give a shit where you're from.

Meredith stares across the table at Valdez like he's done something wrong. Jamison is her right-hand man, and she's the one in charge of the corruption side of things. She's never liked Valdez and doesn't like how he does things. Doesn't like his attitude. Doesn't like him. Not a problem. He's never liked her.

Jamison starts the meeting by asking Valdez, "Would you like a representative? This is an official investigation. You are entitled to FOP representation."

"Am I in trouble?" Valdez asks.

"Would you like time to ask someone to be here?" Jamison asks.

"Why? There's no reason for representation. I didn't do anything wrong."

Meredith speaks for the first time. "Someone did."

"Major Crimes did," Valdez says. "But that's government for you."

Jamison picks up Valdez's tone. "There's no reason to be hostile."

Valdez looks at him hard and yawns, exaggerating his movements, stretching his arms and legs. He pushes his body back into the chair, using the table to his advantage.

Meredith clears her throat. "We want to get things down," she says. "Document what's happened. Clear up some issues that have... just clear things up. You understand?"

No, Valdez doesn't. "There's nothing to clear up."

Jamison creases his charcoal suit jacket as he leans forward, talking with his hands. He spreads them open like he's holding a book. "We want to get everything out in the open. Get the story on record for the State. We want to show that we are team players. Help with their investigation. See if there's anything we can give to them that can help them figure out how this happened."

Jamison pushes a piece of paper forward. The paper has Eddie's name on it. It is the initial police report from the Wagoner County Sheriff's Office.

Valdez points at the piece of paper. "Figure what out, what's there to say? You left him out there. So mark that down there," he adds, tapping the paper with his index finger, "that you let him down, not me. Write that in your report. Let's make sure we get it on record for the State—for cooperation purposes."

Meredith waves her hand over the paper, palm up. "It's not every day an operation falls apart like this." She pauses and pushes forward to pull the paper back. "A lot of work went into this operation, and we can't have this happening again. We want to figure out what happened. Figure out what went wrong. Surely, you can understand this?"

"Which part do you want me to understand? The part where we abandoned a Confidential Informant—we got what we want—so fuck everyone else?"

Jamison holds up his hand. "Let me remind you, we're recording this conversation."

"What's the recording for?" Valdez is having a hard time containing his anger. "I'm a cop. Why do you need to record this?"

"You say that like that might mean something," Jamison says. "The cop part, like you're the only one here that is one."

"You say that like that used to mean something to you, but we both know it doesn't."

"—Valdez," Meredith says, silencing him. "No one's saying you're not a cop. But right now, we need you to act like one and we need you to conduct yourself appropriately, for the recording. There is no reason... we don't need to air our laundry to another jurisdiction. They will receive a complete debrief of your operation—that's what the recording's for."

"I don't think you understand what I'm saying," Valdez says. "That's okay. You will."

Jamison understands. "What Valdez is saying is he's a cop, implying we aren't cops. Not anymore. And I don't need you to remind me you're a cop."

Valdez says, "And I don't need you reminding me you're recording this—so who the fuck cares?"

Meredith reminds the room, "I understand the anger. Eddie was your responsibility."

"That's right; he was," Valdez says. "Mine. I'll be the one that's going to have to talk to his mother. I'll have to answer her questions. I'll have to tell her what happened when she asks. I'll be the one that's going to have to sit there and tell her. No, explain to her how every promise Major Crimes made her boy was for nothing. I'll have to tell her how sorry we all are for what happened, but sorry won't bring her boy back.

"Then there's you all, my department. All you want to do is throw somebody to the media hounds. Give them a sacrifice. Me. That's why we are in this room. That's why you're recording this conversation. So fuck off. At least, me and Eddie will share that because betrayal hurts everyone, right? That's what happens? But let me ask you this. What becomes of those that betrayed the betrayer, who judges them?"

Meredith and Jamison remain silent, processing his outburst.

"I'll tell you what happened," Valdez says. "I know what's happened. I know because I was there this morning, standing on the side of the road, looking in the open passenger door of a black BMW left on the side of a country road. Seeing what was left of the kid. My kid, mark that down for clarity—mine. Doing it because some deputy pulled my fucking business card from the windshield and called me in the middle of the night and started this terrible day. But that doesn't matter; I wasn't asleep because sleeping at that place is fucking impossible. You should know that. Mark that in the things you all should know."

Jamison holds his hand up to calm Valdez. "We know where you were."

"Business card?" Meredith flips through the report. "Your business card?"

"You do?" Valdez says. "Funny, because I didn't get a call from you. I got a call from the sheriff. But fuck all that. And yes, Meredith, my business card. It was left for me."

"Left for you? Why?"

"It was a message, and I know how messages work. I work in a subtle world. This message wasn't subtle. This message said I got the kid into this. And for that, I'm just as guilty of this kid's death as the motherfucker who killed him."

"That was the message?"

"That, and this; fuck you pig," Valdez says. "But you two won't get that. Your world is politics."

Jamison starts to protest that his world isn't politics.

But Valdez says, "Just so we are all on the same page, have everything cleared up. You know, for cooperation purposes. Jamison, you're the worst of you two. Meredith can't help herself. She's a paper pusher, but you should know better. You were a cop once. You seem to have forgotten what cops go through. You can't justify this.

"I want you to know if you're going to put this on me. Understand if Valdez Jones is guilty of this kid's death." His voice grows louder. "Then so too is Major Crimes, and all those involved. It was sanctioned but sure, sit over there on the other side of this table," pointing at Jamison. "Treat me like you did before. This is Frankie Green all over again. Try to brush this aside, saying it's not important. But it is important. Eddie's different. This isn't like before."

Jamison recoils in his seat. "There's no need for that type of outburst." He collects himself. "Let's start with the phone call. The deputy called you, asking you what?"

"Let's start with 'That's not any of your fucking concern,'" Valdez says.

Meredith says, "All we want to do is find out how this happened and keep it from happening again."

"Do you know what you aren't doing? You aren't asking what you should be asking. What the most important question is. Which is this—'Why aren't you holding yourselves responsible?' You sit there asking me what happened. Telling me you want to prevent this from happening again. I know how to do that. Do you? We know who did this, so why don't you let me out of here so I can go find him."

"We don't know who did this." Meredith corrects him. "And there's no reason for this type of behavior. You need to calm down and take a breath." She shakes her head, pointing to the recorder. Her way of reminding him this conversation is recorded, but he just doesn't care.

Valdez slants his head to look at her. "What do you think this is all about? We're sitting here because we have a problem. Instead of facing this fucking problem, you're turning the other way. Ignoring what happened. You happened. This place happened. Cooper happened—excuse me, sit down, don't get your panties in a wad—Sergeant Cooper happened. Why isn't he sitting here? He got the call, and he didn't do shit. He left the kid out there in the open."

Jamison plays stupid to regain control of the conversation. "The kid?"

"Edgar O'Malley." Valdez glares. "Don't you act like you can't keep up. Eddie called in, gave the code words. And yet no one says anything to me about it. So he got to take one for the fucking team, a one-fucking-way car ride to nowhere. That shouldn't have happened."

"You weren't able to be reached," Meredith says. "Dispatch tried calling you, and you didn't answer."

Valdez points at the table, finger pressing down into the fake wood, trying to push his finger through the table. "But somehow, the deputies got me on the first try. So what are you trying to say? You're going to tell me not a single fucking person could call me? Not a single person, whose sole job is to act as a glorified operator, could pick up a fucking phone to call me? Or you know, call the fucking hospital? Not like no one around here doesn't know where I am. I've been there for six months—that's bullshit Meredith, and you know it."

25

Meredith blinks and shuffles in her seat. "They did call your boss. Like it or not, Cooper is your boss. He says what goes and what doesn't. It was sanctioned after Cooper found out you had a CI, and Cooper made the decision here. He was the one that took Dispatch's phone call and he thought the information could wait." She pauses and opens the file under the paper in front of her. "Tell us about how this started."

"Which part? It's a long story. I want to make sure you don't feel like I'm wasting your time since you're wasting mine."

"The arrest," she says icily. "We can start there."

Valdez says, "We'll start wherever the fuck I want."

———

A YEAR AGO

"Sit in that chair," Valdez says, eyes flickering to the side and pointing Edgar O'Malley to the chair in the corner of the room away from the door.

The kid looks small in the orange on white jumpsuit. Hair cut close to his scalp in a well-maintained fade. Tan skin; every bit brown of his Mexican heritage. Green eyes. One of the two things he inherited from his father's Irish roots. The second, his name.

Valdez stands to the side of the square interview room, leaning with his back against the painted cinder block wall—a cream color—one foot up and resting on the wall, knee bent, and the other providing balance. Both in Italian brown loafers. Valdez is a big man with a big personality, brown, gel-covered, slicked-back hair that is longer on the top than the sides, and round eyes with a spark of kindness. A round jovial face, red from his heritage—Irish-Italian—and drinking. His arms are crossed over his large chest, a remnant of another life, a weightlifter. He's not fat, but his chest and stomach strain against the fabric of his purple dress shirt, pressing against the buttons so that his stomach hangs slightly over the brown belt and the top of his gray slacks. His badge and empty holster are on his belt.

The small room isn't like the interview rooms seen on TV. County funded. No two-way mirror. One camera hangs in the corner, which is more for the inmate's protection than prosecution. No audio, either. Simple gray plastic chairs. Some still have all four legs. Three are positioned around the table. One in the corner empty. One across from where Eddie is supposed to sit. And the other waiting for Eddie. A round table sits in the center, made from a cheap compressed composite with a sand-filled base. It is too heavy to pick up off the floor but easy to tip over. The stage is set. Before Eddie arrived, Valdez sat his notebook on the table and positioned the chairs the way he wanted. Being part of the Major Crimes Task Force, Valdez's been here many times, but this time's different. The county jail is named after a dead District Attorney and sits off Denver in downtown Tulsa. It's located next to the homeless shelters—the whole street's a way station for the downtrodden.

If this works, Valdez can get Billy and all of them, so he needs everything just right.

Jimmie Waters, thin-lipped, a farmer-like body, sharp-featured, long-limbed with thin short sandy blond hair and a lean frame, sculpted through religious appointments with the gym and an ironclad diet, sits sunken in his chair, body slack and relaxed. Long legs crossed at the knee, pinky finger in his mouth, picking at his teeth, staring right back at Eddie as the boy takes his assigned seat. Eddie's hesitant to sit, which gives Valdez time to study him. The kid resembles a trapped animal. His hands shake, reminding Valdez of the time he caught an opossum in his garage, eyes wide, teeth glaring. He shot that opossum with his long barrel .22 range pistol. Watched the thing bleed out in the garage. Watched the blood pool underneath his car.

This boy is like that—captured and scared.

Eddie tries to act as if he isn't bothered by Valdez, but Valdez watches the blood drain from his face as it dawns on him who Valdez is when he makes the introductions. "That's Detective Waters," indicating the man slung down low in the seat. "I'm Detective Jones. And right now you're like a scared animal. We could walk away now. You don't have to talk to us. You don't have to do anything. You can end this right now. But Eddie, you could be the key. The key to Gilliam. The key to Billy. The key to my white whale, a RICO case, my career maker."

Without looking, pretending he isn't bothered, Eddie says, "We met, so why am I here?" He even throws his upper body across the table, giving a convict stare to both Valdez and Jimmie, slow and scanning.

"We want to talk to you," Jimmie says, his angular body unmoving.

Valdez adds, "And you want us to *want* to talk to you."

Eddie draws his arms back, off the table, and drops them to his lap. "I got nothing to say to you."

Valdez says, "That's not what you said last week at your momma's house. You were friendlier then. You met with me at your mother's house when I served the arrest warrant. Your mother told me you don't respect anything."

"I got nothing to say to you, man," Eddie says. "I told you that then and I'm telling you that now. What don't you understand? Go fuck off or fuck him. I don't care. I told you that last week, and still, you arrested me. Do I look like I'm in a talking mood? Look like I've changed my mind any?" Eddie pinches the folds of his orange and white jumpsuit, his fingers pulling on the fabric.

Jimmie unfolds his long limbs like an uncoiling snake. "You must not understand English," he says. "We got shit to say to you. Not the other way around."

Valdez waves him off with a slight head tilt. "Didn't you hear? We want to talk to you. Not you talk to us." He holds that statement for a moment, letting it sit so Eddie can think it over and be uncomfortable, using the silence as leverage. "But if you don't want to hear what we have to say, then we're wasting our time and might as well be on our way. Let you take all fifty years because that's what you're going to get with what I have on you. In court on this earth, it's beyond a reasonable doubt, and you're way more than beyond reasonable, you're in motherfucking outer space."

Jimmie stands and Valdez drops his foot off the wall—every salesman needs to be willing to walk away. "Sorry we bothered you," Valdez says as Jimmie scoops up his folder. Valdez turns his back on the kid and puts his hand on the door.

"Wait," Eddie says, "I'll listen. But I ain't telling you two shit."

"Too late now," Jimmie says, "You don't want to talk—we won't talk."

"I won't talk," Eddie sits up in his chair, showing a spine, "but I'll listen to whatever you have to say."

"You know how I knew that?" Valdez turns from the door. "Because you're screwed, and you're too stupid to realize it. Two detectives are standing here telling you you're screwed and that we want to talk to you. Help you out. And all you want to do is pretend you're hard. Pretend you have balls. You don't. I do. I have them right here in my hands. And let me tell you, I'm squeezing them tight. I'll burst them like grapes if I want."

"You're there thinking you aren't fucked," Jimmie says. "But you are. You're fucked. Like you got fifty years' worth of fucking reasons to talk to us, and all we want to do is say some shit to you, but you want to sit there and act like you're hard. Like you don't want to talk to us. But let me tell you what's going on with you. Tell you what your asshole's telling you right now. Telling you it's as tight as it's ever going to get. It's telling you there's nothing it's going to be able to do to prevent the fucking coming down the line and that maybe you should listen to what we have to say because it don't like dick. It won't ever be the same if you let that type of fucking happen. So you're going to talk."

Valdez points his notebook at Eddie and adds, "Of course, you're going to talk. We knew this. Knew it when we walked in and so did you. And when we're done, you're going to sing, and then you're going to beg for more because this is how this works. You're going to be like a battered bitch. That's what you are—right now—a battered little bitch begging us to keep going. You'll be asking us to come back, give it to you again. You know what happens when we stop. You know what happens when we walk away. What's happening now isn't as bad as that. You know that."

"Because that's his offer," Jimmie says. "He wants you to be his bitch." He returns to his seat, slides down in it, crosses his legs, and puts that pinky nail between his teeth, settling in to wait and see what the kid's going to do.

Valdez moves slower not only to build the tension but also because he's a large man and never in a hurry. Regardless, he has the kid's attention. Eddie's watching him. "So what will it be?" he says. "You going to be my bitch or you going to take your chances back there?" He hikes his thumb back, pointing to the door. "For the next fifty years."

"Because that's what you're looking at," Jimmie says, removing his pinky from his mouth to talk. "He's a big man, but he'll treat you right. He lubes up good before he goes in. You will barely feel a thing. Barely feel it going in. Won't hardly bother you any."

Valdez says, "You have one question to ask yourself. Do you want to be fucked here with me or back out there? Now you need to know and keep in mind, I can give you a reach around, give you something for your trouble."

"And when your blood's pumping you're going to want that," Jimmie interjects. "Want something in return. Getting off together is better than being used."

29

Valdez says, "Otherwise you're looking at taking it raw and unloved, but I have a soft touch, and I can help you out in so many ways."

Valdez tries his best to keep a straight face, which is hard when Jimmie is over there with his finger, picking at his teeth, enjoying this, looking like an opossum.

Eddie isn't enjoying this. As he tries to back up in the seat, his eyes are wide, large, and luminous. "You two are messed up. What the hell is this?"

Valdez closes the gap, coming in real close—close enough that he can smell the county-jail-provided soap on Eddie's skin. "This is us talking to you. You don't like what we're saying?"

"I don't want to have sex with you," Eddie says.

"Come on, man," Jimmie says to Valdez. "He's not the one. He's too stupid to pick up what we're saying."

"I'm not stupid," Eddie snaps. "I just don't get your point. You're talking about wanting to ass rape me."

Valdez plays confused at how Eddie could have gotten such an impression. "No one's talking about that. We're not going to rape you. What we are talking about is you working for us. You telling us what's going on in Green Mafia land. You singing a sweet song."

Jimmie looks at Eddie, waiting for the boy to look his way, and Eddie does. "We're going to make you work."

"Because fifty years isn't a choice," Valdez says. "So you'll work for us."

———

NOW IN THE CONFERENCE ROOM

"That's how it went?" Meredith asks, narrowing her eyes. Her cheeks flush bright red. "I can't believe it," mouth open and stammering, "That's... that could get you in some trouble... you can't say things like that."

At the same time, Jamison exclaims, "*Jesus*, Val, what the fuck's wrong with you? You can't talk to people like that. You—I don't even know what to say to you."

Valdez shrugs. "It doesn't matter to me how you feel about it. I had to get my point across. I got my point across."

"Is Jimmie okay with you doing this?" Meredith throws her arms on the table and clenches her fists. "Talking like that?"

Valdez copies her by hefting his arms on the table. "Jimmie's okay with what I tell him to be okay with."

Meredith retracts her hands and puts them in her lap. Jamison places a hand on her shoulder to whisper in her ear. She nods. Jamison faces Valdez.

"At least you have the manhood to do this face-to-face," Valdez says.

Jamison's eyebrow twitches. "You believe that your bond with your partner's stronger than doing the right thing? Do you believe that? And face-to-face has nothing to do with this. We need to understand how you could run an informant off the books, who ended up getting killed. That type of shit is what civil litigation is made of."

"We did the right thing," Valdez says. "That kid turned his life around."

"You had this kid over a barrel," Meredith says. "A defense attorney could say you threatened his client. Threatened to rape him. I mean I can get the physical stuff. Getting rough with him. But Jesus. That's the type of shit that gets cases thrown out of court."

Valdez says, "Now who needs to watch their language?"

"Don't you fucking dare," Meredith hisses, slamming her fist on the table. "If that type of shit makes it on TV, we'd be crucified. The only way Major Crimes works is with the support from the Holy Trinity: the sheriff, the chief, and the mayor. You want to go and alienate all three? You be my guest. But I'm responsible for Major Crimes, and I'm not going to have my officers act this way."

"How do you think the public thinks we are going to stop crime?" Valdez asks. "You think people are going to start talking about the shit they did, to the police, if we don't put some kind of pressure on them? Sure, I get how it can't be like the old days. Where we beat the living shit out of someone or where we hold them under a light and threaten them all day. But at some point, we got to tell the community how it needs to be. How we can't treat people with kid gloves, because these people don't live in our world. They live in theirs."

"What?" Meredith says.

"You don't get it," he says. "And in regard to what my partner's going to think or not think, Jimmie's going to be okay with it because it's the right thing. We helped that kid. He turned his life around. He was making something of himself. That is until you all got involved."

"You can't start an investigation like that," Meredith says, half-standing, ready to launch herself across the table at Valdez. Jamison puts his hand on her wrist to calm her down.

Valdez points a finger at her then changes it to a knife hand, mocking her still. "Like you can fucking tell me how to run an investigation? When is the last time you decided to get out there and do any honest fucking police work? Either of you? When's the last time either of you were real cops?"

Meredith shakes her wrist out from under Jamison's hand and slams her hand down on the table. "We're not the ones being questioned here." The table reverberates. The sound bounces off the walls of the conference room.

Valdez stands, knocking his chair back—the sound louder than her fist. "No, you fucking aren't. Meredith, you're a lost hope, but Jamison, you still have something worth something. Still have some balls. They're just in her purse. I am telling you Gilliam knew. The kid knew he knew. We knew he knew, and we didn't pull him out. So, you know what? Tom Cooper should be the one sitting here, not me. He didn't bother to find me. He knew where I was. He says fuck him. He knew. Eddie's death's on him and you. Not me."

"No one's blaming you for Eddie's death." Jamison urges Valdez to sit.

"That's exactly what you are doing."

"What would you have had us do? What could we have done differently?"

"How about being real fucking cops for once," Valdez tells him. "Go after the bad guy instead of hounding me for doing good police work. How about you stop fucking whatever stick's up your ass and get out there and do some damn good? Your community deserves it."

CHAPTER 5:

KADE

THE SUNLIGHT COMES THROUGH THE WINDOW AND wakes him from his stupor. His arm smacks the liquor bottle next to him and knocks it to the side. It rolls off the bed and hits the floor with a dull thud, matching the pounding headache raging inside his head. He drank the whole bottle last night—or was it this morning?—and nothing's left. Drinking is the only way he can sleep.

Sunlight in the windows means his name's out there now—as true as the grass is green.

But there is darkness in him, in his heart, and it's always been there. The darkness has been in him since the day he shot his father for touching his sister. Kade walked in on him with his hands down her panties and his dick in her mouth, and snapped, grabbed a crossbow from the closet— the only thing his ten-year-old self knew how to handle—and put one in his father's chest.

It was a sad day for the police, DHS, others, but the cops understood they still had to arrest him, so they booked him for Assault with a Dangerous Weapon. The District Attorney wanted Attempted Murder. Then Kade told him what his father was doing. Then the District Attorney understood too.

That and his father failing to cooperate with the investigation after failing to fucking die. He ran off somewhere. Like roadkill, slinking off wounded, frightened, to lie down and lick his wounds. If there was goodness in the world, his father would have died or at least stayed gone, but that didn't happen. Because nothing is good in this world.

They convicted Kade, and he did time in juvenile lockup. The judge ruled he would get out when he turned eighteen. The judge took pity on him, but pity is weakness, and Kirsten paid for that weakness because his father couldn't stay gone. He went after her one last time—this happening while Kade was in lockup—the doctors said it was bad. That didn't matter because Kade would handle it when he was free.

Then he was free—free at eighteen, but not free, not how he expected it to be. The anger held on to him tightly, and his experiences held him captive. He spent eight years of his life behind walls.

Eight years without running and playing like a normal kid.

Eight years deprived of normal social interactions.

Eight years separated from his sister.

Eight years of learning in a classroom with a volunteer teacher.

Eight years in the yard.

Eight years in the dorms learning how to fight. How to stay in shape. Discipline. Crime. Learning what it meant to be Green.

All because of pity.

And it made him the man he is today.

When he got out, he hunted his father down when the law wasn't looking—then his father stayed gone.

Kade started the whiskey after that.

There were others after that, so many more. All sacrifices for the greater good, or so he told himself. Casey, Frankie, and now Eddie. Others too.

The whiskey takes it all away, and tonight he'll need more.

Now in bed, he struggles to sit up. His hands are still in the handcuffs. He pulls at the links, trying to separate his hands.

Kade remembers what happened. Remembers slipping the cuffs to the front, climbing over the center console, and stealing that trooper's car. Remembers driving off, crashing it, and running into the night. Remembers Eddie's death. Blood. Eddie dying. Gunshots, sirens, speed.

Kade sits up, running his hands over the crown of his head, wrists still in the cuffs, thinking of what comes next. He throws the lower half of his body off the bed, places his feet on the floor, and rolls his toes over the carpet, which is littered with clothing.

He needs a shirt. Shawna cut the shirt off his body. He needs to lose the handcuffs too. He'll have to cut them off or see if Shawna's got some bobby pins. Maybe he can jiggle the lock or something. Maybe that'll work but it feels like some TV shit. Or maybe Aaron can come to get him, bring him the keys they keep for shit like this, maybe bring him clothes too.

Kade looks to his side. Shawna's next to him, half-naked, with the sheets covering up half her body and a bare leg sticking out, smooth and tan. Not the Shawna he used to know. That Shawna was a skinny white girl. She's more woman now, healthy-looking, plump.

They hadn't seen each other since after her overdose.

Kade told her she shouldn't do that shit, but she wouldn't listen. She told him it was okay because Ryan was looking out for her. But Ryan didn't look out for her. After the overdose, Kade visited her in the hospital and learned how the cops saved her life by hitting her with the Narcan. Shawna almost didn't come back.

Kade didn't expect that black trooper to come after him in the Lexus the way she did. He can respect that, and that's saying something. He lost her in a turn, just long enough to reach the elementary school behind Shawna's place, where he bailed out of the trooper's car and ran across the playground. He tripped on a piece of fucking playground equipment and landed hard in the wood chips. Then he was up again, running and jumping Shawna's back fence. Shawna seemed happy to see him but surprised to find him at her back door with sirens blaring in the distance somewhere behind him. He was standing there in handcuffs, blood on his shirt. She was wearing nothing but a t-shirt. She opened the sliding glass door and asked him what he was doing there. Kade said she was the closest person he could think of and needed help. Shawna told him Ryan wasn't going to like him coming around. Kade told her to fuck what Ryan thinks. He let that sit with her and said he was glad she was not dead. After that, Shawna smiled as he told her, "The cops are coming. You letting me in or what?"

Kade leaves Shawna sprawled out, wrapped in her covers, and walks to the bathroom, pisses, and examines his face in the mirror. He looks like shit, but the liquor does that to him. He needs to spend some time lifting and running to work the bottle off, but he chose this, chose to be a killer.

He needs new clothes. His jeans will need to be burned with the shirt. Shawna can do that after he leaves, but right now, he needs a ride.

And he'll have to set up a meeting with Gilliam to get the plan back on track—because Gilliam will want to talk things over. Gilliam told him there was more to the plan than just killing Eddie.

Send a message, yes.

Let them know not to fuck with the Green Mafia, yes.

Said killing Eddie was the start, but there was more.

Said something about using this situation to make the move.

Said Gilliam needed Eddie gone so Billy didn't find out because Billy's about to make a move while the boss is in prison.

Gilliam said the City and Tulsa are about to be at war with each other now that Tulsa's boss is locked up and what's left of Tulsa's crews are about to make a power move. Someone will come out on top. Someone like Billy. The City won't like that. Billy told Gilliam his crew needs to be ready, meaning Kade needs to be ready. Meaning it's a good thing Billy didn't know about Eddie.

Another thing Kade'll have to do is face his sister. She's a big girl; she'll handle it. He'll take care of her, even if her fucking boyfriend snitched to the cops. He won't tell her that part yet, but he'll have to say something.

Certain things will have to happen now.

Action and reaction.

Cause and effect.

In the kitchen, Kade finds his jeans and his phone in his pocket. He sees he missed calls: Aaron, Gilliam, one from Kirsten, also a number he doesn't know, a call that came in this morning.

Kade calls Aaron back. The phone picks up and Kade says, "Hey."

"Where are you?"

"Shawna's"

"What the fuck are you doing over there; Ryan's going to flip his shit."

Keeping his voice down. "Might. More if he finds out I fucked her brains out—don't think she's too keen on him anymore."

Aaron exclaims, "You didn't?"

Nodding as he talks into the phone, Kade tells him he did. "I think Shawna liked seeing me."

Aaron sounds relieved at hearing Kade's voice. He sighs into the speaker. "We were worried."

That plucks a string in Kade's mind. Something's not right here. For the moment, he ignores it. "I'll need a pickup."

"No shit, I figured as much; I got a car and some clothes in a bag."

"You didn't leave anything in the Lexus, did you? Nothing that will come back on us."

"No, nothing that means anything, some trash."

"Good, because the cops have it."

Voices whisper off the phone. Sounds like Gilliam, rusty and foul-mouthed. Aaron must be sitting at his feet like a fucking dog.

Aaron says, "Are you good for me to come get you?"

Kade checks the blinds in the kitchen, pushing them apart, peering across the back fence. Police cars are still in position. "No, wait some."

Clarity strikes. He should have seen it before. Gilliam's ruthless, and Kade wasn't meant to come back from that trip with Eddie.

Who would Gilliam have do the dirty work?

Only one answer makes sense, the only person who is close to Kade. Aaron can't pick him up now.

Kade switches to a new plan, but it's the old plan, it's how it's always been; he's on his own.

"We're on the clock here," Aaron says, "you know this. It's only a matter of time."

"He can wait."

Shit, this isn't how things were supposed to go. Fuck Eddie for bringing this all down on him. Eddie ruined everything.

There are more whispers off the phone, and then Aaron asks, "Yeah, but how long?"

Kade doesn't answer.

He hangs up the phone, throws it down next to the sink, breaking the screen. He lays his hands on the edge of the sink and hangs his head, thinking about what comes next.

Eddie fucked him.

Gilliam's fucking him.

Scorched earth.

Kade was supposed to handle this Eddie shit. Then they were going to exploit it, send the cops after the wrong people, and send a message.

Everything's changed.

Eddie changed everything.

What was supposed to be will no longer be.

Gilliam will be coming for him.

Oh well, that's how it goes.

CHAPTER 6:

AARON

AARON ENDS HIS CALL WITH KADE, OR RATHER Kade ended it with him, but Aaron puts on an act, showing he's the one that hung up on Kade and not the other way around, wishing he could hang up the phone like when he was a kid—slam the phone down into the receiver, put on a show to say he's angry, and make the phone go ding.

Gilliam likes theatrics.

The bit about the business card says that.

But that's not what Aaron does because Gilliam's in Kirsten's kitchen watching him talk on the phone, and Aaron has to make this look good. Which should be easy; he's angry. There's no faking the anger.

Aaron deposits the cell phone on the round kitchen table and picks up his coffee. "He's not coming in." He takes a drink of the coffee, waiting to see how Gilliam reacts to the news.

Gilliam crosses his legs and rubs his chin, recrosses his legs, and massages the area around the cleft in his chin. "This is fucking bad," he says. "You know what Billy's going to do? We'll have to fucking tell him what happened."

"No, I don't know what Billy's going to do," Aaron says. "I don't get to be in the same room as you guys. That was always Kade's thing."

"Well, that's your fucking thing now."

"I don't want it to be," Aaron says. "Why's it got to go like this? Kade handled himself alright with the Frankie Green shit. What makes you think he's not going to handle his shit on this?"

Gilliam drops his hand from his chin. Slams a fist against the table. "Frankie was different. Frankie wasn't fucking his sister. Frankie wasn't this bad. Billy took care of Frankie. Better he did it than me 'cause I would have chopped that fucker up and mailed him back to the cops. This is different."

"Kade doesn't know what we were going to do," Aaron says. "Billy doesn't know about Eddie. We don't have to say anything. I'm his best friend—Kade trusts me. Here's what we should do: come clean about what's going on, tell him what we were going to do—what you wanted me to do—and then tell him we'll pretend none of it happened. He'll come back to us."

"Like he's fucking coming back now?" Gilliam says. He points at the phone on the table. "He must not trust you too much to blow you off like that."

"He'll come around," Aaron says. "We just have to explain to him what's going on. You made a mistake. Tell him that. Make him see what happened."

Gilliam shakes his head. "Aaron, you dumb shit, Kade knows exactly what was going to happen. We won't have to tell him a thing. I wanted scorched earth. You didn't deliver. Now there's some fucking radioactive fucking fallout. And if you're not careful, you will end up on the wrong side of this house cleaning. So be fucking careful. Did he say where he was?"

"Shawna's."

"Ryan's not going to like that."

"Kade and Shawna used to be a thing."

"Well, things change," Gilliam says. "I mean, look at your friend, he was on the inside." Gilliam reaches across the table and takes Aaron's hand in his and pats the top of Aaron's hand. "Now you are on the inside, and he's not. We have a meeting with Billy. We'll have to confess our sins and see what he's going to want to do. See where we are in all this. See how we can correct the problem. If you'd fucking done what was asked of you, none of this would happen, but you didn't. Now Kade's out there, and no one knows what he's going to do."

"How do you think Billy will take it?" Aaron asks. "How do you think Kade's going to take it if he knows?"

"He knows," Gilliam says. "He knows what you were going to do. Don't give me that look. He knows. Now it's about figuring out how he's going to handle that information."

"What's Billy going to do? What are we going to tell him?"

"We'll tell him the truth. Billy either accepts it or goes to Mikey. That's the only person Kade won't see coming and the only motherfucker with the balls to take Kade on. But going to Mikey, that's bad for us... if he gets involved—we can't have that. No one needs Michael Collins getting involved. That would just fuck things up. Look, I'm going down the road to get cigarettes. When I get back, we're going to leave. This is your mess. So, you're going to fix this. We'll go meet with Billy because Billy wants to talk about this Eddie bullshit. You're going to explain to Billy how all this fucking happened. Let's hope to fuck Mikey's not going to be involved."

As Gilliam gets up to leave, Aaron catches Kade's sister Kirsten, who's just getting out of bed, standing at the bedroom door, wearing a dirty blue robe, tattered and worn, over a white tank top and hot pink panties, no bra, looking at Aaron as Aaron looks at her. Gilliam notices and stares at them both as he leaves the apartment, slamming the door behind him.

Kirsten yawns and steps out of the bedroom, pushing the tank top strap back up her shoulder. "He's in a good mood—what you two yelling about?"

Aaron shrugs her off. "We're not yelling. Just talking loudly about your brother. You're not usually up this early."

"I had a bad dream, one about Eddie," she says. "I don't know, I guess I just don't feel good. I'm worried about him. I've not heard from him. Have you heard from him? Know where he's at?"

Aaron doesn't want to talk to her about this. He doesn't want to talk about Eddie. Doesn't want to give her his attention because if he does, he might not keep things to himself.

Eddie meant something to her, but Eddie's dead.

"What, are you not talking to me now?" Kirsten touches his shoulder. It's her way of taking advantage of his feelings for her. She's always had a way over him, and he has a thing for her. The only good thing that could come out of this whole thing is that Kirsten's going to be single again. Aaron could make his move.

That'd be something. Move-in on the dead guy's girl.

Bile rises in his throat, and he forces it back.

"Can you get me some coffee, please?"

Kirsten nods and moves toward the coffee pot to grab two mugs from the cabinet. She fills one with coffee and strolls over to him. Then she goes back to the counter and fills the other. With her back toward him, she asks, "Are you that upset with me you're not talking? Or did Gill piss you off?"

"He doesn't like you calling him Gill."

Kirsten twirls around and drinks from the mug while leaning against the counter. "I don't care. Gill, Gilliam, what the fuck does it matter? He still fucks me if I want him to or not."

"Kirsten," Aaron starts to say, but she holds the mug up, stopping him.

"What?" She lets the coffee rest under her nose for a moment before sipping from the mug. "You don't like it, fine, don't like it. Kade doesn't, Eddie doesn't, but it's what it is. Don't tell me what it isn't. Gilliam likes to sample his product. That's what I am, right? A fucking product? That's what you say about all the girls. What am I? Who am I? How am I any different? If it doesn't matter to you then, it doesn't matter to you now. That's your problem. You don't understand. Eddie understands."

Aaron sighs. "We're not doing this now are we?"

"What are we doing?" she asks. "What are you doing? I'm trying to have a conversation with you while I wait for you to tell me whatever it is that you and my brother and that creep were going on about."

"You're being passive-aggressive," Aaron says. "I can't do this with you right now. I don't like that Gilliam messes with you. That's how he is with all the girls," he says, stopping to choose his words carefully." I can't tell him otherwise; that's not my place."

"You sound like a dog; loyal to his master."

"That's not what this is," Aaron says. "That's not what I am."

Kirsten steps forward with the mug held out toward him like she's pointing at him, no, not pointing, accusing him—accusing him of being complacent, of being a dog. "No, he does this shit with me, to me, to mess with Kade. He likes having power over him. Kade and you are better than him—smarter too—just because he's older, been around longer, friends with Billy, he's in charge? I don't get it. I don't get why you two put up with him. He's dumb. You're better than him. He's a sleazeball, but he controls the both of you, makes you two jump when he says. Good thing Eddie's not like that. Not that way. He's small, tiny, but he doesn't have to show how big his dick is every time he opens his mouth."

"Comes with the territory. That's life here. Life with them—Kade, Gilliam, Billy, and all of them."

Kirsten laughs, holding that mug out toward him. "You know what, this life's shit," she says. "Eddie knows that. I wish you would fucking wake up and see that neither Gill nor my brother like you. But you love this shit too much. It's a family to you. But it's not to me. There's more. Eddie wants out of this life. Gilliam and Kade just want to get deeper. You too. You just care about being Green. I don't give two shits about it. Eddie doesn't either. He's a good guy. Different from you and different from my brother. He's better than all of us, and he told me he loved me—you get that?"

"Kirsten, he's a kid, he doesn't know what's good for him," Aaron says. "He doesn't know what love is."

That hurts her. She looks down. "No, he doesn't know what's good for him, but you do."

Aaron does.

Kirsten says, "Kade does. You two need to look out for him. Keep Gilliam from dragging him through this shit. I get this is the life I choose for now, and this is the life Kade loves. He loves being Green. He loves you like a brother. He sees this all like a fucking family, even Billy, and Mikey. I don't know why, but he does. So you think he's going to give this shit up? No, he's not going to give this shit up. But Eddie's a confused kid."

"He's more than that," Aaron says. "He makes his own decisions."

"Sure, you've been pulling jobs, but it's only a matter of time until someone calls the cops or brings attention to you all."

She doesn't know how right she is.

Aaron says, "We'll be okay."

Kirsten asks, "What was with the thing last night? Where'd you all have to go to?"

How does he answer that? What's he going to say—I helped your brother kill your boyfriend? The thing about Kirsten is that she's smart. She's not going to let this go. He's going to have to tell her something.

"I can't talk about it." Saying the only true thing that comes to his mind.

Kirsten sits down at the table. "Can't talk about it?"

"Not supposed to."

"Where's my brother?"

"I told you, I'm not supposed to say."

"Spill."

43

"Shawna's," he says.

"Why's he there?"

Aaron shrugs. "Beats me, probably to get laid."

"Ryan won't like that," Kirsten says, "but that's my brother. He doesn't care what others think. He's just going to do what he thinks is best." She points at him. "Good thing you guys are friends because if anyone were to fuck him over, he'd do whatever it takes to kill anyone that crosses him."

"I know," Aaron says.

"Where's Eddie?" Kirsten asks. "I've got something important to tell him."

CHAPTER 7

KIRSTEN

T HE LAST TIME KIRSTEN SAW EDDIE, HE TOLD HER
she was paranoid, and she told him that paranoia kept her alive. Made her smarter. Craftier. Kept her from catching a bullet.

This was happening in her bedroom.

She said, "Don't tell me how I feel."

"If I can't tell you how you're feeling then who am I to you?" Eddie asked, touching his chest and gesturing to her as he said it. "If I'm not able to do that, then why the fuck are we doing this?"

This is their first real fight, which started after she told him that Gilliam was at the apartment. After she told him Gill went through his backpack. The one he kept in the bottom of her closet. The one no one was supposed to know about. "Gill found something in your bag," she said. "So what was in your bag?"

After that, Eddie panicked when he saw the contents spread out on the closet floor. Turning to her, he said, "I don't know."

"He marched right in here and went to the closet. I asked him what he was doing. He told me to keep my fucking mouth shut. He knew where it was. How could he? I got up and he pushed me back against the door, knocked me to the floor. He pulled the pile of clothes off your bag and started going through it. He dumped everything on the floor. He looked through it all, found a piece of paper. It looked like a business card."

Eddie held up his hand to stop her from talking and called his mother. They spoke in Spanish. Kirsten didn't understand anything he said, but she watched his face and saw it fall.

After the call, she asked him again, "What did he find in your bag?"

"I don't know." He was clearly lying.

"You do, I see it on your face," she said. "Talk to me. Gilliam knows something. Whatever he found, he slipped it into his pocket."

"It was nothing, I'm sure."

"Are you? Are you sure? Because if there's something you're not telling me, now's the time. I can help you, but I can't help you if you don't tell me. Whatever it was that Gill found, it meant something—something big."

"I'm sure it was nothing."

"Don't you do that," Kirsten placed her finger against Eddie's chest, pushing hard into him. "Don't you do that; don't you lie to me, Eddie. Don't mess with these guys. I know things. I've seen things. Jesus, Kade... he's done things. Don't you fucking lie to me. I can't help you if you lie to me."

"I'm not lying," he told her, taking a step back. "It's nothing, I'm sure."

She saw otherwise.

He said, "This life's made you this way. Paranoid. It's nothing. I have to go do this thing. When I get back, we'll talk about it. But I have to go."

She told him she doesn't want this life. "This isn't the life someone seeks out."

He replied to her, "But that's the point. Kade made you this way."

"Kade wanted this life," she said—Kade, her twin, her brother, friend, confidant, protector. Eddie called him her destruction. "I don't want this. He does. We might look alike, but he's not me."

"You're not a little girl anymore, not that you ever were," Eddie said. "This isn't life. This isn't a life anyone should live. You can decide. Make a choice."

"I love you," she said. "Like in the movies type of love. I love you. I have since the day we met. I've loved you that long."

"That's not love," Eddie said even though that was a lie. "Movies say love happens at first sight and unicorns are real. Unicorns aren't real. Love isn't like that."

"It is. Love can happen. It does happen. It did happen. I've felt it. I love you. You came along. You showed me a version of me, more complete than what I was before. Made me care about something other than myself—that's what you've done."

"But you're in the life. I'm in the life. I don't want to be in the life. I want out. Do you?"

"I'm stuck here," she said. "I want out, but I'm stuck here. There's nowhere for me to go. I need you. I need you, Eddie." She cradled her stomach. "Now more than ever."

Eddie said, "Look, we'll talk more about this later. Your brother wants me to go do a thing. Might be dangerous. When I get back... we'll talk about... we'll talk about that. Okay. I want to know, but I can't know right now. Or I won't leave, and I need to go."

――――

SHE HASN'T SEEN or heard from Eddie since last night. Something isn't right. It wasn't right when Eddie left the apartment. He shouldn't have gone.

She told him not to go, but he wouldn't listen. He said he had to. She asked him why, why he couldn't stay with her. He didn't need to go. Whatever it was that Kade wanted him to do, he could sit this one out. Eddie said that's not how it works.

Kirsten leaves the apartment and walks to a nearby McDonald's. She orders coffee so the employees don't call the cops on her. That happened once. She finds a booth and plugs the phone into the wall to power it up. It's slow. She waits, staring at the screen as it cycles through the brand manufacturer's information and comes to life. She flicks through the screens, and she has one text message. It's from Eddie.

[Eddie: Gilliam knows.]

Kirsten replies aloud to herself, "Gilliam knows what?" She checks the other apps on the phone, making sure there's nothing more from him. There's not.

Something isn't right.

Her heart sinks.

Kirsten didn't think to check her voicemail because Eddie doesn't call her. Not on this phone. It would have been off. No reason to call this phone, but he did. Eddie left her a message. What could that mean?

"Why did you call?" she asks. "Why would you call me?"

Eddie's voice through the phone's speaker. *I'm sorry we fought. Really, I am. I've not been honest with you. I'm sorry, but before you start freaking out about it ... thinking I'm not in love with you or anything like that, I want you to know I am in love with you. I love you. I want a life with you. Everything that's happened over the last year has been all for you. So I can spend time with you. I love you, Kirsten. Know that. Know that I love you. Hold on to that because I don't know what's going to happen, but things are changing.*

"*Before you go telling me things are always changing, no, I've not been cheating on you. I've never lied to you about loving you. There's a lot I have lied about, but never lied to you about myself. Except for this one thing ... and I'll get to that, but it's hard because I'm trusting you like I've never trusted anyone before. Thing is, I've never really loved anyone. It's a weird feeling, you know. I get nervous thinking about you. I can't wait to see you. I've done so much so I can be with you. I've sacrificed so much. I'm so sorry,*" he's crying. "*Look, there's something that I've done. I fucked up, Kirsten, and I don't know how to get out. I know you won't understand, but I did it for you. Don't blame me. Don't be mad at me, but I did it for you. Remember that. Whatever happens, remember that I loved you and I did this for you.*"

Kirsten wonders, *What did you do for me?*

The message continues. "*I know what Gilliam found in my bag. My mom put it in there. She shouldn't have, but she did. I'm not sure how it's going to shake out. I know something's wrong, and I've got to do something. I mean look at me, I'm calling you. I never do that. No reason to do that.*"

He pauses and nervous laughs.

"*Look, don't blame my mom. This is on me. She thought she was helping. God, I can't believe I'm saying that. We never got along, but it wasn't her fault. I guess that means I'm a man now. Fuck that, you made me that. I'm accepting responsibility. I finally understand what Valdez has been saying.*"

"Who is Valdez?" she asks out loud.

"*He's told me a lot of things over the last few months,*" Eddie's message continues. "*Tried to teach me. Tried to help me. I've learned so much. I should have listened more to what he had to say. He's a bit grumpy at times, moody at others, hard to get along with, but a good guy. You need to know that because if something happens to me, he'll be coming for you. That was what I told him. I said, 'Valdez, if something happens to me, you got to get Kirsten out. She can't stay in that life. She's a victim. She's not like her brother.' I'm sorry Kirsten, but your brother's evil and...*" He stops talking, takes a minute to regain composure. "*...Valdez will come for you, but you have to survive the fallout. You listening to me?*"

"I'm listening," Kirsten whispers into the phone.

Eddie says, "*You have to survive. I know you know how to do that. We fought about that. You made that part clear. You probably think I'm crazy. Think this sounds like my last message. Like a goodbye.*"

More crying, more nervous laughter.

"*It might be, but I've got to do this. It's important because it's important to save you. I have to get you out. You're wondering what I'm talking about, but when I tell you what's been happening... what I've been lying to you about. You will understand. But maybe, when I do get to see you again, you're not going to want to see me... so bear with me as I work up to this, because it's hard. It's hard to be this honest with someone, even someone you love, after so much lying.*"

"What is it?" Kirsten yells into her phone. The employees look at her. She glares back. She misses what he says, catching Eddie say, "a Cop."

Her heart stops. She pauses the message and backs it up.

Eddie says, "*It's hard to be this honest with someone, even someone you love after so much lying, but I did it for you. I did it to get out of trouble. Look, Valdez is a cop.*"

Eddie says, "*Valdez is a cop. When I was arrested, Valdez got me out of trouble. He kept me from going to prison for a very long time. I'm sorry I couldn't tell you. I couldn't tell anyone. The only person who knew was my mother. Things have been rocky the last month or so with people going to prison. Billy playing at being king and Gilliam being so paranoid about things. I did all that. Billy and Gilliam are next. The cops are coming for them. I feel like Billy knows. I don't know how. When I talk to Valdez, which isn't that often, I tell him I think Billy knows. Tell him it's in the way Billy looks at me. He tells me there is no way Billy knows. But he knows and he's been waiting for proof. I think my mother gave him that proof. I think Gilliam found it in my bag. I couldn't tell you about it.*"

Kirsten wipes the tears from her face.

"*We got in a fight about it last week when I went home for her birthday,*" Eddie says. "*What happened isn't important. I don't know how long I have to talk, but she put Valdez's business card in my backpack. When I called her earlier, she told me. She told me she did it, so I'd remember to be a good boy. Remember that Valdez is helping me. Don't tell her she's the reason Gilliam and Billy have their proof—that'd break her heart.*"

"What about me?" Kirsten asks the phone. "What about me? Why didn't you tell me?" She sinks into the booth, puts her head against the table, and cries listening to the rest of the message.

"I don't know what to do, but I know the first thing I needed to do was call you. Kade's pumping gas right now, then we're going to go do this thing he needs done. Something about hurting someone. He told me I couldn't ask questions. So I'm calling you now because I have a moment. I'm going to call Valdez next, but I don't know if I will get through to him. I don't know what to do. He hasn't been answering his phone calls. I don't know why. Does he know and..." Eddie doesn't complete the thought. *"...we had a backup number. I'll try that, but Kade wants to do this job tonight, and I still have to act like everything's cool until I can get back to you. Then I'm out. I can't do this anymore. I want out, and I want you to come with me— screw everyone else."*

The message ends.

Kirsten cries. She backs the message up to the beginning. *"Before you start freaking out about it ... thinking I'm not in love with you or anything like that, I want you to know I am in love with you. I love you."*

She whispers, "I love you too."

CHAPTER 8:

BARBARA

BARBARA'S WATCH COMMANDER IS THE EPITOME OF what OHP used to be and still wants to be in a day and age where people like her are more abundant than washed-out ideas. He stands at the door with his arms crossed, thin-lipped, and looking like he is ready to render judgment.

The substation is a simple pre-made building, with some heat, little air, and enough space for a few offices and computers. Barbara enters the wood-paneled room with the manufactured feel, saturated with an antiseptic smell mixed with strong male cologne. She knows what the outcome is going to be.

The Watch Commander, with a double or triple chin, gestures for Barbara to have a seat in the chair in front of his cheap desk as he rounds the desk and sits. It is silent in the room except for the cheap A/C and the clicking of a clock on the wall behind her. The Watch Commander says nothing until he shifts forward, unfolding his arms, and he places his elbows against the desk, resting his body in a large intimidating way. He waves his hands across the desk and sighs heavily as if he sleeps with a CPAP machine, deep red lines left under his ear. "Look, we have too much going on right now to deal with this."

"Meaning what?" Barbara crosses one leg over the other. She sits with her hands on her knees, arms straight, and back arched forward, emphasizing her chest and her badge.

Barbara will not back down. She knows what's going to happen, and she knew it when it did happen. The only outcome right now is a suspension. She's already talked to Jamison about it after he called and asked her how she was doing. He said he heard about it on the news.

The Watch Commander says, "Meaning we go show them sons-of-bitches that you don't make a fool out of us."

"Meaning OHP?" she says. "You're really taking this seriously."

He stomps his foot. "Damn right I'm taking it seriously, and you should too." He points at her, hiking his finger to the window on the side-wall. "We can't have that element—as in the criminal element—out there thinking they can do something like this and get away with it. They can't. I mean what would that do to us? What would those sheep out there say?"

"That you're not a shepherd?"

He crosses his arms again, dipping his chin to his chest, giving finality to his words. "Sheepdogs—that's what we are."

"We aren't those either," Barbara says. "We aren't sheepdogs any more than those bad guys out there are wolves."

"See, that right there," he says, "that's your problem." He gestures to a framed black cloth with a thin blue line running through the middle. Words are in white above and below the blue line. He reads the top line. "Sometimes there's justice." Then he continues to read below the blue line. "And sometimes there's just us."

Barbara tells him, "That's ridiculous."

"Ridiculous?"

"Yes. Look, if we want to police the community, great. I'm on board with that, but that right there's saying there's more going on, saying that we're something special—we're not."

He pounds his chest. "We are. We're the goddamn Oklahoma Highway Patrol."

For a brief moment, Stanley is in the room, whispering in her ear, and Barbara hears her husband's voice saying the words along with her, *"Don't take the Lord's name in vain, otherwise, we're going to be the goddamned Oklahoma Highway Patrol, and that's something else entirely."*

"Is there something wrong with you?" the Watch Commander says, turning bright pink. "You know they tell me you're usually good-natured, despite your uppityness."

Barbara tightens her lips and talks slowly so that he will understand. "Nothing's wrong with me, but you're pretending we're something we're not." She delivers the line the way she intended, and it lands the way she wanted; his face grows from pink to red. "We're not special. You want to say we're the elite law enforcement agency, fine, say it. I agree. We are elite. But you want to say we're something above all those people out there. Those people paying taxes, paying for us. Don't, because we're not. There's a thin blue line, sure, and there are wolves, sure. But you damn well know there's a difference between murdering people and driving without a license. You believe one equals the other, and it just don't. There's only *justice*. Not just us. It's never *just* us."

The room's silent for a moment.

The clock keeps ticking somewhere behind her. A computer fan whirs. And then the air kicks back on, making a booming clunk.

He says, "You're on thin ice."

"No, I'm not," Barbara says, "I've fallen through, and you're yanking me out of the water. I'm not breathing. I'm frozen. My lips are blue, and you're deciding if I'm worth the trouble of saving. Let me tell you right now that's what's happening... this is what you need to get rid of a good officer that doesn't fit in with your ideals." She motions to all of him. "Well guess what, there's ideals here that I do believe in and some that I don't believe in. Do I believe we can get this Kade Carradine and bring him in like that boy who brought down that cop killer? Hell yeah, I think that. Do I think that just because I'm short and black and female, the only one fitting all three, that I see the same ideals as you? No, I don't."

He smiles. "I have to say I appreciate your directness. Let me be direct too. You're suspended."

"You don't say," she says, feigning surprise. She knew this was going to happen the moment Kade slid over the center console of her cruiser.

"For two weeks or until we can figure out this mess," he says, delivering his sentence. "Plus, we got that murder investigation going on with OSBI. Concerns some Major Crimes snitch that got himself popped. Sheriff's not equipped for that. Had you not let some low-life, piece-of-shit-criminal steal your vehicle, you might be helping with that investigation. Instead, you're facing a suspension."

The Watch Commander opens the folder, picks up a pen, and forces her to go through the whole thing again, the whole story from start to finish, asking her questions but more condemning her. His way of embarrassing her—an attempt to put her in her place. Going on about how things don't look good. Asking about how could she chase after the guy that stole her vehicle in a stolen vehicle, saying the word vehicle slowly

like a straight-backwoods Oklahoman, putting the drawl in his words. He makes her sit there and take it.

Barbara asks, "We done?"

He nods. "We're done."

She gets up and walks out.

CHAPTER 9:
VALDEZ

VALDEZ DOESN'T CONSIDER WHAT HE'S DOING licking his wounds. He's not an animal, but he's at the hospital and hates hospitals. He's here because she's here—been here, not going to leave here.

That's what they tell him. That's what she tells him. Telling him to accept it, but he can't. He can't accept his wife needs a kidney, and he doesn't have one to give her; he's not a match, and neither is anyone else. He can't accept that because accepting that means he's going to have to accept life without her. He can't accept a life without her because there *is* no life without her.

That's where he is—it's gotten to that point.

Valdez barely leaves her side now, and when he does, it's only for a few occasions—those moments when she says she needs some time alone. It is her way of getting him out of the room, telling him to take a shower or to go out for things like food. And even then, Valdez doesn't want to leave.

He doesn't want to feel human.

He doesn't want to feel.

"What are you going to do when I'm gone?" Charlotte asks, doing that thing where she says what he's thinking. Her voice surprises him. It shouldn't. They've been sitting here staring at each other for the past hour. Valdez thinking. His wife lying there thinking about other things while trying to guess what he's thinking.

She looks small in the bed, fragile, wearing a hospital gown, but she's done her make-up. She told the nurses, who in turn told him, that she wanted to look nice for him when he got back because it was a bad day—her bad day—not his. That's what the nurses told him when he returned. Charlotte's Muscogee Creek Nation and part of the Bear clan—legendary fighters that have imbued her with dark hair, raven black, streaked now with blonde highlights from the last time she went to the salon—their daughter took her because she wanted to make sure mom had a good visit—and flawless skin.

Charlotte turns her head, looking at him, returns his smile, and asks, "What will you do?"

"Excuse me?"

"You are here," Charlotte says, motioning to the room and pointing to her head, "but you're not here. I would appreciate it if you would choose where you want to be and be there."

"I'm here," he says, feeling guilty for letting his mind wander. Then softer this time, "I'm here."

"You don't have to be. You can be out there." She points to the window beyond Valdez. "You could be out there doing good, not here watching me die. That doesn't do anyone any good."

Valdez snatches her hand out of the air, caressing and stroking her hand. "I don't want you talking like that."

Tears form in the corners of her eyes, and she frowns to fight them, but at the same time, her face softens. She says, "Oh Val, please, we need to talk about this. Talk about what the doctor told me."

"There's nothing to talk about," Valdez says, letting her hand fall back to the bed. "You're the most important thing right now."

Charlotte blushes. She fights the schoolgirl smile she gets when he makes her feel important. "I have to talk like this; I'm the one lying here."

"There's still hope."

"There's not. That's what the doctors made clear."

"Maybe they'll find a kidney, statistically there's a chance. The numbers aren't zero."

"Hope left me a long time ago," Charlotte says, echoing what the doctors said and something he doesn't want to hear. "It won't come in time. And even if it did, the chances of it working are too small now."

"I don't believe that; I won't believe it," Valdez says, "There's still hope, damnit!"

"Val, listen to me, I know what's happening. I'm okay with this." Charlotte lets go of his hand, withdrawing into herself.

Valdez stomps his foot on the tiled floor of the room. "Well, I'm not. We can fight this."

"We've been fighting this; it's not gotten any better."

"I won't accept a life without you," he says, snorting through his nose.

"You don't have to. It's going to happen, one way or the other—you don't have a choice. Not in this."

Valdez grows quiet and sullen, and he sinks into the chair, defeated and powerless. He hates it.

Charlotte continues, "You know what you look like right now. Like a sad lonely boxer, sitting in his corner, arms on his knees, breathing heavily, thinking about what your next move's going to be. But, Val, there isn't a next move. Not for me. The bell will ring, and you'll have to get up. Do what comes next. Do it without me. It's been a year. I'm not getting better."

"Sure, falling didn't help. Your knee's a mess, but you can come back. I've seen you do it... I don't know what to do next."

"You don't have to do anything next," she says. "I'm the one that has to go without a kneecap for a while, but you're the one looking like you're dying. I'm the one fighting here. Don't take that from me."

"I could say the same thing about you. I could say there's still some rounds left to fight. Say just 'cause the points have you down doesn't mean you can't come back with a KO. It doesn't have to come down to a decision." Valdez reaches for her, but she pushes his hand away.

"Val, shut up."

Valdez's mind flashes through his day—Eddie with the bullet in his head.

Charlotte asks him, "What's wrong," but he doesn't answer. Louder this time, she says, "Val, are you there? Are you going to talk to me? What's wrong?"

"Nothing," he says,

"That's a lie, it's something," she says. "What happened this morning? Are you going to tell me?"

Valdez tilts his head down to behold her. "What happened was I had to leave your side."

"That's not what I'm talking about," Charlotte says, "You still have a job. One of us needs to work. You have to look at what comes after. You can't sacrifice those types of things because you need those types of things."

"I don't care about work right now." Valdez lies. He does care. It's all he's been thinking about, Eddie, wondering what he's going to tell his mom—the blood on the window, Eddie in the driver's seat.

"You going to tell me what happened?" she asks. "Or, are we just going to sit here and stare at each other, waiting for me to die?"

Valdez groans, deeply frustrated. "You're not going to die."

"You are going to have to accept what's happening."

Valdez shakes his head. "The kid's dead."

Charlotte's hand snaps to her mouth. "Oh, my God, what happened?"

"He got himself killed," Valdez says. "He was compromised, and they killed him."

She gives him a look.

"It's what happened. They shot him, Cher. They shot him right here." Tapping the center of his forehead with his right index finger. "Then put my business card on the windshield."

"Oh, God," she says, "I'm so sorry."

"Nothing to be sorry about," he responds. "The kid knew what could happen."

"Doesn't mean it should've happened."

He huffs in agreement. "No, doesn't mean it should've."

"What are you going to do now?"

"That's the question, isn't it?" Valdez says and drops his chin to his chest. He speaks in a quiet voice with feeling and intention in every word. "I'm going to find the fucker that did it and kill him."

"Don't talk like that," she snaps.

A knock interrupts the conversation and Valdez lifts his head. At the door is Jamison Sterling, knuckles against the frame. He says, "She's right; don't talk like that."

"What the fuck are you doing here?" Valdez is out of his chair and charging Jamison before he knows he's moved, but Jamison stands his ground. "You shouldn't be here. Get out."

Jamison holds his hands up in surrender and peace. "I came to see how you were doing." He talks to Valdez but looks at Charlotte.

Valdez is inches from Jamison, breath coming in ragged huffed snorts, with redness growing across the back of his hairy neck. He puffs his shoulders and becomes aware of the sweat on the palms of his hands. "How I'm doing? Bring me in, interrogate me, ask about a boy I cared about, and you come here, to this place and ask me about how I'm doing?"

Jamison doesn't back down. He says, "Dez, I wanted to see how you were doing. I wanted to come by and say that wasn't me this morning."

"Sure sounded like you."

"That's what I came to say," Jamison says.

"Well, you said it."

From behind him, his wife's sweet voice breaks the tension. "Jamie, come in and sit down. It's been forever since I have seen you."

Valdez's shoulders slump.

Jamison pats him on the shoulder as he steps past him, and then loudly, in Jamison-fashion, walking toward Charlotte's bed, holding his hands out in front of him, he greets her, smiling. "Charlotte, you are looking lovely as always, how are you feeling?"

"Like shit. I look like shit too," Charlotte says. She pats the bed, indicating where she wants him to sit. "Jamie, don't suck up, sit down. It's been a while."

Charlotte is happy to see him.

Jamison takes Valdez's seat at the side of the bed.

CHAPTER 10:

JAMISON

JAMISON GOES DOWN TO THE DUMPSTERS WITH Valdez because Valdez wants to smoke, and hospitals don't like people smoking in their building or on the property, but down at the dumpsters, it's okay. Valdez explains this to Jamison, telling him he made nice with some of the security people who told him about this spot, hidden from every camera. Saying the spot's surrounded on three sides with a ten-foot cinderblock wall, just don't mind the smell. "It's not like the old days when we were kids—you could smoke anywhere—I miss that."

Then the conversation dies, and that's alright with Jamison. He needs to ease Valdez into this.

So they stand there sizing each other up, trying to remember what the other saw in the other. They were friends once. But that was a long time ago; things change. People disagree.

Jamison doesn't normally smoke. He doesn't like the smell that hangs on him for hours. He used to smoke, and his little house in Midtown still smells of it. Sometimes he still smokes socially like he is doing now.

Jamison picks up the conversation. "At least no one is going to complain about the smell."

Valdez, rocking on his feet side to side, smokes his cigarette, jamming it in his mouth, staring at Jamison from out of the corner of his eyes. He inhales deeply and shakes his head. "No, no one's complaining about that."

Jamison says, "My mom—you met her that one time, remember?"

Valdez indicates he remembers.

"We were at this big dinner at that local Italian place. The one where the guy made a bunch of money selling pizzas that tasted like cardboard.

Must have thought, *Hey, I'm doing such a good job selling shitty pizza; I'm going to open this semi-fine-dining Italian place.* Because you know, Oklahomans don't know any better."

"I know the place," Valdez says. "Use to serve bread on a wooden paddle."

"Right," Jamison says. "Well, they used to have smoking."

"Everyone had smoking."

"This was before the laws passed about smoking in restaurants. Before the State said you had to have separate shit. Walls and ventilation. This place had a partition. I would not call it a wall, but I guess you could. Looked more like a fancy wine rack. Lots of wood slanted to the side, making X's and shit." Jamison motions to his waist. "Went up to about here. We were sitting there, all of us, my brothers, my cousins, my aunts, uncles, everyone. We were on the nonsmoking side, but near the wine rack. This woman is smoking on the other side. I coughed. My mom took offense to that. Guess it was because of the smoke.

"So my mother—she's not good at keeping her temper in check—asked the woman, 'Can you put that out?' all nice and shit, you know, trying to be good about it, but her tone wasn't the best. This woman, she looks back at my mom, doesn't say a word. You know the whole thing about actions. Well, this lady, she takes one big inhale off that cigarette and turns to my mom. She blows it all out at her. Smoke crosses the partition in this big hazy cloud and hits our table. The lady's way of saying all she had to say in one motion.

"I thought my mom was going to go at her. But no, my mom, she knows how to make a scene. She's smart enough to know that putting hands on the lady isn't going to get what she wants. Won't have the right effect. So, she picks up that bread paddle and starts waving it at the lady like a fan, sending all that smoke back her way. Embarrassed the hell out of me. Later in the car, my father got on to her about it."

Valdez asks, "You going somewhere with this?"

"I am," Jamison says. "But I'm not ready to tell you my idea yet."

"Trying to soften me up a little bit, huh?"

"Something like that," Jamison says. "How's Charlotte doing? Like really doing, not what she's saying?"

Valdez continues to smoke his cigarette and glances down at his feet. "Not good."

"Not good how?"

"Days, weeks, I don't know, maybe less, maybe more," he says. "Not good."

"That bad?"

"That bad," Valdez confirms.

"How are you doing?"

Valdez snorts. "I'm okay."

He's not, and Jamison sees that. Valdez is red-faced, splotchy, and has gained and lost weight all at the same time. He's worn out, tired, defeated, a walking disaster.

Jamison says, "What's going on? You can talk to me."

Valdez takes a long drag of his cigarette. "I'll tell you a story. You told me one, so I'll tell you about what she'll do. She'll tell me to go get her food, turning her head toward me. Look at me sitting in the recliner as I watch over her. Ask me for her favorite meal, even though we both know she's not going to eat any of it. Tell me to leave; go get the food, bring her something back. Tell me … no command me, 'enjoy it there, eat, and get some sun—you're looking washed out.' Then I'll say something like, 'Is that what you want? You're not going to eat any of it.' Each time expecting her to shake her head no. She just tells me, 'You're right, but do it anyway.'

"And you know what, I comply even when I don't want to. I'll go out for the food. Carry-out. Get it to go, grabbing the minimum amount of fresh air. Feeling guilty about it the whole time. Feeling bad for going alone, going without her. Then I'll race back to the hospital. Try to eat what I can in the car and bring the rest to her. Knowing the food will sit on the bedside table until the painkillers and other cocktails of drugs put her out for the night. Then I'll pack it all up, bring it down to these dumpsters, and throw it out. Down here, at least I can smoke a cigarette. Then I'll go back up to the room to settle into the recliner for the night.

"There are these other times she repeats the process—same as the food—turning to me, saying 'I can smell you.' Waving her hand, with the tubes and tape and bruises, under her nose. Her way of saying she wants time alone. Telling me I can't use her shower, saying, 'You can't use the one in the room—that one's mine.' So, I go home, check on the house, and stare down at the ever-growing mound of bills on the kitchen table. Nowhere to sit. No place to eat even if I wanted to… She does this so she can deal with what's coming, you know? She does this so I can prepare to face life without her.

"That's what they tell me. Tell me that she's fading. Tell me there's nothing they can do. Tell me only she can fight to stay alive. But she's tired of fighting. I can see it on her face. She needs a kidney, and one's not coming—that's how it is."

Jamison says, "Needs a kidney?"

"She did," Valdez says. "Does. Now things are a bit different. Infection. Started on her leg. Lost her kneecap." He knocks his knuckles against his kneecap. "She got hurt. Fell. Won't heal. Now it's gotten worse."

"Will it... will they take the leg?"

Valdez nods. "If that's what they decide. She's okay with that part if she could get a kidney, but the longer we go the greater the risk of the infection spreading. Could make it where she can't do dialysis anymore, and without the dialysis... well..."

"That bad?"

"That bad," he says. "Jamie, why are you here? It's not to talk to me about my dying wife."

"No, it's not," Jamison says. "You were right with what you said."

"Which part?" Valdez asks. "The part where I said that Major Crimes was responsible?"

"We were, but that's not what I'm talking about."

"You're talking about what I said about being cops? Talking about me telling you that you needed to get off your ass. Stop acting like the moral arbitrators of policing. Get out there and do some real fucking police work. You talking about that?"

Jamison nods along to what Valdez is saying. "That's what I'm talking about." He flicks the cigarette butt away. "You were right."

"What was I right about?"

"All of it."

"You're here to tell me you changed your mind, had a change of heart, want to be fucking friends again? Tell me you haven't spent the last couple of years climbing the political ladder? Crawling over everyone else's back. Stomping on people who were your friends so you could get to where you wanted to be? You're here to tell me that? No, you're not here to tell me that. You're here because my wife is dying, and you don't know how to be a good fucking person anymore. Well, guess what, she's been dying for a while, so you can go on your way. You're too late—you're not a good person anymore. You're Meredith's bitch, and we both know it."

Valdez smokes his cigarette.

Jamison doesn't take any of what Valdez says personally. He can't. Not if he wants this to work. He has to put his feelings aside. Besides, Valdez is not wrong. Jamison feels the same. Meredith's a bitch, and he knows it.

So through gritted teeth, Jamison says, "I came here to tell you that you were right and share a story. After the story, I'm going to ask you a question."

"The story about the fucking bread paddle?" Valdez says. "If that's what you were here to tell me—you told me." Valdez flicks the cigarette away. He pulls another out of the pack and jams it in the corner of his mouth. He lights the cigarette, hands cupped around his mouth, talking while he does it. "What's your fucking question?"

After the cigarette is lit, Valdez offers Jamison another. Jamison decides another cigarette sounds good. He takes one from the pack, puts it in his mouth, and lights it with Valdez's lighter. After bringing the cigarette to life, he asks, "Who do you think offed your boy?"

"Kade," Valdez says, withdrawing the cigarette from his mouth and holding it to his side. He shifts his weight from one side to the other in a steady rhythm. "But I'm not sure, I figured it's someone in the crew. Could be any one of them."

"Why Kade?" Jamison asks. "Who else in the crew could do it?"

"You didn't care earlier; why the fuck do you care now? You could have asked me then."

"I cared, but you know how it goes, we don't share information in an active investigation."

"Whose investigation?"

Jamison doesn't answer the question. "You think Gilliam ordered the kid's death or was it someone higher? Who do you think would have done it?"

Valdez thinks on the question for a moment. "My money's on Billy. He ordered it. Gilliam made it happen. Kade did it. He's the enforcer of the group. Aaron's too much a pussy, and Gilliam's not going to get his hands dirty. Billy would have done it himself, but I know he didn't."

"How do you know?"

"I do," Valdez says. "He likes to manipulate shit 'cause he's a manipulative little shit. Anyways, I'd sure like to know who Billy's talking to in our department. That was what Eddie was supposed to find out for us."

"What if I told you a story about a certain Highway Patrol Trooper I used to date?"

"You're going to tell me how you liked to take the nightstick?"

"That's not funny."

Valdez laughs. "You're talking about that Jones lady?"

"I'm talking about the Jones lady."

Valdez, smiling for the first time, says, "No relation."

"What if I told you a story about her, about how she got her car stolen, and what if I told you who stole it?"

"What's any of that have to do with anything?"

Jamison smokes the cigarette, not looking at Valdez. "Ten miles from where Eddie was killed this Jones lady pulls over this car. Nothing about it is too much out of the ordinary, except the car was stolen. Guess who was in it?"

"You want to play twenty fucking questions?"

"Humor me. Guess."

"Who was in it?"

Jamison gives up. "Kade and Aaron, Aaron driving, Kade in the passenger seat. Now, tell me, you think Wagoner County or OSBI have put two and two together?"

"You're saying you put it together?"

"If I ask you who the fuck you think killed your boy, who the fuck do you think killed your boy?"

"They'll put it together," Valdez says. "A matter of time."

Jamison nods. "But that will take time. Time we can't let get ahead of us. You think the State boys are going to work your boy's murder. It's shithead on shithead. No one fucking cares."

Valdez nods in agreement.

Jamison says, "No one fucking cares but you, and you know what, you should. You should fucking care. We all should. We all should care because someone's child's been murdered, and we know who the fucker is that did it."

"You're saying you think Kade did it because he was in the area."

Jamison nods.

Valdez says, "You're saying, you think they killed him, then got themselves pulled over?"

"That's what I'm saying; that's the story. They left your business card on the window."

"As a fuck you, yeah, I got that part."

"You made it clear that's what you thought it was," Jamison says, "but I'm asking you, do you think Kade killed your boy? Do you think he could have done it, because if you do, that's what we cops call a fucking lead."

"You're not a cop," Valdez says, "and that'd be more of a hunch."

"Fuck you," Jamison says, pointing at Valdez's chest. "Fuck off. You know I'm a cop. I've come here to tell you the story because I want you to be clear that what I'm about to do could fuck me over. Worse than it would you. I need you to understand because if you don't understand that, don't appreciate it, then what's the fucking point?"

"What are you asking?"

Jamison finishes the cigarette. "I'm asking, can you step away from Charlotte for... what I guess is... I don't know... three days? More like two to do what needs to be done before the State boys figure their mouth from their ass."

"You're going to go after them?"

"No, you are," Jamison says. "I'm going to look the other way."

"Just me?"

"No, Barbara will want in on this. She's embarrassed—this will help her. You can bring anyone else in on it that you need. Keep it small, there's only so much I'm going to be able to do."

Valdez throws his head at Jamison. "She tell you she's going to do it?"

"Not yet, but she will." Jamison is sure of it. "She will. I know it. I've already talked with her on the phone. She told me she's been suspended. Just a matter of meeting with her, which I'm going to do as soon as I leave here. I'm late as it is."

Valdez throws the cigarette down, stomping on it. "If I do this, I want Jimmie."

"I figured you would," Jamison tells him. "You have him."

"I want you too," Valdez says, "meaning I don't want you hiding behind any plausible deniability bullshit if this goes sideways."

Jamison nods because he figured Valdez might ask that. "I can give you two days maybe three to do what you need to do to prove Kade did it. The sooner the State boys figure their shit out, the harder it's going to be. You have a head start. You already know Kade did it; you got the motive; fuck that's clear, now prove it."

"Let me talk to Charlotte."

"I figured you would need to." Jamison checks his watch. "I have to meet Barbara, bring her on board."

Valdez grunts. "That story about your mother."

Jamison turns around. "What do you mean?"

"How'd it end?"

"The best way to rectify the situation," Jamison says, "is to bring a whole lot of noise and attention to it."

"We're doing the same thing," Valdez says, withdrawing another cigarette from his pack.

Jamison nods and smiles. "We're doing the same thing."

CHAPTER 11:

AARON

THEY MEET AT MIKEY'S PLACE, A DIVE BAR AND GRILL in a rundown shopping center. It is as neutral ground as there is. Aaron sits in a booth off to the side of the room, near the back door, far away from the kitchen, while Gilliam's at the table in front of him with his back to Aaron and Billy Vaughn's sitting opposite Gilliam, facing Aaron. Both men talk in hushed voices, making it hard for Aaron to follow the conversation. He's doing his best to keep his ears open to catch what they're saying—this is all new for him.

This is Kade's thing. Not his thing.

Kade should be the one sitting here, not him. But he feels like he's got a stake in this situation, considering Gilliam wanted him to bump off his best friend. Part of Aaron is happy Kade went AWOL because he's not sure he would have been able to do it and then maybe he'd be dead. Part of him likes to pretend he could kill his best friend, his only friend. Looking at it from this side of things—the next morning—he's not too sure. Not after seeing Kirsten.

Because how would he face her when he goes back after doing the deed? The short answer is he couldn't. He wouldn't have been able to face her; he knows that now.

He wouldn't have been able to do Kade the way Kade did Eddie because he's not Kade. Kade's Kade, and he's a killer. That's clear.

Sleep makes things easier to understand. That's how it's always worked for him. Sleep gives Aaron distance and allows him to think things through. Right now, Gilliam's the one that needs to be thinking things through, but he's fucking stupid. The man's all about reaction. Eddie was a reaction. Kade was a reaction. Gilliam didn't expect any of what he called the fallout. He didn't think about what the recoil was going to be from firing that particular weapon. He sure as hell didn't plan for a misfire.

From listening to the conversation, Billy's thinking a lot about what comes next—more than Gilliam.

See, Gilliam answers to Billy, and in a way, Billy answers to someone else. Like a Captain or a Capo, or whatever the fucking Irish call their people. Like they're in the fucking military talking to different levels of command. Except Billy doesn't like answering to anyone else, and Gilliam doesn't like answering to Billy. And neither man particularly cares for the other. Especially now that the person Billy answers to is in prison—Aaron's unsure how that happened. Kade seemed to think it was Billy's doing and called it a move—so as Gilliam quoted Billy, "'The kingdom's ripe for the taking.'" Gilliam explained it in the car—his Honda Accord. "Segmentation keeps people from knowing others. Don't want anyone knowing too much about things. Otherwise, it'd compromise the whole dick-lick operation, and *the boss* can't have that."

Aaron asked who their boss was.

And Gilliam answered, "You don't get to know those things. As far as you're concerned, I am. I'm keeping you on your leash to look menacing—we both know you ain't got no bite. I want you at the meeting, and I want you to be my backup. That was Kade's job before last night. I'm meeting with Billy to try to un-fuck the situation." He was telling Aaron, "I got this handled, but I need you to trust me on this; we're doing this my way."

Aaron replied, "Yeah sure—your way."

But it took a long time for Gilliam to look back at the road like the man was thinking about how Aaron answered and what that might mean.

Now, he's overhearing parts of their conversation, and Aaron, like Billy, isn't comfortable with Gilliam's way of handling things. Because Gilliam's over there trying to save his ass and trying to keep Billy from shutting down his side of the business, what Billy calls Gilliam's branch of things. Billy asks Gilliam how he fucking allowed this to happen. Then explains what he expected to happen next. "There's heat on you."

From where he's sitting, Aaron can't see Gilliam's face. He hears the distrust in Gilliam's voice as he says, "I've got this handled," sounding like he did in the car on the way over.

But the way Aaron heard it in the car was that Gilliam wasn't completely sure he had this handled. Aaron's not sure he even has a handle on this, which leaves him thinking the man's all false confidence.

"Must be how Custer sounded before facing all those fucking Indians," Billy says. Billy, with his oval face, ruddy complexion, ruthless eyes, piercing and soulless, with a sharp smile. Doesn't look pleased with Gilliam. "If this's your way of keeping things handled then I don't want to see what happens when things go to shit."

Gilliam shifts in the seat. "Things haven't gone to shit," he says, "I got things. We're okay."

Billy frowns. "Not from where I'm sitting." He points at Gilliam and then touches his chest. "Look at it from here—from where I'm sitting. Right now; we don't know what your exposure is on this. But a man is dead, so that's going to bring things down upon you. Things are fucked. The best way to play it is to shut things down for now. Let others take the girls off your hands. You know; take a break. We'll send you someplace nice and warm—take a vacation."

But Gilliam doesn't like the idea. He pounds the table with his fist. "You're not taking those apartments away from me. I make you money. That's not right."

Billy licks his lips. "You can't make me money if you're in jail," he says. He runs his hands through his shaved, smooth brown hair, ruffling the stubble. He rubs the back of his head. "I got people I answer to. People I can't upset. We can't have the City and Tulsa getting upset with you or me. Look—I got things going right now—important things. You know how this works. You sure as hell can't make money if you're dead..." He pauses, thinking of what to say next. "What the fuck were you thinking trying to get him?" He motions toward Aaron. "To take Kade off the board—that was stupid."

Gilliam half turns his head to look at Aaron from the corner of his narrowed eyes and then turns back. "Kade brought that little shit in," he argues, justifying why he decided to do what he did. "I had to have a response."

"You had the wrong fucking response," Billy says. "I told you to make him disappear." So Billy did know. "You didn't do that." He shuts his eyes and licks his lips; his tongue fat and burnt in the dim light of the bar. Calmer now, Billy says, "You don't think about these things. You don't think about what happens next. You're like a twelve-year-old boy

with a girl for the first time. You're too concerned about the immediate moment. You're thinking about getting your dick wet and feeling her heat on you. Thinking about how to kiss her because you have not done this shit before. You're too in the moment to think about what happens after that moment. Think about what happens after." Billy taps the side of his head. "Think about the fucking future. There are more people in this than just you."

"We've been friends a long time," Gilliam says, voice gaining a hard edge. He rolls his shoulders forward like he's going to pounce. "So I'm going to take that into account when I think about what you just said. But you don't get to fucking tell me what I can and can't fucking do as long as I push your product and I earn. I pay my respects, like the old school, and I *earn*. That's my role. I know mine. You fucking know yours?"

Billy matches Gilliam, getting his face close to Gilliam's. Voice low. "You don't get it, do you?" He holds the question over the table, making sure Gilliam hears him—hears what he's trying to say.

Gilliam starts to speak, but Billy silences him with a snap of his eyes, cold and dark.

Aaron is smart enough to know what's happening. Billy's telling Gilliam that he's the boss and Gilliam needs to know his place. Billy waits for Gilliam to decide if he's going to challenge his authority or back the fuck down.

Silence.

Gilliam backs down, slouching in the seat.

Billy, pleased with himself and the outcome of events, stretches his arms on the back of the booth, looking a bit like Han Solo from the first *Star Wars* movie, and rotates his fingers as he speaks. "Think about it. If you can't earn, you can't push my product. You can't pay respect if you're dead or in jail. Don't forget how someone like Kade—God you're fucking stupid—someone like him isn't going to take things well. He doesn't think things through. Even worse than you. But you should know better. Kade doesn't. Kade's a mad fucking dog... a fucking lunatic... a true psychopath. He knows the ins and outs of our organization and you've declared mother fucking war on him. What'd you think was going to happen? Think he's going to take that lying down? And you fucking ask that cunt over there to kill his best friend. You think that it was going to be rainbows and butterflies?"

Gilliam mumbles, "I can handle him."

"Can you?" Billy asks. "Because if you can't, now's the time to say something. I'll get Mikey to do something about it before things get too far out of control. Mikey owes me a favor."

"—I can," Gilliam says, interrupting Billy mid-thought.

Billy pauses, leans in on an elbow, and points at Gilliam. "Don't let this shit get too far out of control. You can't ruin the shit I got going on because I got bigger shit than this fucking small-time stuff. Tulsa's weak. It's time for me to make my move, and when I do, Mikey and I plan on making a big fucking move. Look at all this—we own this whole shopping center and there's an even bigger land deal I got working down by the river. You can't fuck that up. It's like this. We're over here trying to control power, attempt a motherfucking coup, and you're off fucking collecting taxes for the fucking kingdom. There's more at stake than you. Get that straight. Get that through your head. I don't need you pissing off some local shithead wannabe cops. I can't have you out there pissing on some rogue fuck-up—Kade—who's going to try to burn the castle down around me while I'm about to murder the king in his sleep. I want to take over an empire—I got things going—don't ruin it."

"I can control him," Gilliam says. "And if I can't, I got something of his that means a whole hell of a lot more to him than me."

He means Kirsten.

"You willing to bet your life on that?"

The back of Gilliam's head bobs. "I got this. I told you."

Gilliam's silent as he looks out the window. "What's his fucking problem?" Gilliam asks when they're back in the Honda, after the meeting. Gilliam is in the passenger seat, Aaron driving, not talking to Aaron, just voicing his thoughts for his ears to hear. Gilliam kicks the underside of the dash. "What's his fucking problem? How can he sit there and tell me what to do? Who does he think he is? He's doing what?—Off trying to fucking legitimize his organization, what about us... what about me? What's he going to do? He's going to fuck us over. Bring problems down on our heads—that's what he's going to do. Things we don't fucking need. Things that upset the balance we got."

Aaron doesn't speak. He does the easy stuff, he drives. They head south, returning Gilliam to his trailer. Gilliam told Aaron he wanted to go home. He slapped Aaron in the stomach and said, "Take me home. I can't fucking stand this place. I need some time to think things over. You

go back to Kirsten; keep an eye on her. Kade will come for her, and we need to be ready for that."

At the light to the on-ramp, sitting on the overpass, the wind whips against the car. The light gives a green arrow, and Aaron takes a left onto the highway's on-ramp.

Gilliam kicks the dashboard again and punches the roof of the Honda. "Billy's going to get us killed—that's what's going to happen. That stupid bitch is going to push things so far that both the City and Tulsa are going to turn on us, like motherfucking rabid dogs, and then what's going to happen? What's that turd-cutter expect?"

Aaron doesn't say anything because there's nothing to say.

"I want what I want, have what I have—is that too much to ask? Maybe..."

"Maybe what?"

"No," Gilliam shakes his head, indicating he's not going to answer, but then a smile forms, and a wild look appears in his eyes as he figures a possible answer to his problem. "Fuck it—this is what we're going to do—we're going to bring bitch boy Billy down and teach him a thing about being too concerned with his own stuff to fucking ignore me. No one ignores me. That's what he's doing; he's ignoring me. Ignoring our issues. I won't be ignored. I won't be commanded. I won't be heeled like a fucking dog. That's you. You're the dog. Cops want to bring us down, so be it, fuck them, but Billy's not going to care. He will let it happen if it means protecting himself. Well, too much has happened. Just because he's the guy I answer to, doesn't mean he needs to keep being the guy I answer to."

"Sure that's wise?" Aaron is working out what Gilliam means, and what Gilliam means is a potential takeover, which means going to war, which means "scorched earth."

Gilliam smiles. "I'm not sure of anything, but I'm sure that bitch boy Billy will turn on us as soon as he can. Maybe he put that fucker Eddie with us. It's bitch boy who's got the police contact, and I wouldn't put it past him to not only know it was Eddie, since he's the fucker that suggested it, but also to manipulate the fucking situation. Remove you, Kade, and Eddie all in one fell swoop, leaving me with nothing, leaving me weak. I bet he put Eddie in my fucking crew just to remove me without showing what he's doing. Working ten moves ahead, figuring out how to remove me—ME—without upsetting too many others. It's fucking chess not checkers, and bitch boy's moving too far ahead. That's his game. You heard him yourself; he wants me out, wants the girls and the network, but not me. Take a vacation—how about you go fuck yourself."

Aaron doesn't say what he thinks; he drives because that's his role. Aaron has never wanted to go outside the lines because that's when things happen. That's when things go wrong. Like with Eddie. Like with Kade. But his mind works, processing the pieces. Billy's turning on Gilliam like they turned on Kade.

Aaron says, "Billy's got a hammer."

Shifting his body to the side, Gilliam turns to look at him and nods. "Yeah, bitch boy's got Mikey, that's right, but if we take Mikey off the board, then what's Billy got? Nothing, that's what he's got; he's got nothing if Mikey's not around. Remove Mikey from things, and Billy's got no protection. He's a pussy. Deep down, he's no different than Kirsten, and then it's a numbers game after that. And I got numbers."

"We can't just kill Mikey; that'd cause bigger problems," Aaron says, trying to be the voice of reason. "Killing Mikey would upset the cousins out east, and no one needs that happening. The City's bad enough. They don't need the real Irish Mob coming down on their heads. It happened twice before, and the dust took a long fucking time to settle. It might've happened before my time, but it doesn't change the fact that it's happened."

Gilliam says, "Well bitch boy Billy don't like having people answering to him. Says it could upset future business deals. Says he don't want RICO charges coming down from some hot-shot bull-dick trying to make a name for himself. Billy's got me maybe three others that kick things up to him. Then he kicks up the ladder, but if we cut the rungs above him, then who's he going to fucking complain to?

"He wants to make a move on them," Gilliam says, "but if we make a move first then where's the fuck he going to go? Nowhere, that's where. What do I got to lose making that type of play? Fuck him. Fuck the police. That's what we're doing right now. Billy wants to move against Tulsa while the City's trying to figure out who steps up next. Then fine, we'll follow fucking suit and move against him. It's a big fucking game of Hide the Weasel, fuck you in the ass, but at the end of it, we'll be fucking standing."

That's dumb and suicidal and Aaron worries he picked the wrong side. So he asks, "Yeah, but what are we going to do about Mikey?"

CHAPTER 12

BARBARA

ARBARA AGREES TO MEET JAMISON AT HER
favorite diner because meeting an old boyfriend on the day she's
been suspended sounds like the perfect time to visit her favorite diner
with its fifties theme, pictures of Elvis, Marilyn, and Sammy Davis, and
several other dozen personalities from a decade lost to time—white tile,
teal walls, black tables, red booths, about as gaudy and over the top as any
diner can get, and all of it smells like bacon grease, which isn't a turn-off.
She arrives first and orders coffee, and like always, Jamison arrives late.
He's always late.

Jamison surveys the restaurant, his eyes roving over the tables and
people, and when he spots her, he walks over to the booth. Barbara
ignores him and leaves him standing there at the table waiting for an
invite to sit down.

"Finally. It's just like you to be late by the way," she says, picking at
it because it's a pet peeve of hers. "You're always late. You're late to the
party. Late to the date. Late to catch on. Late. Not that you could get
your shit together long enough when we were dating," which they did
after her husband's death. "So why am I surprised that you've not gotten
it together now?"

Jamison shrugs.

"God, you've not changed. You're too much a pretty boy. Too obsessed
with your career. Too distracted by your star to care about the other
people around you. That's why you're late."

Still, Jamison doesn't sit; he remains standing and waits with an
amused look on his face.

"God, you're frustrating—you don't even apologize for being late. You just stand there looking like you want something," Barbara says. "You haven't changed. When I ended things with you—not that they began—I told you as much, you even took it well, as you are doing now, but that's Jamison, that's you. You don't take anything too seriously. You've not changed. And look at you, wearing that smug look on your face, the one you wear when you know you screwed up, but you're not going to admit it—no you've gotten worse."

Jamison tilts his head to the side. "I do want something."

"I know that; I can tell." She brushes past his admittance. "So it wasn't a coincidence that you called to set this meeting up as I was walking out of the substation?"

Jamison says, "It wasn't a coincidence I called. Only that it was after the shit-storm blew over."

Barbara's nostrils flare. "Jamie, I've been here for the better part of thirty minutes... thirty minutes trying to figure out why you called. Do you know what I've figured out? Nothing. I haven't gotten anywhere on it." She pauses. "What could you want?"

Barbara is aware of how her feelings are getting the better of her, and she understands that's a mistake. That's when mistakes usually happen; that's what Stanley would tell her. Barbara misses him, but it doesn't help that the only man she never felt guilty about going on a date with was Jamison. Everyone else felt like she was betraying Stanley, which doesn't make sense because Stanley told her to get back out there when she was ready.

But she's not ready and isn't sure if she ever will be.

Barbara softens some, dropping her shoulders. "Look, I'm thankful you're here, but frustrated because it's the afternoon. I'm tired, and I haven't been home where I can curl up in a ball and cry."

"Not that curling up would make anything better," Jamison says. "Can I sit now?"

Barbara motions to the other side of the booth, telling him to move her jacket. Jamison slips out of his jacket, a charcoal-colored sport coat, and throws it in the booth on top of hers.

As soon as he slides into the booth, Barbara says, "They had me sit on a cold metal bench outside the office. Like I was a kid waiting to see the principal. Like I'm a scared child. Like I did something wrong. Like I'm waiting to hear what my outcome's going to be. Not that I need to hear what it's going to be; I know what it's going to be; I know it's not good—why would it?"

Jamison rearranges his sport coat in the seat next to him. "Surely it's not that bad."

"Make me feel better," she says. "It's that bad. Today sucked. It started bad, got worse, and now I'm suspended. Pissed off too, if it matters to you, but what can I do about it?"

Jamison tells her there's a lot she can do about it.

She disagrees. At least she had the chance to change out of her uniform. Trade her uniform for a tank top, Stanley's old brown leather jacket—now in the booth across from her, under Jamison's sport coat—and blue jeans. The jeans, she's aware, are too big for her in the waist. She keeps this outfit in her "oh shit" bag for times like these when she needs to feel some comfort.

Jamison studies his menu, dropping it some so he can see her. He smiles but doesn't speak.

Barbara picks up her menu, too, even though she knows what she's going to order since she's been here thirty minutes waiting. She pretends to browse the selection, letting him stew long enough, so that she can test him to see if he's going to apologize for being late or explain what he wants.

Jamison merely scans his menu.

Barbara gives in. "It's bad," she says, giving Jamison another moment to apologize for being late or say why he wanted to meet. He doesn't. "After suspending me, the asshole wanted to go through it all again. He told me that, sitting there across from me, tsk-tsking me, after already telling me I was suspended. Like we had more to talk about, like making me go over it all again will change his mind. He just wanted me to go over it again so he could rub it in my face. So, he could tell me, 'You know this is bad, right?' No, I don't know. Why don't you use a bit more condescension? See if I figure it out then... I ordered you a water by the way."

He puts the menu down and pushes it to the side, indicating he knows what he wants. "You didn't say that did you?"

"No, I didn't say that," she says. "I said other things. I was in my supervisor's supervisor's office, trying to explain to him what happened. But he wouldn't listen. It kind of makes it hard to make your case when the guy in charge is sitting there going through the motions. Makes it hard to explain what happened. The guy sitting there looking exactly like what

OHP wants in their troopers. Six foot plus, white, and balding—but twenty years out of date. In other words, not me. Guy reminds me of the prison guards from *Longest Yard*—have you ever seen it?"

"New one or old one?"

"The one with Burt Reynolds, not Adam Sandler," Barbara says, feeling the need to clarify because it doesn't matter which movie it was. "Both had guards that looked the same." She pauses to drink her coffee. "But Adam's not Burt. He couldn't ever be Burt. I used to tell Stanley that he should be happy I married him because if I ever got a chance with Burt, I'd take it. Stanley would say it was the mustache."

Jamison smiles, saying nothing.

Barbara says, "This guy's staring back at me and tells me, 'You let him steal your car,' like I need reminding. I know that's what happened. I wanted to say, did you need the report to tell you that?"

Jamison gives her a closed-lip smile. "What did you say to him?"

"I asked him if that was a question."

"What'd he say to that?"

"He explained it to me in this way," Barbara says. "Told me had I not run toward my vehicle, the tater-tot, my words, wouldn't have been able to put it in gear. Telling me, 'It was the key fob on your belt that allowed him to slip the *vehicle* in gear.' Saying 'vehicle' slowly and very much like an Oklahoman." Barbara demonstrates stretching the word vehicle out. "He said *vehicle* several times that way. Like he needed to highlight it for me. Then he said, 'That's how he was able to slip the vehicle into drive.' Then he asked what I was thinking chasing after him."

Jamison gets comfortable. "You chased after him? What *were* you thinking?"

"I wasn't. I was acting. That's what they trained me for." She stops, but then says, "Why are you doing this? I told you most of this over the phone. You already know most of the broad strokes of the story. I'm sure half the county knows I let a bad guy steal my patrol car. Why are you acting like you don't know what happened?"

He puts the water down. "I want to hear what you have to say."

She wraps her hands around the coffee cup, feeling the warmth seep into her fingertips. "Why does that matter?"

Jamison shrugs and holds his hands out to the side. "You could have defended yourself. Got indignant. Said some things you would have regretted. You didn't. Tells me something about you."

Which leaves her blinking and silent.

Jamison picks up his water and takes a sip. He holds his water in both hands under his chin. "I called you for a reason," he admits and takes another sip of the water, dragging this out. "I need to be sure of some things before I tell you what that reason is."

Barbara says, "So, making me go through my humiliating day is your way of working yourself up to asking what you're asking?"

Jamison holds his hands out wide over the table, his way of giving an apology that's not an apology at all. "In a way," he says. "You chased after him?"

Barbara smiles because she likes this next part. "Yeah, I chased after him in the stolen car."

"Why'd you do that?"

"My supervisor's supervisor asked me that same question. I told him all I was thinking about was getting my car back," she says. "Like a blind rage. I don't know what got over me, but I... I needed to fix the problem... I needed to act. That's what I did. I acted. I chased after my vehicle, flashing lights and all, in a stolen car. Had to kick the other guy out." She leans into the table. "Get this, he got in the passenger seat like he was going on a ride-along. Said, 'Let's get the f-er.'"

"What'd you say to him?"

"I told him to get out."

"Your boss—how'd he take it?"

"How do you think he took it?" Barbara asks. "He said I better be happy that I didn't work for a city, telling me the media would crucify me. Not that the troopers won't do that anyway. That's what this suspension is. It's my moment in the garden, a time to come to terms with all the ills I've brought down upon their oh so holy name. They're going to use me as a scapegoat, use this as a way to put me out of my misery."

"Good thing for you, you know. They don't release pursuit details to the media. Be thankful OHP feels the citizens of Oklahoma. A right to know State, meaning they have a right to public and open records. Don't think Oklahomans have a right to know about what the Highway Patrol is doing? Which nine times out of ten is them covering their asses."

"Agreed."

"So, there's that small miracle," he says. "A bright side if you will. But I'm here to help you see it."

Jamison pauses and stares at her, doing that thing where he hijacks the conversation. Where he wants something. And now he's turning it from what happened to her to what he wants, and damn is he good at it.

"What could you have done differently?"

Barbara thinks about his question for a moment, running through all the options in her head, which isn't anything different than what she's been doing all day. Despite all the different scenarios, she keeps coming up with the same answer. "My supervisor's supervisor asked me that very same question. I told him, 'Well, first off, I'd have violated policy and put the son-of-a-female-dog in the back seat of my *vehicle*.'" She says the word "vehicle" the way she demonstrated before, slowing it down. "But seeing they don't train us that way. Everyone else seems to have figured out that particular officer safety problem. Putting people in handcuffs in the front seat is dangerous as hell. I told him, 'I'm glad the media's not involved.'"

"What did he say to that?"

"What was there for him to say?" she says. "He knew what I was saying because he leaned back in his chair. Rubbed his bald head with skin that looks like he has a permanent sunburn."

Stanley used to tell her she was being mean, saying those things about that man.

"It's not his fault God made him the way he is. Stanley would say I'm being mean because I'm angry. And damn right I'm angry. Stanley, he'd ask me, 'What's to be angry with? God's got it.' Then he'd say, 'So no worries.' But I have worries. Just like I have bills. I need this job. I can't think of what might happen if I'm not doing it."

"So, you're saying, you think they're going to hang you out to dry?"

Maybe it's because he's a supervisor. Thinks that way. He would do that to someone. Maybe it's for other reasons.

"But if they do, you're going to make their life a living hell. Right? Go public, talk about all the ways the Highway Patrol could improve. Go on TV and drop all those ear-perking types of words that white men in power love to hear like race and gender?"

Nodding, Barbara says, "I could. I thought about it. I'm the only black female. But I don't know. He kicked me out of the office after suspending me, but I like to think I left."

The waitress comes to the table to take their order, interrupting them. Jamison starts to give her the order, asking for coffee, ordering coffee the way Barbara likes it—which is frustrating. No other man she's dated since

Stanley can even remember her favorite color. Jamison can. Jamison, the man she let down "oh, so politely." Who took it all in good stride. He not only remembers her favorite restaurant—he suggested it—but also how she takes her coffee.

Jamison looks at Barbara. "This place has good pie." He folds his hands in front of him on the table, smiling. "That's what I remembered most about this place when we were dating—the pie. You know, a day like this calls for pie. You want some pie?"

"No, I don't want pie," she says.

"You sure? Pie's good for feelings."

"You know what, sure, why not? It won't go with the ice cream I plan on drowning myself in later."

"A la mode," he deflects.

The waitress writes it all down and walks away.

"What I want, I want to spend the next three days drinking and eating myself into what Stanley would call a 'stupor.' Which was his way of calling whatever it was I do during times of depression," Barbara says. "I did when I miscarried the first time. Did the same thing after he died."

Jamison says nothing as the waitress disappears from view and earshot.

Grimacing, Barbara says, "I'm suspended, so what do you want?"

CHAPTER 13:

JAMISON

JAMISON EXERCISES THE SKILL BARBARA SAID SHE couldn't stand about him, and he does it without knowing he's doing it. She told him he did that when they were dating and told him how she couldn't stand it, turning any conversation into something about himself. She accused him of being narcissistic. And told him how she couldn't see herself dating a man that did that all the time. But it is not like he has much control over it. It happens without him thinking about it. In the movie business, they would call it charisma.

Now, Barbara accuses him of doing that very thing. "You're doing that thing now. What do you want? You've made me ask twice; I don't want to ask again."

Still, Jamison says nothing.

Now that he has pie, it will be easier. He swipes his knife across the top of the pie, removing the whipped cream, and dumps it on the side of his plate.

"Jamie, what do you want from me?" she pleads. "We've sat here patiently while we waited for the pie because you said you wanted to talk after the pie came. Well, it's here. Catching up with you and going over my day was nice, and it's nice to see you—we should do this again—but I don't like you doing this now, turning my bad day into something about you. What I feel like doing is going home and sleeping … until I decide I can show my face again. So forgive me when I say, the pie's come, and my patience has run out." She puffs a short blast of air toward her nose. "Are you going to tell me what that is? Or, are you going to make me guess?

If I have to guess, I'd have to say it has to do with that poor boy of yours getting his head blown off in the country."

"You had it right." Jamison stabs his fork into the pie, smiling, but he still doesn't explain. He lets Barbara sit in it for a good moment, stringing her along. "This pie is really good," he says, pointing his fork at her. "I forgot how nice this place was. I don't come here. Not after you and me... I just don't come here very often. I think Valdez likes to eat here, but I don't come here."

Barbara, annoyed, takes a sip of her coffee, smashes the mug down, picks up her fork. She takes a piece of pie off his plate. Chewing while talking, she waves the fork in the air. "I know some boy that had something to do with Major Crimes went and got himself killed and seeing you called me up hours after that event and my event, you must think they are connected. But what I can't figure out is why you are here trying to win me over. Or why you let me vent like we're a thing," she says, moving her hands back and forth. "We're not a thing. So, there's no reason for you to be dining me, which means you want something. So, what do you want, Jamie? What's the reason for this show? You made me go through all the horrible parts of today so you could lead up to something. What are you leading up to?"

"I wanted to see where you were at." Jamison taps the side of his head with the handle of his fork. "Like what sort of headspace you were in and to figure out how you felt about things... and... and to hear the story from you. Hear what happened. When you hear that type of story, you want to know if it is as bad as it sounds—true."

Barbara steals another bite of his pie and washes it down with a sip of coffee. "Okay, now you've heard. I've told you."

"Valdez was right." Jamison leaves his words at that. "Part of what I wanted to talk to you about was to tell you, you were right about me. That's hard to say, but I guess admittance is the first step in acceptance. I didn't see it then, and now, someone else told me something about myself that I don't want to believe. He said I wasn't a cop. He told me I haven't been for a long time. But I want to change that."

"What are you talking about?"

Jamison puts a piece of the pie in his mouth. "I told you; you and he were right. I realized he was right—it bothers me."

Barbara raises an eyebrow. "Who was right?"

Jamison forks another piece of the pie, breaks the piece off, still chewing the first, and adds this piece to the one already in his mouth. He chews, slowly.

"Jamie, what are we talking about? We were talking about something, come back to that conversation." Barbara rolls her knuckles on the table. "Don't you dare keep doing that thing, where you turn everything back on you; we're not doing that today—today's about me."

Jamison swallows. "I'm not turning it back on me. I'm admitting to you, you've been right about me all along. I'm telling you something important and embarrassing. Like you told me. I'm telling you he was right. He said I wasn't a cop anymore. You want to know what I'm talking about, that's what I'm talking about."

"What are you talking about?" Barbara uncrosses her arms, using her hands to motion to him. "That doesn't make any sense. Are we going to keep talking in riddles? Or are you going to talk about what we were just talking about? You're frustrating, and I can't figure you out, or for the life of me, why I thought there was something between us. Or why I agreed to meet with you. I knew you would do this. I knew it the minute you were late, and yet, I still sat here hoping you changed. Being late should have been a clue—you haven't changed."

"You said there wasn't anything between us," Jamison says, ignoring half of what she said, doing that thing she keeps accusing him of doing again, flexing his charisma, his charm, but he means to this time. "You said that we aren't a thing. Are we a thing? I mean, I feel like there's something here, something between us, but I don't want to be the only one feeling that. So, what are we, Barbs? What are we?"

Barbara is quiet for a moment, her face saying she can't believe he just asked that. "If this is how it's going to go, I'm leaving. You come here; you make me go through my day. Yes, alright, there's something here between us. But you know what, it'd never work out. I find you super frustrating, and I've grown past the chasing the frustrating guy phase in my life. Jamie, I'm not young. I'm not inexperienced. I know what I want, and I know what you want. They are not the same thing. I'm glad you realize I was right."

"What do I want?"

"You want what they all want, sex. You all do. But I've lived some. I have grown kids. I have a dead husband. I buried him. What do you have? Nothing but your damn charisma, and it's super freaking annoying,

especially now with you sitting there, talking in riddles, and I can tell you are meaning to do it. You like theatrics, and … well, I don't. When you turn on the charm to cover up the fact that you were late, that's annoying. When you refuse to apologize, that's infuriating. The fact that you have made me re-live this horrible day is heartbreaking. And now, you're over there teasing me with something, but you won't say what it is, which is just plain sad and pathetic, because do you know what the worst of it is? Me, who won't get up from the table because I want to hear what you have to say—that's the most frustrating thing of all."

Jamison says, "He said I wasn't a cop anymore."

Barbara groans, nostrils broadening, and clears her throat, squeezing her lips tightly together. "Are you even listening?"

"I'm listening." Jamison chuckles. "I've heard everything you said."

Barbara bites her lower lip, glaring at him. "But you just don't care about it, right? Well then, I might as well just go home if you're not going to tell me anything, and you're going to treat me this way."

Jamison seizes her gaze, extruding the charm, forcing it out of his body and for it to flow across the table. "But yet, you're still sitting here." The effort is exhausting, and he'll be insecure about it later, and maybe he feels bad about manipulating people, but not that bad. He licks his lips, smiles, and takes another bite of his pie. "This is a good pie. Do you like this? Or should I have gotten the cherry? I can never decide."

Barbara picks up her cup of coffee, sips it, and cradles it underneath her chin, delighting in the heat on her face. "Who are you talking about? What are you talking about? Who said what, and why are we here?"

"Valdez. Remember him? I think you met once."

Barbara shakes her head, puts the cup of coffee on the table, and picks up her fork. She takes another bite of his pie.

"Valdez said… no… told, that's better. Valdez told Meredith and me that we weren't cops anymore. He's wrong. I'm still a cop. I bleed it. I was raised with it. I don't know what else I'd be, but damnit he said it, and now my mind's rolling it over and over. And I can't get it out."

"But you aren't a cop."

"You say that, but you don't know."

Barbara shakes her head. "No. no, I know, you're more about what looks good, what makes you look good. That's what you are about. You're about appearances. Cops, real ones anyway, aren't about that. You say you're a cop, but I say, you want to look like a cop being a cop. But you aren't a cop, not anymore."

"That hurts."

"Good, you need to hear it."

"You're wrong."

"Am I?"

Jamison's quiet and then says, "I'd like to do something about it, prove you and him wrong, but I wanted to see what was going on with you. What I'm about to do might end my career, and I haven't come this far to *only* come this far. I don't want to come just this far."

"What happens if you succeed?"

"If I succeed—it doesn't hurt me. I have everything to lose and little to gain beyond catching the criminal who killed a criminal. But if I fail, well, I would ruin everything I've worked for."

"Then why come to me? Why play this game? Why do all this?"

"I told you, Valdez said I wasn't a cop anymore," he says. "I had to see what you thought. I had to see if I could enlist you in what I'm about to do because I'm not going to be able to do it without you. Not officially. Not the right way. Valdez knows I want you in it. He's okay with that. I talked to him already. He's okay with not doing this officially, which is one reason why I need you, but I know this could ruin you both too. He's good with that too. I mean that's him. He's outside the lines on a lot of things, but you aren't." Jamison motions to her. He takes a sip of his water. "You're a good person. You're the best person I know. You're good-hearted. Smart. Courageous. You do what needs doing without sacrificing the right thing. I need that. Valdez needs that. He needs you in a lot of ways. I... you can help him. So, I had to see how you felt about maybe not doing the right thing for a couple of days."

"Why do you need me?"

"Valdez knows who killed the kid, the one you know worked with us."

"Who killed his informant," she asks. "How would he know that?"

"He knows because his business card was left on the windshield of the car when the kid was killed."

"Like as a message?"

Jamison nods. "It gets better." He takes a bite of his pie.

"How so?" Barbara asks. "And none of that says why you need me or why you're telling me."

"The guy that took your car, he's the one closest to the dead kid," Jamison says. "The one that brought the kid into his shitty life of crime... was the kid's best friend, and who Valdez thinks pulled the trigger."

"The tater-tot who stole my car?"

Jamison nods and asks, "So are you interested in helping or not?"

CHAPTER 14:

KADE

AFTER SPENDING THE MORNING TOGETHER, KADE and Shawna left her house because Kade told her he couldn't stay there; it wasn't safe. They went to a cheap hotel, smoked some weed, and had sex until neither one of them could stand. Then Kade asked Shawna to help him find Ryan, and after a few phone calls, she did.

She found him hanging around at Harjo's Pool Lounge. A place a couple of miles out east in Wagoner County, just across the county line, the same county where Kade took Eddie. The place is where Jobe holds court and Ryan watches his back. Both deal drugs out the back door. Harjo's is for anyone needing to blow off steam without worry, a neutral ground for the retarded one-percenters, those who never get along with the other sorry sacks, who like to feel the power between their legs because they don't have the power there to start with.

Kade's seated at the bar, which fills the center of the room, talking with Jobe, an old friend, who explains how Harjo's, under Jobe's management, works. Kade knows Jobe from high school. Jobe played baseball all through school and looked good doing it, but that's the last time he worked out too. He could have gone somewhere had he had the drive to do so. Easy money, from pushing drugs, combined with the infamous family reputation, a Harjo, kept him planted at home. Jobe's not a fat man; he's a bit bulky, in a deflated overweight baseball player way. Most of America has someone like him in their town. Someone small-time that used to be big enough to inspire.

Jobe takes off his baseball cap and rubs his head of hair cut to be styled in a Mohawk. He tosses his thick black hair. It sticks out at all angles, but under the house lights, instead of looking native, he looks red-faced and bloated. Kade can't tell if he's splotchy or both. He knows Jobe avoids most drugs in favor of getting downright blackout drunk. Something appropriate for his ethnic heritage, and he's on his way there now. Jobe takes a drink from his glass.

Kade waits for Ryan to finish using the restroom and Jobe goes on, "See I'm not affiliated with you all, you Green fuckers, being my family's native, but we're not affiliated with many of the tribes either."

Kade says, "Something Gilliam's hated since you took over, but something he's tolerated, although not well because he's fucking Gilliam. The man can't accept anything as being good unless he sticks his dick in it and fucks it. He accepts it because Billy tells him to. Billy considers all of Gilliam's assets to be in his *sphere of influence*. Like he's some fucking superpower cutting up some third-world shitty ass country. Gilliam sees it as some personal insult. He hates that this place exists and doesn't pay him for protection."

Jobe drinks whiskey as he talks and fills a glass for Kade, pushing it across the top of the bar. He tells Kade to take a drink and points at the bottle. "The great thing about the state changing liquor laws means we get liquor here now. Those percenters," Jobe holds up one finger, his middle one, "they like coming here but before the change, they really liked coming here because they liked the beer; the only thing we had going on. Easier to ride on a motorcycle that way. Now the laws have changed, and my front stoop looks like a fucking schoolyard with all the empty bikes abandoned at night."

Kade says nothing.

Jobe says, "They say some things are happening in your neck of the woods."

Kade remains quiet.

The place is thick with the smell of smoke. Shawna's at the jukebox. He can't help but glance in her direction.

Jobe studies Kade's face. "Keep that up, and Ryan might have something to say about it."

Kade brushes the comment off. He's got plans for Ryan, and they don't involve giving a fuck what he thinks. "I need to set up a meeting with Billy."

"That's a tall order," Jobe tells him. "The way things are, the things I'm hearing, I don't know if you'll be able to make that happen. I can ask, but I don't like it."

"That's why I'm here," Kade says. "I want you to do it—maybe you can reach out to Mikey."

Jobe holds his hands up. "Look, I got a lot of respect for you, and I know you're good for things, but that's not something I can do. You aren't hearing what I'm hearing. You should hear what they're saying. Did you shoot that kid, your friend?"

"Things are changing. Shifting, that's how Billy would describe it; he talks like that. Talks like he's playing this grand game of chess or some shit but isn't."

Kade's not a fucking pawn.

"Still," Jobe says, drinking some whiskey. "Billy's put the word out that we're—people like me—supposed to avoid people like you. Word says we are to not get involved in your mess—keep the peace is the word."

"Gilliam must have talked to him."

Jobe smiles and then throws back all the whiskey left in his glass. He sets the empty glass on the bar. "Hear it was tense, but what I'm telling you, whatever's going on with Gilliam and him, don't concern you. The word on the street is you've been infected, and no one wants anything to do with you. Gilliam wants you dead just the same. The only reason we're standing here talking is that Shawna's a good woman. I owe her a lot, but I don't owe you anything... and it's going to stay that way. I take my neutrality seriously, so you need to leave."

"I'm not leaving."

"My granny's place is a good place to come to blow off steam, but listen to me, I'm not going to be able to protect you if—"

Ryan Horn steps out of the bathroom, strung out, skinny, white, pale, with wispy blonde hair. Pimples and sores on his face—the look of a meth and heroin user, a walking wight.

Shawna turns from the jukebox and spots him. Ryan notices her. Then Ryan sees Kade. Or better Kade finds him.

Kade leaves Jobe at the bar mid-sentence and crosses the room, walking directly toward Ryan and the pool tables, looking at him the whole time. As he passes the pool tables, he plucks the closest pool cue from the table, and before anyone can say anything, Kade attacks Ryan with it; first striking him in the face, then across the midsection,

then finally breaking the stick across his back, sending wooden shards exploding in all directions. The last blow knocks Ryan to the floor where he doesn't move, groan, or even attempt to get up.

Kade kicks him and stares down at him. He turns his head to Shawna, who nods, chewing gum, blowing a bubble. Kade walks back to Jobe sitting at the bar and throws the broken pool cue on the bar.

"I don't need you to protect me." Kade drinks the whiskey and slams the glass on the bar. "Set up the meeting."

Jobe tells Kade to wait; he'll make some phone calls. Kade says that's all he wanted. Shawna goes to help Ryan off the floor, but he angrily pushes her away, which gives her reason to kick him as hard as she can in his side, sending him back to the floor. Kade decides to wait outside. It's too warm here.

Kade, remembering a time when stars were brighter, looks up into the night sky. The air feels cool outside and cools him off some. He drinks a beer and smokes a joint while standing next to the dim fire-pit, working at keeping his nerves down to a minimum, replaying the conversation with Jobe. He could have handled things differently, sure, but he handled them how he handled them, and he can't change that.

Shawna touches his side. "You shouldn't have beat Ryan so badly. He's a good guy once you get to know him. You know, there's a lot in common between you and him."

"Sure there is, we used to be friends."

"Why aren't you friends now?"

"Because of you."

She kisses him on the cheek after that like he's in school all over again. Then she goes inside to use the restroom and get him another beer, leaving him staring into the fire with the heat of her kiss on his cheek. It makes him smile again. The weight she's gained since coming back from the dead looks good on her. Makes her ass look good. He drinks his beer.

"You could have handled that differently," Mikey Collins, standing behind Kade, says over Kade's shoulder.

Michael Collins runs things differently than Gilliam or Billy. Mikey's Green but not Tulsa Green. Not prison green. He's old-school Irish Mob Green, all Irish pride, Boston, and heavy drinking green. How he got that way, no one knows, because Mikey's a bit of an enigma. His father was a police chief in Tulsa several years ago and for a long time, but he and his old man don't see eye to eye—Mikey doesn't explain it, and people know better than to ask about it. He reminds Kade of a gangster version of Wooderson from *Dazed and Confused*. With his long hair brushed back and held in place with some sort of hair product. Lots of it. Sounds like Matthew McConaughey too.

In the firelight, Mikey's face takes on a menacing look that goes with his menacing personality. He's wearing his uniform, blue denim jacket, white shirt, and jeans over black work boots. His neck, wrists, and hands adorned with gold chains and rings. Stands there with his hands on his hips looking down at Kade. Nodding. His way of saying he understands what's happening. "You didn't have to beat the poor boy almost to death. They think he has broken ribs. Sure as hell has a broken nose."

"Jobe call you?" Kade asks.

Mikey nods and steps closer. "Said you caused some problems. Said some other things." He takes a seat on a stump next to Kade. "You know what I do? I mean you know what my role is here? Here in Tulsa?"

Kade tells him he doesn't, but he knows he's killed more people than all his fingers and toes—way more than Kade has.

With his elbows on his knees and his back bent, talking with his hands, Mikey speaks softly, making sure every word carries a certain weight. "I keep the peace." He pauses and points at Harjo's then sweeps his hand across the fire until he's pointing at Kade. "This is my town. I don't want you forgetting that." Mikey raises an eyebrow, his way of telling Kade to keep up and show respect. "So do you know what I do?"

"You just told me. You keep the peace."

"In a way," he says. "I mean I did tell you that, but what I do and what I *do*, those are two different things. I got my way of doing things. Ways I don't think I have to get into because, well, my reputation precedes me. A reputation I've worked hard to cultivate. But now, you got to ask yourself, why am I here if I got this reputation. And if you are here asking for a meeting with Billy. Then you have to ask yourself what's going to happen next because I don't work for Billy. I don't work for any of you. So why am I here?"

"You work for yourself," Kade says. He takes a drink of his beer. The wood smoke makes his eyes sting. He wipes his hand across his forehead. "Like me."

Mikey chuckles. "Everyone works for someone. Who you work for, that's going to cause problems if you don't work for the right people. Me—I've trusted your philosophical brothers out east, sympathetic to

your cause, to help you out. I've been left here to make sure no one does anything stupid to hurt what we call our pride. Think of me as a governor, Billy says that, but that's because that's essentially the idea. Now, that's a tall order, seeing your group does whatever the hell you want. We still operate under the old rules, but you bunch have no rules. You'd think that'd cause some problems." Mikey pauses and shrugs. "But that's why needing to carve out a reputation is so important. Maintaining that reputation's essential."

The smoke fills Kade's nostrils. He waits for Mikey to finish and takes a sip of the beer, staring into the fire. "You know, you talk a lot."

"Only when it suits me." He leans back, straightening his back, and slaps his knees. "I don't prefer it."

"Me either."

"Before I tell you why I'm here, let me ask you, why'd you want to meet with Billy?"

"Set things straight."

Shawna returns carrying a bucket of beers. "Michael, so nice to see you."

Mikey looks at her, seemingly searching his memory to see if he knows her. "And you."

Shawna smiles, brushes her dark hair off her shoulder, and sits on Kade's lap. She wraps her hands around his neck—he can smell her, and she smells good like summer clouds. "What you two talking about?"

Kade says, "Mikey was about to tell me what he's doing here."

Shawna blows a bubble. "Were ya?"

Mikey nods. "I was."

"Want a beer?" She motions to the bucket sitting at Kade's feet. "You can have one. I'd figure we'd need to share to keep things down, you know?"

Mikey reaches down to retrieve a beer, uses the beer opener on the lip of the bucket to pop the cap off, and throws the cap in the fire. He takes a long pull of the beer, quiet, preferring to drink in peace.

Shawna massages Kade through his pants. He likes it, but she needs to leave. "Shawna, why don't you go get another bucket, take it to Ryan, and save me a pool table? You said something about kicking my ass, and I want to show you that's not going to happen."

Shawna nods and gets off him as he slips her a twenty. She goes back inside Harjo's. Once she's gone, Mikey says, "She's a good-looking girl—that why you did the boy the way you did?—makes sense."

"She's an old friend," Kade says. "He tried to kill her."

Mikey smiles and then, after a time, asks, "What do you want with Billy?

"To set things straight, tell him how it is."

"How you see things." Mikey tips his beer bottle toward Kade. "Not necessarily how things are. There's a difference."

"Billy's been holding court in your bar," Kade says. "So let me tell you how things are, how I see them," he adds, putting some venom in his words. "Billy's going to make a play for Tulsa. He's said as much. And he's got your support in this matter. Meaning he's got the support of the guys out East. As long as he's got that support, he's going to make a move that's supposed to be supported, but also means whoever had your support before don't have your support no more."

Mikey stands and unzips his jeans right there in front of Kade. He pisses on the edge of the fire in full view of whoever's outside, and he talks as he pees. "If that's right, what do you think that means right now?"

"Means, a couple of things."

"Like?"

"Like, Billy's making a play, but who could he be making a play against? My guess he's consolidating his power. He's always going on about this being Green Country, so why not make this *Green* Country. That's not going to be alright with others; that'd upset a lot of people and a lot of things, so he's got to take care of them."

Zipping up, Mikey says, "Keep going."

Kade takes a beer out of the bucket, pops the cap, and throws the cap into the fire. He takes a drink. "So, what Billy can't afford are cops coming down on him. That doesn't mean he's not unwilling to let the cops feel good about a few things. What other way is there to ensure the heat's low, like on simmer low, is to turn it up on another burner? He'd look the other way if it meant getting what he wants."

The fire silhouettes Mikey as he sits back on the stump.

"So, Billy's supposed to have all these contacts, and well, I took someone out," Kade says. "Someone I cared a lot about. Someone who's supposed to have been talking to cops. Now that don't make me feel good. But when I did it, I did it for the better of all Green everywhere. I didn't

expect my friend to want the same done to me. That's not how things are done. There are rules. That's not what happened with Frankie Green. Billy's smarter than that, so it wasn't Billy who ordered it. Do you get where I'm going with this? That was all Gilliam."

"I don't think Gilliam's paying much attention to what Billy wants."

"Gilliam's stupid, and he and Billy are about to have a falling out. I want to stay alive, so I'm choosing a side."

"You were forced to a side," Mikey says. "You're not choosing anything. You're you; I know what side you're on."

"Fine, I want to tell Billy I want to stay alive. I didn't have nothing to do with that kid talking to the police, and I'm as pissed as everyone else."

"Billy would like to hear that," Mikey says.

"Billy needs to hear it," Kade says. "Needs to hear it from me. Not from you. From me. So why are you here?"

Mikey shrugs. "To ask you that. Sometimes Billy and I screen things for each other. He wouldn't want to come here and catch a bullet from you to win favor with Gilliam."

"Fuck Gilliam."

"Glad to hear that too, but still, Billy doesn't know what you're thinking. I can tell him some of what you told me. I'll see if he'll meet with you so you can tell him. Because you're right, you got to say it to him. That'll be tomorrow though. The way I hear things, Gilliam's got guys out looking for you tonight. So stay alive until tomorrow, and I'll get Billy to sit down with you at my bar. You know where that's at, right?"

"Yes. And that's all I want."

Mikey, pleased, stands, finishes the beer, and then turns the bottle upside down, tossing it into the fire pit. The glass breaks, and they both stare at the fire watching the logs burn and the flames dance.

CHAPTER 15:

VALDEZ

VALDEZ SHOWERS WITH THE CROWN ROYAL BOTTLE, drinking and washing at the same time, which reminds him of his time at college, pondering all the work he will have to do in the morning, ruminating on his time with Eddie, and speculating what needs to happen.

After the shower, he calls Jimmie and says, "You up for some work?"

He hasn't talked to Jimmie since he talked to Jamison. He figured if he's going to demand that Jamison bring Jimmie into this then he better make the call to Jimmie.

"You drinking?" Jimmie asks. "You sound drunk."

"I am," Valdez says, sitting on the foot of his bed, wearing a white towel around his waist. He inspects the bottle in his hands. "Crown."

"How'd things go at the hospital. Your kid called, said the doctors said it wasn't going good." He means Valdez's daughter, and she needs to know when to not contact her uncle. "Need me to come over?"

Valdez grows quiet for a moment. Takes a drink of whiskey. "No, I think I'll just be me tonight, watch some movies or something. I feel guilty sleeping in my bed. That's messed up."

"You should watch some porn."

"No," Valdez says. "My wife's in the hospital."

"Yeah sure, but you haven't had sex in what, like six months, I mean rightly so, but you know, a guy's got needs. You should, you're wound tight, release some steam. It'd make you feel better."

Even Charlotte has talked about not being a good wife. He's had to argue with her and tell her she's been in the freaking hospital. Still, it didn't stop her from insisting on giving him a blow job last week, but he's not going to tell Jimmie that. Valdez says, "I'm not you."

"I can't help that I know how to take care of myself," he says, "and know how to take care of you."

"Gross." Valdez lies back in the bed, holding the phone to his ear, and changes the subject. "Jamison surprised me today."

"Because he admitted he's doing porn?" Jimmie asks. "You remember doing jumping jacks with him at in-service? Like a piglet with an apple in its mouth."

"Is that all you think about—Jamison's cock?"

"No, it's the Colombians in the porn that I think about."

"You just want to see what Jamison's packing."

"You caught me," Jimmie says. "What'd he do?"

Valdez sips the whiskey. "Wants to go after whoever killed Eddie."

"My guess is Kade killed Eddie," Jimmie says. "Or another one of the crew, but I'd say Kade. He's the enforcer. Aaron's a pussy."

"That's what I said. So, you want in?"

"Do I like Colombian porn?"

"No, you like seeing the big cocks going at it."

Jimmie chuckles. "What do you need from me?"

"I'm meeting with Jamison in the morning. He said the timeframe's tight, so we need a game plan."

Jimmie's voice sours as he says, "You're asking me to do the grunt work, aren't you?"

Valdez studies the Crown bottle, reading the label. "I've been drinking. I can't do it."

"How do you know I've not been drinking?"

"Because you'd be working out if you had. You don't drink."

"Fine, what do you need?"

"Eyes on."

"Who's the most important?"

"Good question. Let me sleep on it, and I'll get back to you."

Jimmie sighs. "You want me to start tonight or what?"

CHAPTER 16:

BARBARA

BARBARA STANDS IN THE HALLWAY OUTSIDE THE
room before the partially open door. It's late, and she holds a piece
of paper Jamison gave her, checking the room number on the paper
against the room number on the wall. Jamison had told her she could
find Valdez here and explained that Valdez's wife needed a kidney or
something. Barbara takes a deep breath, thankful to find the right room.
The breath's more of a sigh because she's not sure why she came here, but
it's not like she had anything else to do except go home and sulk. Jamison
told her as much. "What else do you have to do, go eat ice cream in bed,
this will be better?"

He is right. She hates that he is right, but he is. So, she's here to intro-
duce herself because for the next few days she and this Valdez are going
to be close. That's how Jamison explained it to Barbara, asking her to be
Valdez's compass, telling her she needs to know what type of man he is.
More importantly, what type of cop he is. Jamison told her, "You have
to meet Valdez to know what he's like. I can't do him justice." But that
wasn't good enough for her.

From inside the room, a female voice calls out to her. "Are you coming
in or not? You've been huffing and puffing out there for some time, and
I'd like to get some sleep."

Barbara, tentatively, pushes open the door and enters the room.
"Sorry, I wasn't sure if this was the right room."

"That's bullshit," the woman in the bed says. She's small, darker than
Barbara imagined her to be, Native, contrasts with the white covers pulled

up to her chin. "If you had the wrong room, you wouldn't be out there thinking so hard to yourself so much so that I could hear you in here."

Barbara remains standing at the door.

The woman in the bed introduces herself as Charlotte. "You're at the right room, so why don't you come and sit down? Jamison told me you might stop by."

Stepping into the room, Barbara asks, "Jamison told you I was coming?"

How could he have told this woman she was coming when she didn't even know she was coming?

Reaching over to the table for the remote control to the TV, Charlotte nods and mutes the TV. She tells Barbara to sit down in the chair next to the bed.

"Jamie's a nice boy," she says. "He was here earlier to meet with Val. Then he visited with me some. Told me he might have a friend stop by later to meet Val, but that he wasn't sure he could get you to agree to it."

"Figures," Barbara says.

"You don't want to be here?" Charlotte asks. "That wasn't you that he was talking about?"

Barbara leaves the comfort of the doorway, rounds the bed, and takes the seat at Charlotte's bedside. She falls into the recliner; there's a nice impression, must be where Valdez sits. She readjusts, bringing her feet underneath her. "No that was me alright, but... you know what, it's nothing."

"It's something."

"See the thing about Jamison is—"

"—he has a way of turning things toward himself?" Charlotte steals Barbara's words. "Yeah, I know that. Valdez hates it when he does it. Calls him a manipulative little shit, which he is..." Charlotte holds a finger up. "But he's good people. Otherwise, you wouldn't be here, no?"

Barbara asks, "Did Jamison tell you anything else?"

"Sure, but nothing to do with you," Charlotte says, grinning. "If I had to guess, I'd say you and him have some history, and I'm not talking about working together. No need to tell me one way or the other. It doesn't matter. If that's the past, it's the past. But it means Jamie trusts you, especially if he sends you to me. Although Val and he have always had issues, they tend to see eye to eye on a lot of things. Jamie's always been career-driven, much more than Val. My Val's a cop because he wants to be. Jamie's a cop because he's good at looking like one."

"Ain't that the truth," Barbara agrees.

"But Jamie's good at it too," Charlotte says, "being a cop." She looks down at the sheets. "Jamie's always liked me. Sometimes I wish Val was more career-driven. More like him, you know, to promote and things, make more money, be home more, home on holidays, that sort of thing. But he tells me that promoting for money's stupid. Leads to being unhappy. I guess he's got a point, but I always ask him, what about the holidays?"

Stanley and Barbara used to have the same arguments.

"Let me guess, he doesn't defend that," Barbara says, leaning forward.

Barbara introduces herself. She extends her hand out to shake hands with the little woman in the bed. Charlotte takes Barbara's hand. The hospital ID band hangs loosely from her wrist. Skin slack with sudden weight loss. IV cord making the whole process harder than it should be. She seems so weak and fragile. The pictures on the side of the bed show her loving life, healthy, laughing, drinking, being social. The woman in the bed seems to be a shadow of that person.

"It's how the conversation ends." Charlotte pats the top of Barbara's hand. "Val's a good man. But I'm biased. We've been together since we were eighteen." Pride brightens Charlotte's cheeks. "That's a long time to be married, no? Two kids: a girl and a boy. I have grandkids; I don't feel old enough to have grandkids."

"I have grandkids."

"I didn't think you to be old enough. But I guess that's what I get for judging you by your looks—I don't see a ring."

"Widow," Barbara says.

Charlotte squeezes her hand.

Barbara examines the spot on her finger where the ring had been. She took the ring off last year. Her daughter had said something about how men weren't going to want to hit on her if she had that ring on her finger. She told her it hadn't mattered before; it's not going to matter now. Told her how she didn't think she was desirable, how she didn't care. But she did care.

Tilting her chin down, Barbara draws out the chain, showing the ring to Charlotte. The little woman studies it.

"Well, Jamie's working further ahead than I give him credit for," Charlotte says.

"What do you mean?"

Taking her hand away from her, Charlotte takes great care in picking her words, adjusting for the weight of what she's about to say. "You can help Val when I'm gone. Help him deal with me being gone."

Barbara doesn't know what to say. She's not sure she heard Charlotte or understood what she meant. "Is Valdez here?"

"No, I sent him home to take a shower. Told him not to come back tonight. Said I needed some time to myself—was like throwing rocks at the puppy who doesn't want to leave your side." Again with a smile of sadness. "I'm dying." She puts it bluntly, but it takes the breath out of her body. "Val won't accept it, but it's not up to him. Like accepting it means anything. It doesn't... won't stop it from happening."

Charlotte shuts her eyes, trying to hold the tears back.

"I'm dying, and he's going to have to face that soon enough. I'm not okay with it... but I'm coming to terms with it..." Eyes still closed, tears fall down her cheeks. "I don't want to die, you know, who would, but I know it's happening. I can't change that any more than he wants to change it. He's going to have to accept that... that he has no control over it."

Opening her eyes, Charlotte looks up at the muted TV. Her thoughts seem to shift to someplace else. Barbara decides to share a part of herself to bring the woman back to the room. "My husband's name was Stanley— it was cancer."

Charlotte's eyes are red and wet with silent tears. "I'm sorry."

Barbara shakes her head, telling her don't be sorry. "We were together almost as long as you and Valdez. He brought me to Oklahoma. We were in Chicago before. When I think of Stanley, it always makes me smile because thoughts of him always bring warmth to my heart. Deep down, I know he's in heaven waiting for me. He was a good person; that's where he was going to go.

"He was a preacher and got a job offer he couldn't refuse. I went from Chicago PD to the Highway Patrol, talk about culture shock. We raised our kids here in Oklahoma. I like it here. My kids, they're adults now, as much as I don't want to think of them that way, but they are—live in town. I guess after Stanley left me, I didn't know what to do or where to go, so I stayed.

"Two years after Stanley *transitioned*, I met Jamison through a mutual friend." Barbara sighs, wanting to say more, to lie to the little woman in the bed, go on telling her how the mutual friend set up the first date, but Barbara's not a good liar. "Well okay, to be honest, my daughter set us up."

Charlotte laughs and comments on Jamison's abilities with the young ladies.

Barbara shakes her head, embarrassed. "Not like that." Voice bounces quickly over her words, explaining how her daughter set them up. "She works for the city and met him at some fundraiser. She's a nice girl and thought of her mother. She set us up on a blind date. She's a very loving daughter, and he's very charming."

"Very charming," Charlotte says. "He's also very full of himself."

"That too." Barbara blushes. "We went on a few dates, hit it off, but my heart wasn't in it. He was very understanding about it all. We remained friends."

"That's the Jamie I know," Charlotte says. "Valdez and he used to work shift together. Went to Major Crimes together. Jamie's a legacy, you know, his father was a cop, and so he's a cop." Charlotte laughs to herself. "Val's father—well, that's a different story—Val's been happy doing what he's doing. Jamie's been around us for a while, used to be very close."

Charlotte's face changes shades like something heavy came upon her. There's deep pain there. Barbara watches as Charlotte pushes the pain to the side. "Things change." She waves her hands in the air, dismissively. "They had a falling out. Some sort of disagreement. You know that type of disagreement friends never really get over but don't necessarily stop being friends over it. Things... things aren't like they were before, you know? Everything's different?"

"I know what you mean," Barbara says. "What was it, the disagreement?"

"Val doesn't talk much about it, but we don't keep secrets," Charlotte says.

Stanley and Barbara never kept secrets either.

"I don't know all the details," Charlotte says, "but I didn't ask for them either if you know what I mean. There's some things he has to keep to himself, as I think there are some things you keep to yourself. It comes with the job. Used to bother me some when we were younger and he was starting. But I had another officer's wife sit me down and tell me how it was going to be. See, no one in either of our families were officers. It's something you don't know until you know. Luckily, I had someone sit me down and put it to me straight. Told me that this is a thankless job—not him being an officer—me being his wife. Tell me that divorce happens, but it doesn't if the wife knows some things, like to not put up with his shit."

105

Barbara laughs, thinking of all the officers she knows who have divorced. Also, the ones that haven't. Then of Stanley, who causes her heart to shine just a little brighter.

"That wife told me that I couldn't put up with him being him, being a cop, at home," Charlotte says. "Told me that I'd have to get control of him, pull him by the ear, and all that; said things might get heated. That he'd get arrogant and things, but there were times when he couldn't tell me everything. Not because he didn't want to, but because he couldn't. Not able to. Like he wouldn't want to think about them, even to himself. It's a 'burden'—that's the word she used. He carries that burden."

Barbara says she knows what she means and tells her there are things she's seen. Things she had a hard time coming to terms with. Things even Stanley knew not to ask about, but at the time, she just figured a lot of that came from Stanley being a pastor.

"Deaths were always the heaviest burdens," Charlotte says. More tears form on her cheeks. "You know, kids were always the hardest. He would talk about some of them, and some he wouldn't. Suicides bother him because he doesn't understand them. He's very much you make your own decisions in his thinking." She pauses. "I don't know it all, but I know with Jamison and him, their disagreement involved a death. It happened after the move to Major Crimes. Jamie was a new sergeant." She smiles big. "And was actually over Val and Val hated that, but again, I don't know it all. I know that someone came into Major Crimes with information. Val talked with the guy. Thought it was worth something. Jamie told him no. Jamie was acting as a new sergeant, he didn't know better—but, he told Val he didn't think the guy was credible. Told Val something about the guy having to come back with better information and dismissed the guy outright."

"Sounds like Jamison," Barbara says. "That's pretty standard. Supervisors like to play it safe."

Charlotte nods in agreement. "Yeah, but Val didn't like that. Maybe it had to be with Jamie being a new sergeant. Maybe it had to do with the feelings Val gets. Guess that makes him a good cop. Says they're in his gut. I don't know. He tells me it's how mothers feel about their children. I tell him he's not a woman and ask how's he going to know what I'm feeling, don't tell me what I'm feeling. Number one thing I tell him during a fight. Don't tell me what I'm feeling. You aren't me. You don't know. Maybe it had to do with Val wanting to make a name for himself in Major Crimes like he had to prove himself. I don't know. He never told me, and I haven't asked. I do know he disagreed with Jamie's decision. So, Val took the guy outside and told him what Jamie said. Told him if he recorded something on his phone or was able to gather more information, then somehow someone in Major Crimes would listen to what the guy had to say. Val wasn't telling the guy to do anything, but that didn't matter, because a couple of days later the guy ended up dead. In a way, Val thought that was a message, one that says the guy snitched. But he didn't. Val felt like it was his fault for telling the guy to get more info, thought the guy was doing something that looked bad. Something. Got killed for it. Blamed Jamie for not listening to the guy when he came in to talk."

"That's heavy," Barbara says. "You know a lot for not knowing a lot." But then things click in Barbara's brain about Jamison's motivations, and this might be why Jamison's doing this, trying to make amends with an old friend.

"After that, things weren't the same," Charlotte says. "They drifted apart."

"Yeah," Barbara says, "I can see it happening, knowing how Jamison is. And it seems, Valdez, the little I know about him, has a strong personality. I can see both men telling the other that they were right when both of them were wrong."

"It's a shame because I like Jamie, and I'd love to see them work through their issues. But I'm not sure it's going to happen." Charlotte grows quiet. "Or that I'll be around to see it."

CHAPTER 17

AARON

ARON RETURNS TO THE APARTMENT BECAUSE that's what Gilliam told him to do. He enters and sees one of the girls sitting on the couch, taking selfies. She's nude. The girl looks over at the open door and sees Aaron. Between pictures, she uses her index finger, with its expensive looking-manicure, to shush him. He shuts the front door, slamming it as hard as he can. She stares at him as he walks by, then goes back to taking revealing photographs, snapping away like he wasn't there, posting them online.

Walking past her, Aaron realizes he doesn't know her—all the girls run together now. They come and go. He comes and collects. He doesn't know this one's name any more than the next, and he barely knows which apartment he's at. If it wasn't for his feelings for Kirsten, he wouldn't be at this one.

If he could, he would go away. He would run. Kade would call him a coward for thinking like this, but cowards live, and he wants to live. He's not a coward. If he were a coward, he wouldn't be here at the apartment because he has to protect Kirsten—protect her from Gilliam. Doing so means he can't be a coward. Cowards don't have plans. And there's a plan, but he's not sure if it's going to work. The plan requires him to be at the apartment.

Next to Kirsten's kitchen table, he inspects the scratches and dents from the drinking games, like quarters, which have left scars and blemishes on the tabletop, evidence of a history of friends and family. A different life, smattered under leftover bowls of crusty food and overturned beer bottles.

Aaron asks the girl taking photographs, "Why don't you clean up?" The girl on the couch stands, nude, and tells him she's working; she doesn't clean while she's working. Aaron tells her no one wants to look at pictures with trash in them, calling her trash. The girl gives him the middle finger and leaves him in silence.

Time jumps forward, and now Kirsten's entering the apartment and standing in the middle of the living room. She brushes a tinge of blonde hair out of her eyes, tucking it behind her ear, to keep it from falling again. Her skin's pale—which is how Gilliam likes it—and her eyes show the telltale clue she's been crying, red and swollen. She's wearing the same t-shirt he saw her wearing this morning.

"Where have you been?" Aaron asks.

Kirsten says, "Out."

"Where?"

The sadness in her face collapses into anger. "You don't get to ask me that until you tell me where Eddie is," she says. "Can you do that? Can you tell me where he is? Because I know where he is."

She sounds like she's scolding a child.

"If you can't tell me, how about you tell me how he got there? Because I know how he got there."

Aaron steps forward but then thinks better of it and stops, stepping back on his heels. "I don't know what you mean."

Kirsten cracks him hard across the cheek.

The slap stings, and Aaron deserves it. He holds his hand on the spot as Kirsten finishes crossing the space between them and presses a finger against his chest, ramming her finger against him. The finger bounces with her words.

"No, don't you do that. Don't you lie to me. I know you know. Are you going to have the balls to tell me or did Gilliam take those from you too when he neutered you? When he made you his lapdog?"

Aaron pleads his innocence. "I don't know what you know, but I can assure you, you don't know..." His words don't come out right and don't sound right. He wants to tell her everything, how Gilliam's going to war against Billy. There's nothing either of them is going to be able to do about it. Ask her what she expected when her brother and Gilliam found out her boyfriend was working with the police. Plead with her to run away with him, get out, get out now ... because this is the moment.

110

After tonight, they'll be locked in this; he knows this, and he won't be able to leave. She won't be able to leave.

Dropping his hand from his cheek, Aaron seizes her shoulders and shakes her. "Kirsten, come with me. If we leave now, we can be in Texas or Kansas before anyone knows we are gone. We can get out."

But her face is a mangled mass of confusion. She doesn't understand, and it breaks his heart.

Kirsten ducks out from his hands and bucks backward away from him, shaking her head. Aaron tries reaching for her again. She needs to understand. There wasn't a choice about Eddie, but about this, they have a choice. They can leave and be safe, but she slaps his hands away, leaving behind a notable sting.

Aaron knows even if he told her what happened, she wouldn't forgive him.

"You took him," Kirsten says, bitterness and grief gnawing at her face, eroding whatever composure she still maintained before walking into the apartment. "You and Kade and Gilliam—you took him, and now he's dead."

Kirsten slaps him again, hard. Same as before. The smack of her hand echoes in the kitchen. The resounding blow surprises her, and she recoils, her hand snapping to her lips as if she's going to apologize. Like she's going to recognize she's overstepped an invisible barrier between friends.

As the pain settles and slowly dissipates, Aaron accepts the mark and doesn't raise his hand to feel the tingling prick under his eye this time.

Kirsten shakes her head, repulsed by him. "You and my brother are full of shit."

Aaron starts to say, "I don't—"

"—NO, YOU DON'T GET TO DO THAT," she yells and chucks a bottle at the wall behind Aaron. "Don't lie to me ... because I know." She cries harder now, the table holding up her body. "Tell me the truth. Tell me what happened."

Aaron doesn't tell her what happened because he can't. He wants to. She needs to see that. He wants her to see it, wants her to know it, but he knows she won't. And she won't understand.

So, Aaron leaves, shuffling out the front door as she yells, cries, and screams at him, trying to goad him into telling her what happened; she insults him, calls him names, says she never wanted him around, hollers

Kade wasn't his friend, screeching everything she has, every vile, nasty, shrill comment she can shriek, but Aaron says nothing.

For an hour, Aaron meanders around the apartment complex, plodding, plotting, and chipping away at the fire raging inside him, speculating if he should go into the apartment and tell her everything. If he walked in, would she be sitting there staring at the door, waiting for him? What would happen? He'd open the door. She'd cry, and he would hold her. He would tell her everything. She would love him for it. They would hug. That won't happen. None of that would happen.

Aaron returns to the complex because he still has a job to do. Wait for Kade. He doesn't dare enter the apartment. He can't be around her again. He wouldn't be able to take her questions, her accusations.

Sometime after 2:00 a.m., he sits in the dark under the stairs, outside the apartment in a lime green lawn chair, smoking a cigarette and drinking a beer, clasping the beer at the neck, eyes on the apartment door, staring at the numbers.

Gilliam said, "You don't have a choice in this, you know that, right? You're on my side because Billy's not going to take you, and if you're not on my side, then I'm going to kill you."

So, Aaron doesn't have to choose a side because his side's already been chosen. There's no going back now. Not now. Aaron's stuck on Gilliam's side. He'll have to help, otherwise, he's as fucked as if he didn't. He doesn't have a choice.

In the darkness, Kade comes, as Aaron knew he would.

"I thought I'd find you here," Kade says.

The voice originates from his right, where Aaron can't see him, beyond the light. Aaron feels him there as much as he can see him, and he's not sure how long Kade's been there.

Aaron says, "You're not supposed to be here."

Kade steps closer. "Where am I supposed to be?" He emerges into the pool of light coming from the bare bulb above the apartment, revealing the white t-shirt and blue jeans, a sledgehammer in his hand.

Aaron's eyes are drawn to the hammer. "Somewhere other than here."

"I was," Kade says, "for a time, but my sister's here."

"That's why I am here."

"Well, I've come for her and you're here to protect her. Gilliam put you here to prevent me from getting her. To kill me if I came here."

Aaron, weaponless, looks from the sledgehammer to his friend. "I can't do that; we both know it," he says. "I suppose you could kill me, but I don't think you want to either. I think you came here to say something, so say what you want to say. I know you could cover that distance from where you're standing with one swing of the hammer. A sledgehammer would do a lot of damage."

Kade says, "The world isn't black and white, isn't Gilliam or Billy. There are other sides, other choices."

Aaron chooses. "Gilliam's going to war with Billy."

There's no anger in Kade's response. "Gilliam's doing all sorts of things."

Aaron sips from the beer bottle. "I was supposed to kill you, but things didn't work out like that. I... I didn't want to do it... if that matters."

"It doesn't."

Kade rests the sledgehammer against the brick wall of the apartment. He stands there with his hands down at his side like he's working through a decision. And Aaron doesn't move from his spot. Smokes his cigarette, drinks his beer, and keeps his eyes on Kade. Kade breaks the stare and reaches in the pack of beer, withdrawing a bottle. Aaron throws him the bottle opener. Kade catches the bottle opener and pops the cap off the beer, saying, "You wouldn't have been able to do it."

That's that. Kade's forgiveness. He's right of course. Aaron wouldn't have.

Aaron drinks his beer. Kade drinks his beer. And they're two friends again, drinking together. No one else would know what just happened, nor would they understand the depth of their bond, but it's there.

"There's no going back, but there might be a way forward," Aaron says. "What happens next?"

"We'll see," Kade says between sips.

CHAPTER 18:

VALDEZ

VALDEZ RETURNS TO CHARLOTTE'S HOSPITAL ROOM the next morning, and through the open door sees a woman asleep in his chair, a pillow supporting most of her weight. The woman hugs the pillow against her body, her chin against her chest, with the zipper of her leather jacket leaving an impression across the lower half of her face. Dark lips droop, her arms hang loose wrapped around the pillow, with feet curled up underneath her. She's well-shaped, cute.

Valdez can see what Jamison must see in her, and without having to give it a moment's thought, he knows exactly who she is and why she is here.

Barbara seems comfortable for someone sleeping in a recliner, and that's assuming the recliner's comfortable. It's not. Valdez has slept in it for the last few months; he knows. Valdez peers around the open door. Charlotte's awake, sitting up in the bed, watching TV on mute with close captioning on, trying her best to not wake their guest.

She doesn't sleep anymore. Not here, not in the hospital. In the hospital, she says she can't sleep, doesn't sleep. Tells him it's because she'll get plenty of time to sleep. Not finishing the part about it being because she's dead. That starts arguments. Valdez doesn't want to hear that type of talk. He tells her that line's been used before, and it wasn't funny the first time.

It usually ends with her sticking her tongue out at him.

Valdez knows she's awake because of the pain. The pain makes sleep difficult. The hospital makes it impossible. He knows when he's absent— the drugs hit her hard, drugs for the pain—she sleeps. Sleeps most of the day away.

Valdez enters the room, and Charlotte's smile means his world is complete, the sun has risen, and everything's going to be alright.

Except it's not.

In one hand, Valdez holds two cups of coffee in a drink carrier, and in the other, he has a brown paper sack with two bagels. He picked the bagels up on the way over. He thought it might cheer Charlotte up. Breakfast with his wife is his daily mission. Has been since the beginning of her latest stint in the hospital. And with the thought of death looming over every moment, he's tried to have breakfast with her in the morning. Has to have breakfast with her. Has to see her every morning because he can't accept a life where that's not possible—he's not ready for that.

Her death has become the topic of discussion because death is something that he's going to have to talk about. They have talked about it. He doesn't want to talk about it anymore. The doctors tell him it's inevitable if the infection spreads or worsens. Inevitable if she doesn't receive a kidney.

Charlotte blinks, then rubs her eyes with her hands and pretends to be surprised to see him. She checks her wrist like she's looking at a watch and mouths to him that he's late. Valdez looks from her to Barbara sleeping in the chair.

"Shush," she says in a low voice. "Don't wake her up."

"What's she doing here?" Valdez asks, stepping into the room, standing at the foot of Charlotte's bed. He doesn't whisper well.

"Jamie sent her," Charlotte says, throwing the covers down to her stomach.

"What do you mean Jamie sent her?" he asks. "Why's Jamie sending people to my wife?"

Charlotte smiles at him again. She is always beautiful in the morning, even in the hospital, where she tells him no one looks beautiful. "Because I think I'm going to die at any moment."

"Don't talk like that." Doing his best to avoid an argument.

"It's a joke, Val. Lighten up. What did you bring for me today?"

Valdez hides the paper bag behind his back. "I'm not telling you until you tell me why she's here."

"I did tell you. Jamie sent her, and she wasn't coming here to meet me. She was coming here for you."

"But I wasn't here."

Charlotte uses the, *I'm smarter than you voice.* "No, I sent you home."

Valdez pauses to think about what she said. "You sent me home—you knew she was coming?"

She smiles brightly. "I told you that Jamie told me."

He foolishly argues with her. "You didn't tell me that Jamie told you she was coming; you told me that Jamie sent her here."

"If you keep arguing with me, not only will my one splurge for the day get cold," she says, referring to the coffee, "but you will wake her up. Now, if you want to continue to deprive your dying wife of her one bright happy moment of the day, continue to stand there and argue with me. If you love me." She gives him pouty lips, large and full, a dull red, almost the color of cherry wood. "And if you hope that I get better, why don't you get over yourself? Get over the idea that you could ever be right. That's never going to happen by the way. So come here and give me the coffee and the bagel that you're hiding in that bag behind your back."

"What about a kiss?"

"Yes, you can have one of those too," she says, smiling.

Valdez steps forward and hands Charlotte the paper bag. She happily accepts. Then he hands her the coffee cup. She puts it on the table next to the bed. Valdez reaches into his pocket and pulls out two sugar packets and two cream cups, and she hands them to her too. Charlotte opens the lid of her coffee and hands it to Valdez. She puts the sugar and cream in the coffee. Valdez hands her a plastic-wrapped toothpick, which she uses to stir the coffee. She gives him her trash in exchange for her lid back, but she sets it on the table, preferring to hold the coffee under her chin. She closes her eyes to take the aroma in, which fills the room. It fights the antiseptic smell.

Charlotte tells him, "Thank you."

Valdez sips his coffee, sans cream or sugar. "I see you awake over there. I'm sorry for waking you up."

Charlotte shifts her gaze to look at Barbara, who has one eye open peeking at them.

"You didn't wake me up," Barbara says. "I needed to get... what time is it?"

"Morning time," Valdez says.

Charlotte swats at him, telling him to be nice. "It's just before eight. You slept here all night, and I couldn't bear waking you up—you looked so peaceful."

Rising in the chair, Barbara checks her watch and wipes her mouth. "I'm sorry; I didn't mean to impose on you." Her fingers find the zipper marks and trace them to her ear. She's embarrassed.

Charlotte throws her covers off her legs, her left knee wrapped in discolored gauze. "You're not imposing. You looked like you needed the sleep."

Valdez looks down at his wife. "But you tell me I'm imposing all the time."

Charlotte raises an eyebrow. "No, I tell you you're wearing out your welcome and that I want you to go home. That's different."

"Yeah, but by using the word imposing."

Charlotte rolls her eyes and shoos him away. "So, I say imposing," she says, "I'm trying to be nice to our guest, but I guess you can't do that. See why I make you leave?"

Barbara grins. "You two are cute."

"I look like shit, and he's ugly," Charlotte says to Barbara. "But I understand what you mean."

"She's not much of a morning person," Valdez tells Barbara, then back at his wife, "I'm not ugly, it's Irish."

Looking up at him, nodding and smiling, Charlotte says, "Same thing. The good thing about being in here is I never have to go to sleep. They won't let me. They come in here every couple of hours to check this and that. So, I'm never cranky in the morning."

Valdez says, "Yeah, but have you been with yourself when you wake up from a nap?"

Tears appear on her face, and her skin grows red and bright. He's gone too far.

"Barbara came here last night to meet you," Charlotte forces her cheeks back into a plastered practiced smile.

"Jamie told me I could find you here," Barbara says. She sits up in the chair, unfolds her legs, and drops the pillow to the side. "I wanted to come to meet you, ask you a couple of questions about what's going on, but you weren't here."

"She sent me away," Valdez says.

Barbara turns her attention to Charlotte. "So she said."

Charlotte commands Valdez to sit, stay awhile. "We got to talking last night. I like her. She's nice."

Valdez doesn't sit. He crosses his arms. "What did you two talk about?"

118

"We have a lot in common," Charlotte says. "We talked about you; we talked about life. I don't know. I guess being cooped up in here, I forget about the world out there. I mean you come; you sit with me. The family comes, and they sit with me. My friends come, and they sit with me, but they all are focused on me. It was nice to talk to someone new who wasn't focused on me, you know?"

Valdez thinks he does; he props himself against the wall, putting his left foot on the wall, and sips his coffee.

"So, we talked about life and death. About her husband." Charlotte rolls through her words. "She lost a husband—oh, I hope you don't mind me telling him."

Barbara shakes her head. "No, it's fine. It's not like it's a secret." She tells Valdez, "His name was Stanley."

Charlotte, nodding, says, "Lost him to cancer a couple of years ago. Did you know she dated Jamison?"

"I did," Valdez says and takes another sip of the coffee.

Barbara says, "It wasn't dating. We went out a few times."

"The kids call that dating," Charlotte says. "Says her daughter set them up. Isn't that funny?" She turns to Barbara. "Guess if you two started fucking then it would be called something more than dating."

Barbara blushes, crossing her legs, and tugs at her jacket. "We didn't get along—"

"—he's too full of himself," Charlotte says. "Besides, I've heard he just tries to get in your pants."

"Agreed," Valdez says.

Charlotte quickly turns to him. "He's tried to get in your pants?"

Valdez rubs his neck and shakes his head. Barbara's quiet for a moment, looking from Charlotte to Valdez. Charlotte's embarrassed Barbara, and she appears to be embarrassed about falling asleep in the chair. Valdez senses the tension in the room. Charlotte's verbal sparring is her way of dealing with stress.

Barbara chooses her words about Jamison carefully. "He is a gentleman. He means well."

Charlotte waves her hand at Barbara and spills some coffee down the front of her chin. She jumps in the bed and wipes the liquid away. "He is all about himself," Barbara says. "But he is cute and supposed to be good in the sack. Or, at least, look good without his clothes on—that's what I've heard."

He says, "He's not that cute. I'm cute."

Charlotte smiles at Valdez. This smile is a real one, something he hasn't seen in months. It gives him hope. Charlotte tells him, "You're Irish."

"That's what I'm saying."

"That's the problem."

CHAPTER 19:

KIRSTEN

KIRSTEN SITS WITH A CIGARETTE BURNING IN THE corner of her mouth, her back slumped, facing the door. Aaron didn't come back. He left her sitting in this chair all night. Left her staring at that door. Lights off and then lights on, the other girls coming and going from the rooms to the living room and back again. Life is happening around her, but none of it matters.

Eddie's mother called and told her he was dead. She told Kirsten the sheriff's deputies had just left the house. On the phone, she cried, screamed, yelled, and cursed God. Then prayed to God and then asked for her to come to her. Be with her. Kirsten told her she couldn't come to her because she didn't have a car. So, Maria cursed her too, telling Kirsten that Eddie was dead because of her, that it was her fault. Told her it was her brother's fault. Blamed her, blamed God, and then blamed herself. Told Kirsten, her boy didn't deserve that. Said she had nothing left and asked Kirsten, "What now?" But when Kirsten couldn't answer, she hung up on Kirsten.

Eddie's dead.

And Aaron's weak.

Her brother has told her that, that Aaron's weak. Her brother said that Aaron's good at playing Follow the Leader but wouldn't survive in this world without him. Course, Kade's said the same thing about her too. She just thought it was her brother's way of playing the macho dude, but maybe he was right. Maybe Kade is right about Aaron.

Kade told her, "Aaron can't give you what you need—can't give you the protection you need."

Kirsten checks her phone now and sees there are messages from Gilliam, an edict, saying that no girl is to leave the apartment. He can't guarantee their safety. They are to continue to work from the apartments, and he'd check in tomorrow, let them know what's going on. The statement goes on, something about a disagreement, leaving her wondering what's going on.

But she knows. Her life is disintegrating around her.

She hasn't heard from her brother since yesterday.

Eddie's dead.

And Aaron knows more.

There's a knock at the door, and Kirsten stubs out the cigarette, half-hoping it's Aaron. Maybe he's back to tell her what happened.

Kirsten crosses the living room and opens the door to find Shawna standing there. Foot stomping a cigarette out with a sandaled foot. Her tone leg twisting her ankle to the left and then to the right on top of the spent butt. Shawna wears short jean shorts and a simple black tank top. A leather bag is slung over her shoulder. Her hair is a dark brown curly mess. Dark sunglasses hide her face, hide her eyes. Shawna tips her chin to her chest to peer at Kirsten over the top of the sunglasses, her eyes revealing that she hasn't slept either. "Kade in there?"

Kirsten shakes her head. "What are you doing here?"

"Looking for Kade." Shawna sticks her hand out, introducing herself, but Kirsten tells her she remembers who she is. "Have you seen him?"

Kirsten leaves Shawna's hand hanging there.

Shawna bites her lips and retracts her hand, peeling off her sunglasses. Her eyes are red and burdened. "Can I come in?"

Kirsten pushes the door open wider. She notices the lime green chair moved from the storage area under the stairs, the cigarettes and the beer bottles.

Aaron is weak; he can't even face her, but he can sit out there all by himself. It makes her feel better to know that he didn't leave her completely.

Shawna steps through the door and drops her purse on the couch. She scans the apartment.

Kirsten shuts the door behind Shawna and throws the lock. "What are you doing here?"

"I'm looking for Kade. He left last night, and I've not heard from him."

"Well, that makes two of us."

"You haven't heard from him?"

"You can check my phone if you want," Kirsten says, holding the phone out at her side.

"No, that's fine, I just figured he might be here, you know, I know you two are close."

"We're twins."

Shawna cocks her head. "You look alike, I mean if you had a dick and short hair—"

"—or he had tits and pussy, yeah, I know what you mean. I've heard that before."

"It's weird," Shawna says, moving through the living room, picking up a bra from the end of the couch and tossing it to the side. "He always said you two were identical, but I don't know, I guess I never really thought about it. You look so much like him—it's wild is all."

"I've heard that."

"You haven't heard from him?" Shawna asks, looking at the two closed bedroom doors. She throws a thumb toward the doors. "He's not in there sleeping with someone else? I mean you can tell me if... I'm a big girl. I don't know what we are, but I know we aren't that committed to each other."

"Kade doesn't sleep with the girls that work here," Kirsten says. "One of the few rules Kade has for himself. Tells me he doesn't shit where he eats. I'll say it's an apartment. He says then he doesn't fuck where he sleeps. He says, 'it's a good way to catch a knife.'" Kirsten pauses. "He's not here, Shawna, what do you want?"

Shawna studies the shelves filled with pictures and mementos placed to soothe prospective voyeurs. Most of these were chosen by Gilliam. He makes the girls hang shit on the walls to make the place appear more than what it is. What it is, is a place to fuck.

Shawna points to the couch. "That safe to sit on?"

"Everything happens in the rooms," Kirsten says, meaning the girls don't have sex on the couch.

Shawna nods and sits on the couch. "I'm worried about him."

"Who?" Kirsten moves from the door. "My brother? You shouldn't worry about him. He's fine."

"Yeah, but you haven't seen what's been happening."

"What's been happening?"

Looking up at Kirsten, Shawna says, "You really live here?"

"It's my apartment."

Shawna rolls her eyes, motions to the apartment, and says, "I mean, not really. It really isn't yours. Gilliam pays for it. You really live like this, do the things Gilliam wants you to?"

"It's my life."

"It doesn't have to be."

"What's it to you?"

"Just, you know," Shawna pauses, "you're... you're his sister. You two look so much alike. He wouldn't let anyone tell him what to do, or who to fuck."

"You don't know my brother," she says. "And you don't know me. You don't know what you're talking about. You don't know what we've been through or not been through."

Kade's all Kirsten's ever had.

Shawna sucks on her lower lip. "You two are pretty close?" As much a statement as a question.

Kirsten tells Shawna they are and had to be since they were kids. "Growing up, we only had each other."

Shawna rocks back and forth on the couch.

Kirsten asks her, "What's going on?"

"I'm not sure." She tells Kirsten about Kade's meeting with Mikey.

"He say anything else about anyone or anything?"

Shawna studies Kirsten, unsure if she's trustworthy. "No," she shakes her head. "Who would he have mentioned?"

Kirsten thinks about the message Eddie left. "Never mind, don't worry about it."

"How'd he grow up?" Shawna asks. "Like, how'd he get the way he is? He scares me you know. Sometimes I look at him, and there's no one there. You know, in his eyes. Sometimes I look, and they're glazed over. Like he's a machine or something. Then I look over, and he's back. But he's not himself, you know? Like there's something there that wants to do me harm, something not good, and then there are the other times when he's him. What made him like that?"

"I don't talk about the past," Kirsten says. "It's easier that way." She doesn't think about it either.

Shawna tries to tease information out of Kirsten. "Something did happen, then?"

"Talking about it is pretty worthless, doesn't change what happened. There's no use bringing it all up."

Shawna nods, stands. "I guess I'll go. I see you don't want me here."

"It's... I want my brother," Kirsten says. "I don't want you."

Shawna doesn't take offense to Kirsten's comment. "I'll be going," she reaches for her purse. "I'm sorry I came here. I'm worried about him, you know? I thought... I don't know what I thought. I'll go."

Kirsten sighs. "Wait. You have a car?"

Shawna tells Kirsten she does.

"Can you take me someplace?"

CHAPTER 20

BARBARA

VALDEZ ASKS BARBARA IF SHE WOULD LIKE SOME
coffee. It's his way of getting her out of his wife's hospital room.

"Only if you're buying."

Valdez shrugs and tells her if it gets her out of Charlotte's room he's buying. He doesn't need them conspiring anymore against him. Charlotte tells Barbara to ignore him, that he can wait; the girls can discuss things without him. She says how nice it was to meet her, winking. "When you're done with my husband, come back to visit. I think there's something special about you."

That's the first time anyone's told her that since Stanley left her. Barbara tells her she will be back and thanks her for letting her sleep.

"I must have needed it," Barbara says as she leans in for a hug.

Hugging her from the bed, Charlotte says, "Sometimes we need to trust people." She holds the hug, squeezing Barbara.

Valdez and Barbara leave Charlotte's room, Valdez in front, pounding down the hall ahead of her. Silent. Between sips on his coffee, he stops to make small talk with several of the nurses and he is very polite. He introduces Barbara as Charlotte's friend. Although, she's not sure what to make of that or how to take it. The nurses talk to him, not to her, and mention how happy he looks this morning and how good that yellow button-up shirt looks against his skin. All the while, Barbara stands idly by. Dumbfounded, she fell asleep. Not only did she fall asleep, but she slept all night in a stranger's room.

Why did Charlotte let her, a stranger, sleep in her room?

It's embarrassing.

Barbara doesn't remember falling asleep. She only remembers how warm and comfortable, how inviting the room was even if it was a hospital room. But perhaps, the comfortableness had nothing to do with the room and everything to do with the little woman confined to the bed.

Barbara can see something in Valdez that she recognizes in herself, pain. He's in pain, because, like her, he's facing a life without his best friend, and he doesn't know what to do. Then, add in all the baggage that comes with this job, and you have someone that looks like him, who very much resembles what the Highway Patrol wants in their troopers. However, Barbara doesn't get the impression any of that sentiment means anything to him. Jamison said Valdez is a cop's cop. Charlotte said the same thing. She said he's about doing the job. About doing the right thing. Both spoke about his mission to bring justice to those that deserve it, being a voice for the victims. He reminds her of Stanley, and that compassion gives her chills.

Although Valdez doesn't look like Stanley, he is very much the red-faced Irishman, five-ten, whereas Stanley was black and over six feet tall, slim, a marathon runner. Stanley wasn't bulky or full of muscles like Valdez, but lean and long-limbed. She's not sure what aspect of Stanley Valdez represents the most, beyond the compassion; perhaps it's the devotion to his wife. Stanley was always good to her. They trusted each other completely even when they were mad at each other. She detects the same devotion in Valdez and sees how devoted he is to Charlotte—as Charlotte is to him.

Stanley.

Barbara touches the ring on the chain around her neck.

Perhaps, what reminds her of Stanley is the way Valdez carries himself, so sure what he's doing is the right thing; like Elwood Blues, he's *on a mission from God.*

Stanley carried himself that way too. So sure of what he was doing, so sure he was right. So sure God wouldn't lead him astray. *Blues Brothers* was his favorite movie, and his actual brother used to ask Stanley why he liked watching a movie about a couple of white guys pretending to have groove. Stanley would tell him, why wouldn't he like a movie about a bunch of people coming together over music? Didn't matter who they were, what they looked like, or where they came from—Blues brought them together. He'd say, "Wasn't that what Martin Luther King wanted? Us coming together, not celebrating our differences. Celebrate what we have in common." Then, he'd quote Elwood's famous line with a smile on his face, perfect teeth, and lips, saying he's, "on a mission from God."

Now, watching Valdez talking to the nurses about their lives, asking about the people close to them, she glimpses fragments of the real man hidden under all the anguish. He tells them he doesn't want them to feel like it was always about him and asks Susan about her mother's health; Nathan how his baby is doing; Ethel if Lucy was a handful—making a sly joke about *I Love Lucy*, telling her that was the best joke he could come up with; and then asks about Ethel's husband's wood projects. Ethel's husband's name is Steve. Valdez finishes up with the nurses by pointing to Barbara. "That's the lady that fell asleep in Char's room."

Stanley was like that. He always cared more for others than himself.

Barbara remembers her husband's face. She's heard people forget what their dead loved ones used to look like, but that's not been her experience. She remembers him as he was, not how he was at the end, but how he was, day in and day out. In Chicago, when they were newly-weds. On the side of the basketball court, watching their boy play ball. In the driver's seat of the moving truck, on the way out here. At her OHP badge pinning. On stage at his church, hands up, people smiling, beside her in bed; she remembers him as he was, not the end. Cancer made his face look longer than it ever had, ashen and gray stretched out like her son's putty left on the couch cushions. His ears and nose appeared bigger than they were. Like when she saw the photographs of Patrick Swayze before he died of the same type of cancer. That's how they knew it was bad. How they knew Stanley's time had come. Throughout it all, Stanley didn't seem to mind, but Barbara did, she minded a lot. Stanley would tell her how happy he was, how special he was in an upturned tenor, a symptom of his undying humor. "What other preacher gets the supreme opportunity to go meet their boss?"

Stanley died with a smile on his face, his hand in hers.

At the elevators, Valdez punches the button for the ground floor with his knuckle. "Why did you come to the room?"

Barbara shoves her hands in her jacket pockets. "I came to the room to find you." The elevator arrives, the doors open, and they get on the elevator. "But you weren't there." He gives her a sideways glance. "Jamison said you would be there. Said that's where you normally are."

The elevator doors close. "Did he tell you about yesterday's meeting?"

Barbara nods. "He mentioned some things about it."

"What'd he say?"

"That you were angry," she says, trying her best not to answer his questions. "But I had some of my things going on, so I didn't pay much attention to Jamison talking about himself."

Valdez snorts in laughter. "Yeah, he's a bit like that, but I was too harsh on him. He's a good—"

The elevator doors open to reveal Jamison, wearing that gray suit and those dark glasses. She likes to joke with him, call him Poindexter; the glasses with the suit make him look so nerdy. He has a folder under his arm. Jamison blinks a few times; he rubs the back of his head. "Morning?"

Valdez exits the elevator, throwing a thumb back toward Barbara. "She stayed the night," he says and then walks past Jamison, "said you sent her to find me."

Jamison looks confused, repeating the word, "Night?"

Barbara hugs Jamison, holding the hug for longer than either expected. "I fell asleep in his wife's room."

"Asleep?" Jamison asks.

Valdez turns his head. "She slept in the room, in the recliner."

Barbara says, "It wasn't very comfortable."

Jamison repeats, "Recliner."

Barbara lets go of the hug. "Val's going to buy me coffee. He offered. You want something?"

Jamison says he does, commenting that he's hungry and hadn't had breakfast. Valdez tells them to follow him to the lounge.

CHAPTER 21:
VALDEZ

VALDEZ STANDS BEFORE JAMISON IN THE SMALL lounge at the hospital; Jamison in his gray suit, with horn-rimmed glasses and fresh haircut, displaying every bit of time he took to look good, typical. Jamison drops the file on the table without saying a word. Leaving Barbara and Valdez staring at the file for a full minute in silence before he says, "That's Wagoner County's Murder Book for Edgar O'Malley."

Valdez's eyes stay on the file lying on the table as Barbara exclaims, "It's so slim." His thoughts exactly. His murder investigations fill a large three-ring binder and then some. "This thing's nothing."

Jamison sticks his hands in his pockets, relaxing, and speaks to Barbara's comment. "More, a pamphlet, if anything."

Looking at the file, it reminds Valdez of Frankie's file. Valdez had gotten a hold of it after the boy's death. That file looked like this one. It was nothing, too.

For a long moment, no one says anything about the file because there's nothing to say. Everyone leaves it there, Valdez thinking if they ignore the file, it will go away or maybe it will metamorphose into something they can use.

It doesn't because this is reality, and reality doesn't change no matter how hard one wishes it so.

At a vending machine, Jamison slides his credit card into the slot to pay. Chooses some sort of breakfast sandwich that requires the microwave. The machine drops the sandwich into the drawer with a loud *clank* and *thud*. He retrieves the sandwich from the vending machine and crams the sandwich into the microwave.

Valdez promised Barbara he would buy her a cup of coffee, so he puts money in the automatic coffee machine. The machine drops a white Styrofoam cup and starts to fill the cup with hot brown liquid, trickling at first before transforming into a streaming gush then collapsing into a dribble. The machine finishes with a whirring noise and sputtering hot water. Barbara retrieves her cup from the machine and steps aside to a table to fix her coffee with sugar and cream.

While she does that, Valdez picks up the file Jamison put there and flips through it. His fat fingers grip the sides of the file as he reads it, and his cheeks grow red as he processes what little information there is. He flips back a few pages, studying them, and then closes the file and throws it back on the table.

"That's fucking nothing," he says. "Nothing to go on. Nothing."

Behind him, the microwave dings and Jamison retrieves his food. He drags his sandwich from the microwave, still hot and steaming, sets the sandwich on the table next to the file, to let the sandwich cool, and asks, "What'd you expect?"

Valdez doesn't know what he expected. "I expected more than that," he says. "We know who did this. Let me go after Kade. I don't need a file of nothing to tell me what I already know. Kade killed Eddie. That's the only way this makes sense."

Jamison whistles to himself and then apologizes for not eating breakfast and having to eat in front of them. "That's one way to look at it."

"Is there another?"

"Yes," Jamison says, "you could look at it like you want to take the law into your own hands." He takes two big bites of the sandwich. Mouth full, talking while chewing, he mocks Valdez. "What, you think because Major Crimes is going to come down on you anyways you might as well take him out, huh? Is that what you think? I thought you were smarter than that. Yesterday should have ... woken you up to the fact you can't do things like that."

Valdez says, "What do I have to lose?"

Barbara reminds him, "Your wife." Her tone says she agrees more with Jamison than Valdez. The tone causes Valdez to glance at her, and for the first time, he sees her as a cop.

Valdez says, "This file's too small to have any proof of anything. I have all the proof I need. This doesn't have anything. There's nothing here."

Jamison finishes his sandwich, crumpling the wrapper into a ball, and throws the wrapper in the trashcan.

Barbara leans against the side table and sips her coffee. "That's what I was thinking." Her head turns to Jamison, and she continues. "Seriously, that's all they have?"

Jamison rolls his eyes and motions to the file. "It's something." And then looks at Valdez as he picks up the file and waves it in his hands. "That's what the sheriff managed to put together. It's not much. I get that. But it is something. ME's official report will take longer, but the autopsy was done this morning. Eddie was killed with a 9mm round, shot here." He prods a finger against the middle of his forehead.

"I don't need the report to tell me where he was shot," Valdez says. "I saw him. I saw where he was shot. I saw the car. I was there."

Jamison places the file back on the table and patiently like he's teaching a class, says, "Look, I know things got heated in the interview room, but that's a different thing. You were right. Is that what you want to hear? You were right; I'm not a cop, haven't been for a while. I am a cop. I want to be a cop. I want to get justice, if not for anything other than that's what this kid deserved. No one deserves to die like that, alone."

"He wasn't alone," Valdez says, spearing the file with a finger. "Someone killed Eddie. Someone he thought was his friend, someone he thought he was close to, someone that he trusted." He pauses. "That file. Do you know what it is? It's fucking nothing that's what."

"It's what the sheriff has," Jamison says.

Valdez sighs and rotates to face the vending machine, hands on his hips. "You know what this is. It's them thinking it is shithead on shithead, so it's going nowhere."

Barbara says, "Sounds like the sort of investigation the sheriff would run."

"How can this be all there is?" Anger builds inside Valdez.

"Look, I agree with you, but that's what the county has on the murder." Jamison adjusts his sleeves. "I jumped through hoops to get that. Give me some credit here."

"Of course, you want some credit," Valdez says, slapping the side of the vending machine. "Credit—all you ever fucking want is credit." The machine rattles in place. Something falls from the shelf to the drawer.

In the reflection of the machine's glass front, Jamison steps forward and hesitates. "I want you to recognize I'm trying, Dez."

"If this is you trying, then I don't want to see you working hard."

"I'm trying. Do you see how toxic your fucking attitude is?"

Barbara plants the coffee on the table beside her and says, "Stop."

Jamison cocks his head to the side, and Valdez turns around to look at her. He crosses his arms and stares down at her.

Then in a voice sharper and more commanding. "Stop." Her arms, in that leather jacket—too big for her body—motion to both men. "Either you two figure out how to work together, or you consider me out."

"Fine," Valdez says. "I didn't want you here anyway."

Jamison starts to say something, but Barbara holds up her hand. "Do I look like I am done talking?"

Her eyes park on Valdez as she steps closer, nose to his chest, talking down to him, but might as well be talking up to him.

"Listen, don't be a condescending asshole. Jamie asked me to help him with this. I want to help, but I can't if we are trying to rip each other's heads off." She takes a step back, points to herself then at each one of them. "We each bring something to the table."

"Any leads we develop—ones that we can 100 percent prove—will allow Major Crimes to take over the investigation. Meaning, we can make a difference," Jamison says. "I'm giving you a shot."

Valdez motions around Barbara and the file. "That's not much of a shot."

Jamison rolls his eyes and swipes the file to the floor, pages and photographs float through the air. "Fine, be mad at me about that. Be mad at me that this wouldn't have ever happened, and Eddie wouldn't be dead if I had acted before. But this ain't before. That's the past. We can't think about that right now. Maybe later. Maybe never. But right now, I can make up for this. I get why you're mad. You were right to say what you said before, about me not being a cop, but you're going to have to work with me."

Valdez steps to the side of Barbara and sits in one of the chairs at the empty table. His body sinks in the chair; he uses the table to hold himself up. "Frankie Green is Eddie and Eddie is Frankie Green. You see that, right? And if you had acted then, the first time around, this wouldn't be an issue. Eddie would be alive."

Jamison bends at the knees to scoop up the papers on the floor. Then he's up, shaking the papers. "You're right. Is that what you want to hear? You're right, Dez. This is a fucking disgrace." Fistful of paper in his face.

"We can do better. Look, if I listened to you the first time around, Kade would be in prison, and the Green fucking Mafia wouldn't be a thing. We could have dismantled the whole damn thing, but that didn't happen. We can't change the past."

No, instead, Valdez found out about Frankie Green's murder, and it felt like he killed him. Now, he feels like he did the same thing to Eddie.

Barbara steps forward, nodding. She agrees with Jamison but sits next to Valdez. She places the coffee on the table. "There are some things I don't like about the Highway Patrol. But I'm going to tell you, when I get a hold of Kade, there are some things from the past that I'll be grateful still exist."

Suppressing his feelings, Valdez crosses his arms. "Kade's not going to get away with this."

"He won't," Jamison says. "That's why I brought Barbs in to help us. She's good at her job. Trust her, Dez. You have to trust someone at some point. I asked her to help because Kade took her car, and she can put him in the area at the time of the crime, and because she's not me."

"Trust her?" Valdez says, pointing at Barbara. "I don't know her. Why the fuck do I care about anything having to do with her? So what? So what if she can put Kade there? He took her car."

Barbara dips her chin. "He embarrassed the shit out of me," she says in a quiet voice. "He stole my car. I'll never live that down." She twists in the seat, leans to the side, and withdraws a piece of paper from her back pocket: a photograph. She slams it on the table. "But I'm going to make him pay."

"What is that?" Valdez asks, not looking at the picture.

Barbara turns to Jamison as he puts his hands flat on the table to lean over and look at the photograph. He tells Valdez, "It's a gun."

Valdez's eyebrow rises. "A gun? What are you doing with a picture of a gun?"

Jamison says, "Looks like a 9mm. Can see it written on the frame."

Barbara crosses her arms. "I get that there's some history between you two. I'd have to be blind to not see it. You two had a falling out and never got over whatever it was. Jamie asked me to be here. I talked to your wife. She told me a little bit about what happened, so we have to figure out a way to make this work. But I'm going to find Kade, and I'm going to arrest him."

Valdez shudders, jostling his head. "Don't bring Charlotte into this."

Barbara picks up her coffee and takes a sip. "Charlotte knows what Eddie meant to you. She knows what you're going through right now. Eddie deserves better. That's what I get from you. That's what I got from Jamie. That's what you think. Eddie deserved better from you. Jamison's giving you a chance."

"I thought we were on board," Jamison says, "Dez, we talked about this."

"You told me a story about your mother, and you promised me I'd be able to go after Kade. We can't go after anyone with files like that," Valdez says.

Jamison nods and removes a seat from the table; he turns it around and straddles the seat. "I promised that we could bring a whole helluva lot of attention and noise to this," he says. "We can; we just have to prove it. She's here to make sure we get him."

"It's not like we don't know who killed him," Valdez says. "That part isn't hard to figure out."

Before Valdez can say anything more, Jamison gestures to the room. "Who killed him? Can you prove it?"

"You know Kade killed him."

"I may know it, but can you prove it?" Jamison taunts him. Valdez dips his chin under the burden of the challenge. "Prove it was him, and I'll get the power of heaven behind us and bring it down upon his head. How are you going to prove it?"

Barbara asks, "Yeah, how are you going to prove it?"

"I know he did it," Valdez says. "That's enough."

"Enough for who?" Barbara asks. "Not for a court. Do you want to take the law into your own hands? What's that going to do for Eddie? What's that going to do for his mother? For anyone? For Charlotte?"

"Don't talk to me about Charlotte," Valdez tells her again. It bugs him that she keeps hammering on it.

Barbara puts her hand on the paper on the table and taps it with the tip of her finger. "This is the gun. This gun right here. This is the gun recovered from my passenger seat." Barbara is grinning now. "Well, under my seat. This will help you prove it."

"No way," Valdez says, "I don't fucking believe it."

Jamison turns to her. "From where?"

"My car," she says. "I recovered the gun after I recovered the car. I took a photograph of it that night. The gun's in our property room."

"No fucking way," Valdez says. "No way that's the gun."

"So Val, are you going to be able to work with him because we can solve this thing? You're going to need to pull your head out of your ass and start acting like an adult."

"I thought your husband was a preacher," Valdez says.

"He was," Barbara says. "He taught me how to cuss when it was righteous."

CHAPTER 22:

KADE

MIKEY CALLS SOMETIME AROUND TEN AND TELLS
Kade to meet him at his bar before it opens. He says something
about him not needing trouble with customers being around, that he's
keeping up appearances.

Aaron drives him in his beaten-down, red pickup truck to the bar.
It isn't far, and once there, they park in the shopping center parking lot.
The place is deserted during the day. Retailers and restaurants have fled
from this intersection. What's left are dollar stores, small businesses, and
a second-hand clothing shop, aka Shitsville, USA. And Mikey's bar is a
hole in the wall, sandwiched between the second-hand clothing shop
and some shitty insurance agent under a dentist who has the top floor.

They enter the bar. The house lights are on full, showing how ugly
the place is, how dirty, how much of a dive bar it is. Mikey's behind the
U-shaped bar, wearing a black button-up shirt, the color faded, collar
disheveled, wrinkled, with blue jeans. He leans against the bar, his arm
under his chin, a gun sitting in front of him, and a nonalcoholic beer.
He slicks his hair back. His face is stone. Besides Mikey, there are a lot
of people in the bar. Billy's at a booth, looking like a younger version
of the *World's Most Interesting Man*, and near him, there are several of
Billy's men scattered and standing throughout the bar each in various
positions: Paul Anders, Frances Gillespie, Larry Marlow, and Christopher
Burkhalter. And Billy's girls are here too, Renee Deal and LuAnn "Lou"
Franks. They work part-time for Mikey as cocktail waitresses and bar-
tenders. When Billy's having a meeting, they are his bodyguards. Keep
Billy safe without making things too obvious with opposing parties. For

Billy, everything has a role. Everything in a box. Everything with a place. Kade shudders and lets the door close behind him. The place darkens some. Aaron fans out to the side next to the pool table.

Kade asks Mikey for a beer, holding up two fingers.

Mikey reaches under the counter and brings up two beers. Kade walks to the bar, picks up one beer, takes a sip, and then picks up the second beer and passes it to Aaron. He doesn't drink his.

Billy smacks his lips and nods toward Kade. "Others are coming," he says. "Mitchell and Bonnie will be here in a little bit. Renee's sister Adele is coming too. So, say what you have to say. My time is short, but know Peter's gone too far." He means Gilliam—Peter is his first name.

Gilliam told Kade once his parents liked a book written by some British dude that was the anti-James Bond. They told him that they liked one of the characters so much that's how he got his name. Later, Kade read the book and had two questions for Gilliam: one, he wondered how Gilliam felt being named after a sidekick, and two, he asked him how he felt when they made his namesake gay for the movie.

Kade moves to the booth. "Forming a war party then?" He knows better than to sit. He'll wait for Billy to offer the seat at the booth.

Billy bows his head. "Something like that," he says. "Not like there's going to be much of a war. Carlos is supposed to be coming too, bringing a rep for the North Tulsa crews. We want to represent all sides—funny how they can agree on some things. They're sending one guy. Then again, we're dumb shit white people. No need to waste everyone else's time. He said something about needing to know what's about to happen. Unfortunately, Carlos said Santiago sided with Peter. So East Tulsa might be a problem."

"So, you're circling the wagons; this war shit's real. You know the Ambassador's not going to like a war in the streets. He doesn't like things like war. It upset his business."

"The Ambassador is an old man and only runs Tulsa in name. He may broker peace deals between different groups, but he doesn't have the muscle to enforce his rules." Billy pounds the tabletop with a fist. "He don't run the city. No one owns this city. But that will change. I will."

Kade points his beer bottle at Billy. "Like to see you say that to his face." Then, testing him, he asks, "Why don't you go tell that to the police, tell it to the City?"

Billy bites his lower lip, acknowledging. "Yeah, well the City will learn who's who soon enough. The Ambassador will have to accept what's new, you know? Things change. People go to jail and others step up to take charge. That's all I'm doing. Peter wants to make a mess of things. "

"Things change."

Billy motions to the seat. "Sit." Kade sits as Billy says, "I'm glad we could have this meeting. Mikey said you wanted to talk about some things." He turns toward Aaron, "I saw you here yesterday."

Aaron nods.

Billy continues, "Choosing sides, huh?" Then he looks back to Kade, leaning into the conversation, talking about how things are going. "Guess my meeting with Peter didn't go to his liking, and he's got a big mouth. From what I hear, he's called his banners. I hear a few have answered. A few haven't. And some aren't choosing sides, which means they're choosing sides. Heard the old fucker Bronson said he's sitting this one out. He's telling people he's too old, just likes to steal shit, doesn't matter who's buying it. Louie said he would have to wait and see. Said he wants to move product. The others, I don't know. Like I said, I heard Santiago made his decision. I told you this. But the others, they aren't anything. But you know, I have to take them into account because a crew at the wrong place at the wrong time can still throw a kink in things."

"If you look at it from the other side, they could be in the right place at the right time, so to speak," Kade says. "Depends on how things shake out." He adds, "Gilliam's nothing."

"He's enough to cause me problems. With Vanderbilt going to jail, Tulsa's up for the taking. Sure, his people won't like it, but fuck them. Gilliam must be thinking, oh Billy's focused on this thing over here." Uses his hands to illustrate his point. "Then I'll come over here, make things happen. Might have Mikey take care of him, but what would that say about me." Billy pauses, rotating his body in the seat. "Mikey what would that say about me?"

From behind the bar, Mikey says, "Weak."

Billy twists back to Kade. "Shows weakness, see, and that's something I can't have. Now's not a good time for war, but I guess war can be like that. Shit, you think those fuckers at Pearl Harbor knew what was going to happen?"

"The Japanese did," Kade says.

Billy stares hard at Kade and then requests a beer from Mikey. "And not any of that nonalcoholic shit." Then he's back talking to Kade. "I don't know why he's always drinking that stuff. Like what's the point? You drink to get fucked up. He says he drinks for taste. Have you had the nonalcoholic shit? Who wants to taste shitty beer?"

Mikey brings a bottle to the table. "My kid brother got me into it."

"His brother doesn't drink, so he's got him into not drinking," Billy says, explaining to Kade. "You know who his brother is? A cop, go fucking figure. You ever hear about his daddy? What your daddy think about what you do?"

Mikey doesn't answer. He turns his back on Billy.

Billy says, "Says he hasn't seen his father in seven fucking years. I tell him he's on the TV all the damn time. He's running for mayor, saying he did such a good job being police chief, why not let him run the city—fuck—or the state. Heard the mayor shit was just preamble for governor."

Kade heard the stories about Mikey's family.

"River and Joaquin Rio will go to Gilliam. They're his brother's protectors," Kade says. "I can't stand those two. But you know who he's not going to have." Kade pauses and then touches his thumbs to his chest. "Me."

"So you say," Billy says. "So you say."

Kade puts his bottle on the table and lays his hands out flat, to lay it all out. "I can end this."

Billy takes a long drink, letting the mood settle some, the tension release and relax. "Can you?"

"End it before it starts, but I want you to know that first," Kade says. He takes a drink. "I want you to know what I'm offering before things get too far because, if you're not interested, then we'll be having a wholly different conversation."

"Because you don't do nothing for free?"

"Just so we are clear, what's happening here?"

Billy clasps his hands together. "We're choosing sides; that's what's happening here," he says. "I know what side I've chosen. I bet your side is something like that. But this isn't kickball; this isn't the last man standing off to the side feeling sorry. Fuck that. This is going to be war. Then this war will spread because, well, shit's on the move, and it can't be stopped, so I fight two fronts."

"—But I'm saying you don't have to—"

Billy holds up his hand. "Look, I get what you are offering. I get what you're saying. I don't have to fight two fronts, but you were honest about what you're offering, so I'm being honest with how things stand. If we have a war, the fucking city will rip itself apart, and I want you to know that."

Kade nods and says, "I know it."

Billy brings his hands together on the table, crossing his fingers. "Good, I'm glad we got that out there." He pauses, licking his lips. "So, you're offering to do what, kill Gilliam? That could happen. But then again, Gilliam don't think in straight lines. So, I'm going to have to think about your offer. Might mean you need to do something for me. Show your loyalty and all that shit; do something that I know you wouldn't do if you were still his lapdog—why would you do it? You'd have a choice."

"You don't know me very well," Kade says.

"You'd have a choice." Billy closes the distance. "What I'm saying is you don't have a choice right now because I'm not letting you fucking leave here alive. Why would I do that? Like who would do that? You're like that general that rides out in the middle of the field to parlay—No! Fuck that! You're the fucker that goes in the besieged castle to talk shit over. Do it under a white flag and all that." Billy showing off his history knowledge the way some guys talk about sports. "Well, I'd be fucking stupid not to cut your head off with my sword when I have the chance. I'm in a position of strength. Besieging me will take months. But ... if you can kill the general. Well then call it a fine fucking day, have a feast, and get on with watching the walls."

Kade wants to say something, but Billy holds up one finger from his crossed fingers.

"But you come to me, you say, 'Hey I don't want war; I can end this for you.' Now, that gets my attention. How could it not? I don't want this war, either. I've got other shit going on, and here you are like the angels have fucking delivered you right to me. Hark, the herald of good fucking news. So, what should I do? Waste this opportunity to end this before it starts? Do I trust you? Leave myself open? No, removing you from the board is the smartest play."

Silence sits over the table for a moment.

Kade finishes off his beer, looking at Billy as he does it, and then sets the bottle on the table, empty. "You set Gilliam up."

That gets Billy's attention. He tries to hide the sly smile like he doesn't know what Kade's talking about, but Kade knows Billy knows what he's talking about. He's done a lot of thinking on this matter, and after talking with Aaron, he knows what happened.

"Whatever do you mean?" Billy plays stupid, but the guy can barely contain himself.

"I mean, with Eddie, you set him up."

"How would I have done that?" Billy asks. "Why would I even do that?"

"Because you're taking over, and you need the peace of mind, and Gilliam doesn't bring anyone peace of mind."

"Okay, okay, I can get on with that, but that's the why. Tell me how."

"How?" Kade says, shrugging. "Could be many ways. Look, I know you got people in the department. Maybe you put a call into one of those people, tell that guy—cuz cops are mostly guys so it's a guy—to send the kid in? But how would they know Eddie'd be accepted in Gilliam's crew? How do you put Eddie in with someone like me? So no, that's not how you did it, but it's a way."

"Go on."

"So how would you do it? You call the guy up, you say, 'Hey anyone working anything on Gilliam?' You'd come out and ask the question just like that. Your guy says something like, 'Of course, they fucking are, it's Gilliam,' and you say, 'Great, tell me who.'"

"That's a way, but how does that benefit me?"

"Couple of ways," Kade says. "Way I see it, this guy you have, and mind you, I know he's not some low-level guy."

"So, he has rank?" Billy says. "He has a rank."

"Rank, and he's smart, too," Kade says. "Dirty even. He knows how to do this. You and him have done this type of thing before. I've been here enough and listened to Gilliam talking to you to know that you're smart. You'd have this guy of rank, possibly even directing the investigation. You drop hints on anyone who might have a link to Gilliam that'd get in with Gilliam. So, when the kid gets arrested, you see the opportunity. You tell the guy of rank to say hey this kid might flip. If he doesn't, it doesn't hurt you. You know the kid's loyal. If the kid flips, then you know that you're going to insulate yourself from the top, fuck Gilliam. So that's what happened."

"Why'd I tell Gilliam the kid was dirty?"

"Gilliam's too hard to control. You let this card sit for a while. You wait. The guy of rank calls you if the police get too close to you. If everything stays with Gilliam, then Gilliam's the only one that goes down. They didn't make a move on Gilliam, took too long, whatever, so you made your move."

Billy likes what Kade said. His intelligent eyes watch him as he finishes his beer bottle. "I'll consider your offer, but in the meantime, prove your worth. Go kill the kid's sister and mother, and we'll call that Good Faith."

CHAPTER 23:

VALDEZ

VALDEZ TELLS JAMISON AND BARBARA, "I HAVE TO go talk to Eddie's mom. I owe her that much."

Neither one of them argues.

Barbara tells Valdez, "I'll come with you."

He knew she would.

Jamison, determined and like-minded about getting to it, picks up Barbara's picture of the gun and says, "I'll see what I can do about fingerprints."

Valdez still can't believe Barbara found the gun in her car. There's no way Kade was stupid enough to leave it behind in the car, but it's there so it has to be true.

Then the phone call comes as he's leaving the hospital. Tom Cooper calling him on his work phone, telling Valdez there was a girl at the station waiting for him. So, Valdez holds up a finger to tell Barbara to hang on a minute. Barbara stops and stands by patiently. He stops walking through the halls and puts that finger in his ear.

"Who was it?'

"What am I, your secretary? I don't know who it was... *a girl*."

"What she look like?"

"I told you a girl," Coop says, "What that don't do it for you? Want to know if she had tits on her? She was alright, blonde thing, skinny, looked like she might be a bit rough. You like it rough?"

Valdez sighs. "Did she leave a name?"

"No," Coop says. "You didn't answer the question. You like it rough? Like them to look rough? I bet you do."

Valdez ignores him. "She still there?"

"No," Coop says. "What am I supposed to do? Tell her you will be right back, fuck that, I haven't seen you all morning. I told her that too. She was here though, waited awhile. I told her I guess he's taking his sweet time coming in—so she left."

Valdez says, "I'm working on something, you know, something you don't do, it's called a case."

"I work cases."

"Yeah, well get off mine."

"What's your problem?" Coop asks. "First, I hear that you were unhappy with how I handled your idiotic kid's call-in. Me not calling you. No one knows where you are half the time, and the other half the time, you're in the hospital. So, I took your kid's call. It's my fault the guy couldn't keep from getting killed for two fucking hours while I worked on finding where you're at? That's my fault? Now, I'm hearing from up yonder you're upset with me because I didn't jump to like a house..." He breaks off. "Listen, you complain, and I adjust. So, I'm calling you, now. That not good enough for you?"

"She leave a number?" Valdez shakes his head.

"Oh, no, we're not doing that. You dodged one question; I'm not letting you dodge this one."

Valdez dodges the question. "She leave a name?"

"You going to continue to act like I'm not talking to you."

"I know you're talking to me. I'm just not going to answer you while you're acting like a jackass."

"Man, you're too uptight," Coop tells him. "You need to loosen up."

"Coop, I don't have the patience for this. She leave a name or number or not?"

"No, she said she'd be back."

"She tell you what it was about?"

"People don't tell me nothing," Coop says. "Like your kid, he didn't tell me he was compromised. Hell, had he done that, I'd have scooped him up, you know? He didn't say that. Said he needed to talk to you. Pass on a message. So, you know what, next time you set up a code you might let a sergeant know. I didn't know that's what he was saying. I didn't know he needed out," Cooper adds, sounding like he has to defend himself. "I'm calling you now 'cause they told me I had to."

"Who told you?"

"You know what; you aren't answering my questions, so I'm not answering yours now."

"Can you tell me anything about the girl?"

"She had another girl with her. That help?"

"No," Valdez replies. "Anything else?"

"No, she was cute though," Coop says. "She didn't leave a name, and she didn't feel comfortable giving me a number. She said it was because I'm a cop ... like she can't trust a cop."

"You can't."

"Yeah well, she didn't want cops having her number. She said she knew how to get a hold of you. Guess she'll try you later. That help you any in figuring out who it was?"

"No," Valdez says.

"Didn't think so, but then you had to go on and make me give you a play-by-play like it would have made a damn difference. She was here. I told you. I've done my part."

"Gone real far out of your way," Valdez says.

"Screw you," Coop says. "I'd say go fuck yourself, but you might take that as an order. Then I'd have to take you not doing so as insubordination, so I figure I'd say that."

"Real big of you," Valdez says. "You done?"

Coop laughs into the phone. "I'm done. Seriously though, I didn't know about the kid's code, and the girl wouldn't leave anything."

"I appreciate the call."

Coop hangs up without saying anything else.

Valdez tells Barbara, "That was Cooper calling to say some girl was waiting at the office for me."

"She still there? Do we need to put off what we're doing and go talk to her?" She asks like they're partners now.

Valdez guesses in a way they are, but it doesn't sound right, them being partners.

He shakes his head and says, "No, she left, wouldn't give Cooper anything that would help us get in contact with her. I guess we'll focus on what we got to do."

———

IN THE CAR with Valdez driving, Barbara asks him if he guessed who the girl might have been.

Valdez says, "I do."

Barbara asks him who.

But Valdez doesn't say. He doesn't want to ruin the surprise.

So, she sits in silence and then, after a few streets, Barbara guesses at his thoughts. "What if it was the sister?"

"Whose sister?"

"She was there for you. He told her about you."

Valdez says, "Eddie's sister wouldn't come to me."

Barbara chortles, "You're dense—I'm not talking about Eddie. I'm talking about Kade's sister—what'd you say her name was?"

"Kirsten," Valdez says. He does think it was the sister and lover, but he doesn't know who she would have been with. "Not sure how she would have known anything about me."

"Eddie might have talked about you," Barbara says. "Might be Eddie told her to come to talk with you."

"That'd be stupid."

"Could be how they found out, you know?" Barbara's mind rolls with the thought. "Maybe this... what'd you say... Kirsten..." She says the name like it doesn't sound right. "...this Kirsten told her brother. Finked on your boy."

"Finked?"

"I'm black; I get to use that one."

Valdez turns his head from the road to her. "Finked? That's what you're going to go with?" He turns back to the road.

Barbara nods, going on like he didn't interrupt. "I see it like this. Kirsten finds out about Eddie. That's where the card came from—the one on the window. She finds out, she feels betrayed, and she goes to her brother. He loses it, thinks the best way to go about dealing with this is by killing the kid and giving you the middle finger."

"If that's the case, how'd the kid know he was compromised?"

Barbara is silent for a minute. "I don't know."

"Because the kid knew. That's what Cooper said."

"I don't know," she says.

"That's right, we don't. We don't have enough information. I hope his mother will tell us something."

Then quietly, Barbara says, "It could have played like this. His mother put the card in his bag or something. You know, like as a reminder to be a good kid, and this Kirsten found it and did all those other things?"

"Does sound plausible," he says. "But we won't know, so there's no sense thinking on it. We need more."

Barbara shakes her head. Disagrees. "That's what police work is." She uses her arms, straight, to lift herself in the passenger seat. She folds a foot underneath her, sitting up higher. "For me, at least, that's what it is. I take what I know. I start trying to work it, like a puzzle, but you know, I don't have all the pieces, so some things are guesswork. A new piece gets revealed, and I add it to the puzzle. Like a computer game when the map is all clouded out and as you move around, it reveals things. So, things change, and you work those things in and see what you come up with. If you came up with what you had before, great, you work that. But if you don't then great you work that."

"I know what *you're* saying." Valdez's voice betrays his annoyance. "But what I'm saying is the kid's dead. We know who did it. We need to figure out how it happened, but we don't need to figure out how he got compromised, not yet, that will come, though."

"You sure about that?" Barbara places a hand on his arm, voice all concern. "I mean, what if it doesn't come, how are you going to handle that?"

"I'm going to find out," he says, softening. "That's what I'm saying. I'm going to find out, just doesn't mean I want to sit here thinking about it while we don't know and I'm going to find out anyway."

"I get it." She removes her hand and looks out the window. "You think Eddie knew it was going to happen? Like, when he was driving out there, you think he knew what was coming? Think he went out there anyway, like in *A Tale of Two Cities*? In the end, the guy knows he's going to die, but still decides to go out there. Even could have stopped it, tell the truth, avoided it, but goes out there anyways—you think he did that?"

"Hard question, easy answer," Valdez says, "When I first met the kid, he was that, a kid, nothing—"

"—and?"

"—and the man he became." Valdez nods his head. "Yeah, he would have because that's what needed to be done. He was a good kid. Got down on himself at times, didn't have anyone to show him any different. No dad, no male figure to look up to, just a mom who works two jobs to put food on the table. So yeah, I think he would have. I think he would

have done it to keep his cover. Done it for me. He was a brave kid. Good kid. A better man."

Barbara's quiet for a moment. His answer satisfies something inside her. "You're taking his death hard, aren't you? Like you think it's your fault?"

"You wouldn't understand."

But looking at him now, Barbara says, "No, but I'm starting to."

CHAPTER 24:

KADE

BILLY TELLS KADE HE'S SENDING MARLOW WITH
him. "Marlow will drive to make sure you do what you need to do.
If you can't or won't or don't—it doesn't matter to me which—Marlow's
going to put a bullet in your forehead. Then he'll bring your body back
to me so I can mount you on the wall. Give me a trophy."

All Kade has to say about this is, "Aaron drives," putting it out there
like a challenge.

Billy shoots him down. "Well, Marlow's driving today."

Kade concedes. "Sure, whatever, it's not like I'll have a choice anyways."

Billy savors his agreement and claps his hands together. "Good, we'll
keep Aaron until this thing's done."

"Like a hostage?" Kade doesn't like that part, but that's the plan
and has been the whole time... Aaron's idea. He knew it might happen,
but still.

Billy corrects and says, "More like a ward. Like a way to make sure
you do what needs to be done." He uses his history lingo again like people
use sports metaphors. It's stupid, but what's Kade going to do about
it. Nothing.

Even though this is part of his plan, Kade knows from Aaron's face
that he doesn't like the agreement. Kade walks over to *his friend*, puts his
hand on Aaron's shoulder, and whispers in his ear.

Billy yells over at them, "Hey, this is what happens when you play
with the big dogs. No one fucking cares what a little dog thinks or likes
or doesn't like—little dogs don't fucking matter."

Kade pats Aaron on the shoulder and tells him not to worry about it, doing the act. He tells him he'll be back and then turns back to Billy, looking over at him then over at Marlow. "Got a gun I can use?"

Billy throws his head to Marlow. "Marlow will get it—Marlow get the man a gun."

————

IN ARRON'S TRUCK on the way over to the house, Marlow's driving and telling Kade how he'd do it. He's saying she'd open the door, meaning the mom, and he would blow her head off.

Marlow's idiotic. Worse than stupid. Kade's had enough of this, listening to him drone on since leaving Mikey's bar.

Kade asks what Marlow would do about the sister?

Marlow says he'd blow her head off too.

"What if she isn't home?"

"Then I'd wait."

"What if she was upstairs, a gunshot might scare her."

"Then I'd go upstairs."

Kade says, "And be around when the cops showed up?"

"Well, then how the fuck would you do it?"

Kade says, "First, get them in the same room."

Marlow nods like he likes that.

Kade says he'd get the girl to come down. That might tip the mom, but he'd put it to them this way. He would say he wanted to talk to them both. Say how sorry he was about Eddie being dead. Tell them both how sorry he is—that might work.

Kade would be saying all of it while holding the gun Marlow gave him. A little 38 snub nose revolver, barely enough bullets to get the job done. Silver, tarnished, no serial number, nothing but a tool for a job.

Marlow says, "Yeah well that's a lot of talking for something that don't need nothing more than two bullets."

Marlow parks down the street. Kade gets out of the truck and walks up to the house. At the front door, the kid's mom opens the door. She's a mess with makeup running down her face, hair frazzled, and splotchy skin. Still, she looks put together in her black dress with lace and shit, poised, even if her world's coming apart. *Mourning.* The word sits over the conversation. That's how she describes herself at the door: "I'm in mourning. What are you doing here?" Then, she tells him to get lost, saying she doesn't want him here. She doesn't like him.

He tells her he wanted to come to check on her.

Eddie's mom accepts his statement and invites him in, pushing the door open, allowing him into the house. She tells him to sit on the couch and asks if he wants tea.

Eddie's mom goes into the kitchen to get him some tea. He could get up right now, put an end to this act, put the gun to the back of her head, pull the trigger. That's something he could do. But something in him tells him not to. Says he can't. Sure, he can kill a kid like Eddie, who did something, but Eddie's mom did nothing.

The gun's in the small of his back, like when he did Eddie. Like on the drive out there. His mind tugs at him, wanting to go back to that night. There's something about killing that makes him think about killing. Maybe the ghosts might be trying to tell him something; he's not sure.

Doesn't matter.

There's whiskey, and that's good.

Kade watches the woman in the kitchen, listening to her mutter prayers to herself, all in Spanish. Nothing he understands, except for *Dio*—he knows that's God. Does she know he killed Eddie, and if she does, why did she let him in the house? She moves about the kitchen, slowly, like someone who's lost everything. In a way, she has. She's wearing that nice black dress with white pearls. The pearls make him think about Bruce Wayne's parents. Batman's mom wore pearls like that when she died. He chastises himself for thinking about comic book shit. That's kid shit—this is real life.

The mother comes back into the room, carrying a tray with tea. "Hot tea. Hope you like green tea."

Something in her voice puts him on edge, but Kade plays along. Smiles even.

The woman looks a bit better. Something changed in her in the kitchen. She found some strength somewhere. Maybe she found God's grace or something. That's what all that praying was for, God's grace. That's something he's never going to have. Knowing that makes things like this easier.

She sets the tray down on the low coffee table. The tray's got a pot, two cups on saucers, a plate with some lemon wedges and cakes, and a very large knife. With the tray down, she pats at her dress and sits, taking

the seat across from him, plastic crinkling under her. "He liked you, you know," she says. "Always looked up to you."

Brown eyes stare at him—there's something behind them.

Kade tries to ignore that look. "He liked my sister more. They had a connection. She says she was in love with him." Aware of how his voice sounds, coming out too smooth, too accepting—no remorse, no sadness—his act.

But she's performing an act too, feigning a welcoming attitude. She tilts her head to the side. Shakes it as if she's saying "No, that's not right." She pours the green tea into a cup that's sitting on a saucer: fine China, white, delicate, but old—stage props.

Kade perceives she's trying her best to keep things together—this is a show.

He's sure of that, now.

Is she going to snatch up that knife and stab him with it? That's what he'd do if he were her.

Then Kade's mind pulls him right back to the car. Eddie's eyes, like hers, the same but different colors, staring at him, and now he wonders if she knows why he's here. If she does, she's doing a good job not showing it. But that knife, he can't keep from looking at it and he half expects her to grab the handle and launch herself across the coffee table.

With shaking hands, the woman picks up the saucer with a cup of tea, asking if he wants lemon or sugar in his tea. Kade tells her, "No, straight's fine."

She hands the cup and saucer to him, which forces him to leave the gun tucked in his waistband and use two hands to accept the tea. He thanks her and uses one hand, pinky finger up, like he's seen on TV, to drink from the cup.

She smiles at him as he does it.

Is it poison? No, it's not poison because then there wouldn't be a need for the knife.

Kade tells her it's good.

Eddie's mom pours some tea and takes a sip. "My boy liked you," she says, sipping, the cup and saucer at about chest level. There's something proper in the way she does it. "Always thought you were something. He used to talk about you. He said he was having fun hanging out with you. Used to tell me how I had you all wrong. I always thought you were a bad influence."

"He was a good kid," Kade says, not sure what to say. He didn't expect there to be any real talking. He's not good with conversations, and he can feel Marlow's eyes on him, watching him through the window from the truck. Kade glances that way.

"I wasn't wrong." Her tone brings his eyes back to her. "I think you're not a good kid. I don't think you are good at all. You know how I know? God told me. He came to me in a dream last night. After the deputies left, God came to me, told me you killed my boy."

Kade starts to say something, tries to defend himself, but she cuts him off.

"I used to take Edgar to church—a Catholic Church; it runs in the family—my brother's a priest. Edgar used to love going to church, used to look up to his uncle. His sister and I still go, but Edgar stopped going a long time ago. He was so angry when his father died. You know that? Maybe that's why he stopped going to church. I don't know; he wouldn't talk to me about it. His father died. You know where his father died? In prison, that's where. The only thing Edgar got from his father was those green eyes. I used to tell him they were emerald, but..." She pauses to wipe tears from her left cheek. "...but, Edgar had my eyes, not the color, but the emotion—true eyes." She pauses to sip some of the tea. "God is good and grants miracles. You know what they used to call miracles?"

Kade tells her he doesn't.

"Signs," she says, putting the tea down on the table and crossing her arms across her chest.

Something's not right here. She's leading up to something.

She reaches for the table again, and for a moment, Kade thinks she'll go for the knife. But she doesn't, so he doesn't dare pull the gun, not yet. Not because he can't do it, but because he wants to see where this is going and find out what she has to say.

Her hand hovers over the tray and then drops under the table, and she pulls out a pack of cigarettes; the pack is open and worn, the type of pack old women hide for times like this when things are bad and decisions tough. She withdraws a cigarette and a disposable lime green lighter from the pack.

She sticks the cigarette in her mouth, squashing her lips around the end as she rams it between them with her one hand, nearly bending the stock of the cigarette, while she says, "Well God came to me in my dreams and gave me a sign. He came after I'd cried, and drank, and nearly tore

my hair out." She tries to light the cigarette, but she's shaking too badly. She tries again, getting it this time. Once the cigarette's going, she lets out some smoke and continues to talk with the cigarette hanging there. "There I was on the floor, a broken heap, a mess, curled up in a ball, broken, and God told me you killed my boy. Don't say anything; I know better. I know what sort of person you are. You're not going to be with God. You know it. I know it, and now Edgar knows it."

She uncrosses her arms and pulls the cigarette from her mouth. Tears fall down her cheeks. She supports her cigarette arm with her hand on her elbow. She blows the smoke out the corner of her downturned mouth. Smoke twists and swirls in the air.

"Now, the deputies say my boy was shot,"—voice cracking— "Said only shot once. I know because I asked." She pauses to take a short drag of the cigarette. "I had to find out what happened—it was hard to ask. But, for him to be shot once and die, it had to be a life-taking shot. So in my dream, God showed me that you shot Edgar in the head. Did he look at you when you did it?"

Kade stares at her.

"Or did you just put the gun to the back of his head and pull the trigger? Why didn't you do that to me while I was in the kitchen? You could have."

Kade could tell her, tell her he coughed, put the gun to the kid's face, pulled the trigger. Is that what she wants to hear? Hear how he thought about killing her. How he wouldn't have a problem with it.

She leans forward and extinguishes the cigarette in her teacup. She's been building toward this moment.

She's going for the knife—he's sure of it. She's doing it slowly like she has to overcome something inside her. That's what separates people like her and Aaron from people like him; he doesn't have to overcome anything.

She bends forward as if she's in pain, her hand above the tray. "Don't answer; it doesn't matter. God showed me what happened. Edgar looked at you. You looked at him. And yet you still pulled the trigger. That's what was in my dream. So that's what happened." She chuckles nervously. "You know the funny part about this? Although funny isn't the right word. The funny thing is it was your kind that killed his father. Want to know why his father died? Because he betrayed his race. That's what their letter said. The one your kind sent me from the prison. You green bastards killed him because he loved a Mex-i-can." She puts a southern drawl to her voice. "Because he loved me."

The sound of car doors slamming outside catches their attention and causes them to look out the window. Her hand brushes against the handle of the knife and retracts. He's back looking at her as she stares out the window and collapses into a sniffling and crying fit, her arms crossed, body sinking into the couch, defeated. He hears the truck start up and catches the sight of Marlow's truck as it drives away. Then the trooper from the other night gets out of the car.

CHAPTER 25:

BARBARA

VALDEZ PARKS THE CAR ON THE STREET BESIDE THE little house with the one car garage. Parks so close to the curb that when Barbara opens her door, the door gets stuck in the grass, scraping an ugly scar in the yard.

Exiting the car, Barbara surveys the house and spots a car in the driveway, sun shining off the black paint. She notices the front door is open, screen door keeping nature out of the house. The blinds are open to the living room, showing two seated figures sitting, a male and a female. The male's wearing a white t-shirt and blue jeans, blonde hair cut short, tattoos visible on his neck and arms. Kade. Looks like he did the other night. The female's talking, and she's wearing a black dress with a white necklace—Maria, Eddie's mother. That's what Valdez called her when he told Barbara about her.

Eddie meant something to him. He's having a hard time dealing with the kid's death. She can see it. He's having a hard time, and Barbara thinks he shouldn't be here—he's too close. Valdez lacks the distance necessary to deliver news like this.

Valdez slams his car door, causing both figures in the house to look out the window. He walks around the front of the car, with his hands on his hips, his gun and badge on display, and starts up the driveway.

Now with his weight out of the car, Barbara's able to shut her door. She uses her foot to brush over the ugly scrape in the grass and notices the beat-up pick-up pull away from the curb on the opposite side of the street, the driver trying hard not to look their way.

Back in the window, the woman's up and moving to the front door as Valdez reaches the halfway point of the driveway. Barbara hustles through the grass to the front porch to catch up to him, but she stays off the front step. Valdez takes the step of the porch like he's climbing a great mountain, hand on knee, hauling his body forward, forcing his spirit onward. He doesn't knock or ring the bell. The screen door opens. The crying woman stands before Valdez, staring at him. She utters an ugly cry—her makeup is askew, black streaks running.

Valdez steps forward like he's going to hug her, but he stops inches from her. The crying woman rears back, slapping him hard across his left cheek. Loud enough that Barbara hears fingers cracking against his skin. Then the woman collapses into Valdez's arms, crying harder. He hugs her, pulls her close, and whispers in her ear. She sobs and says words in Spanish. The woman points at the open door. Valdez hugs her tightly and steps back from her, breaking the hug.

In the window, Kade hasn't moved, Barbara's been watching him as he sits there sipping on a teacup, staring at her. Something in his eyes tells Barbara they interrupted something. She says, "He's pretty damn bold to be here."

Valdez moves around the woman and steps through the door, telling Barbara to "come on." Barbara steps up on the porch. The woman steps to the side to let her pass and looks at Barbara. She stays outside on the porch, sobbing and shaking.

In the house, Barbara hears Valdez's deep voice say, "Kade, you checking in on your dead friend's mother? How nice of you."

Sounding like he did the other night, Kade says, "Glad you remember me. And here I was thinking of you, and I feared we wouldn't get a chance to meet—formally."

Barbara finds herself in the living room, framed in the front window. From his chair across the room, Kade looks up. "Oh, it's you. Did you get your car back?"

Barbara says nothing.

Shifting to Valdez, Kade throws his head toward him. "Why are you here?"

Valdez steps around the chair, toward the coffee table between them. He sits in the chair opposite Kade. The seat is covered in plastic and crackles as he sits. Valdez says, "There's a lot to talk about."

Barbara scans the room. There's a large knife on the table. Kade's hands cradle a teacup. "That don't tell me nothing," he says. He sips the tea with his eyes on Valdez, ignoring her. "But that's alright, I guess you got my message."

"I got your message," Valdez says. He pulls his gun on Kade. "Let's keep it simple. Keep the tea in your hands and don't make any sudden movements and all that."

"Jesus," Barbara says. "Val, what the hell?"

Valdez doesn't look at her as he speaks. "Barbara, I need you to sit down and let what's about to happen, happen." He keeps his elbow bent, gun resting on his leg pointed at Kade, voice calm, body relaxed.

Barbara gauges the situation. Both men, maybe five feet away, the distance most gunfights happen. Both men challenging each other. If she doesn't find a way to stop it, someone will get shot. But she follows Valdez's advice and sits on the plastic-covered seat next to Valdez, warning him, "I can't let you shoot him."

Kade says, "Like you have a say in the matter."

"He's right you don't," Valdez says. "There's nothing here about you stopping me." The gun flickering in front of Kade. "Isn't that right, boy? We've gone beyond that."

Kade sips the tea, playing like the gun doesn't bother him. "That's right."

But it sure does bother her. How could it not bother him?

Valdez rocks forward in his seat. "See, he knows what the score is," he tells Barbara. "If I wanted to shoot him for shooting Eddie, I figured here's the best place for that to happen—they'd call it poetic."

"They'd call it murder—"

"—they'd call it righteous," Valdez says. "Justified even."

"I can't let you shoot him," Barbara says, sweeping her arm back, putting her hand on the butt of the pistol at her side, but then she hesitates. She doesn't want to draw her gun from the holster. If she does, something bad could happen, and then she'd be the one that forced it. It would be her fault. So, she doesn't draw. Leaves her hand on the butt of her weapon. "He's unarmed."

"He's not unarmed," Valdez says, still not looking at her, but the tone in his voice tells her to stop, leave it alone.

Barbara's not one to let a cop do something wrong. It's not her nature. There's got to be a way to stop all this from getting out of control.

She glances in Kade's direction, leaving her hand on her gun in the holster. Shoulders tight with tension. Mouth dry. Barbara asks, "What, he's going to assault you with a saucer?"

Kade's locked on to Valdez and his gun—so much so he doesn't seem to even be aware she's still in the room—he says, "So it's true then, Eddie was working with you, that's why you're here?"

"If by that you mean I had a personal stake in Edgar O'Malley then I'd say yes, that's true. But if you're asking me if he was working for me and if I say no then it would seem pretty silly. Considering that's the reason you killed him."

Kade says, "That doesn't answer the question."

"No, it doesn't," Valdez says, agreeing with him. "But I'm not here to answer your questions. Or ask you questions for that matter—that's not why I am here."

He's here to kill Kade.

Barbara should have known better, seen this coming, but how could either one of them know he'd be here? She still can't believe he's here and she's sitting here.

With his eyes still on Valdez, Kade finishes the tea and places the cup back on the saucer. He leans forward, making like he's going to put the saucer back on the coffee table.

Valdez clicks his tongue against his teeth. "Don't put that down unless you want a bullet in your stomach."

The threat stops Kade for a moment.

"You won't shoot me," he says, confident like he believes it. He leans forward and places the cup on the tray on the coffee table. The cup makes a noise as his hands slip out from under the saucer.

Valdez doesn't shoot him. Barbara breathes a little easier, and only then does she realize she'd been holding her breath. She also realizes her gun's halfway out of the holster.

Would she have shot him?

Kade's eyes flick her way. "See I told you, he wouldn't shoot me," he says, smug, smiling now. So sure of himself, using that criminal confidence that runs through him; runs through most criminals, the real ones at least. Barbara's seen it in enough people, and she remembers it from him from the other night. Even in the face of impossible odds, he's arrogant.

Valdez says, "If you make a move for that gun shoved in your pants, I'll shoot you dead."

"Who says there's a gun in my pants?" Kade asks with his hands out and his cheeks pulled back in a forced smile. The tattoos are visible on his arms. The clover on the side of his neck, green.

"The lady of the house seems to think you were here to kill her," Valdez says. "Says she saw the handle of a gun shoved down your ass after she let you in the house. You're lucky she didn't shove that knife in your neck."

Kade motions to the knife on the tray, swinging his hand over the tray, testing the situation. "I figured that's what it was for—me."

"Why don't you go for it and see what happens," Valdez says, testing him, and then pauses. "She'd have done it too, you know? You killed her boy; it'd only be right."

"So she said." Kade's smile doesn't break, but his voice does a bit. "She call you?"

Valdez leaves that question right there.

With her gun teetering on the edge of her holster, Barbara says, "You can't kill him."

The corner of Valdez's face shifts her direction. "I can't just arrest him. I need to stop him."

"But you can't kill him," Barbara says. "Not here, not now—think about what you've got. You can arrest him. Put handcuffs on him and call it good. Killing him won't bring Eddie back."

"Yeah, think about it," Kade says. "Think about your career. Think about my message. We both know there's only one way this is going to end. I made sure of that. Be better if we do this now. Think about your wife—you got one of those right? What'd she think of you gunning a defenseless man down for no reason?"

Valdez's face flushes red, anger brimming behind his stare. "Fuck you. Putting you down will solve a lot of problems—pull on me, boy!"

"Valdez, stop!" Barbara says. "He's right to make you think of your wife. Because I know if he pulls, you will kill him. But you're enough of a cop that you have to have some sort of pretext. The problem is he might give you that pretext."

Bent at the waist, his hands in front of him, head swerving from side to side like a snake, Kade spits his words out like venom. "I'm ready to pull when you've got enough balls to shoot."

"I'll give you a fair chance." Valdez readjusts his position in the chair. "Go ahead. Make the move. We'll make it fair." He relaxes the gun.

Kade sits back. "I'm supposed to believe you? How do I know you won't shoot me anyway?" Then he scoots forward in the seat, allowing for room between his back and the seat, keeps his hands on his knees.

"Either shut up or pull your gun."

No one moves.

Barbara watches Kade think about what to do next. His mind's working all the ways this could go down. All point to one end. He could pull the gun now, get shot. Could get up and walk away, but Barbara will try to arrest him, and then he'll pull the gun and will get shot. She could pull on Valdez. Try to stop him. But that'd mean either he'd pull his gun and shoot one of them, or he'd pull his gun and get shot. Either way. He knows this, Barbara knows this, and Valdez sure as hell knows this. It'd give Valdez what he wants, which scares Barbara because this version of him scares her.

She says, "Think of Charlotte," making one last attempt to get Valdez to step off the edge and away from this mistake.

From outside the window, the whine of car brakes shatters the brittle tension. Both Kade and Valdez turn to look out the window, and thankfully, Kade doesn't make a move for the gun.

Barbara waits long enough to look to make sure his hands stay clear. Then she turns her head and sees a beat-up Honda Accord with broken windows and dents all over pull up to the curb, nearly bumping the back of Valdez's car. Three men in the car. All three men get out. Each with a weapon. The driver has a sawed-off shotgun. The others carry handguns with extended magazines. The man with the shotgun walks around the front of the Honda, stepping over the bumper of his and Valdez's car, and all three men line up on the curb outside the house.

Kade curses under his breath. "Gilliam."

Barbara glances back at him. Kade's up, out of the seat now, at the window. She sees his mind working as he nibbles on the tip of his tongue.

From outside, the stranger with the shotgun who must be Gilliam, yells at the house, while watching them through the window. "You know what we're here for."

Kade doesn't move. Valdez doesn't move. But Barbara does. She stands, withdraws the gun out of the holster, keeping it low at her side, and tells Kade not to move or Valdez will kill him. "Things have changed. We don't need a shootout." She's showing she's in control now. She looks out the window and moves over to the front door, using the corner of the wall to shield herself. She yells out the screen door and asks the figures outside, "What are you here for?" watching them through the open door where she sees Maria frozen in place, her back against the wall of the porch.

The one with the shotgun says, "Kade."

Barbara glances back at Kade and past him at Valdez's gun still at his side and pointed at the floor.

There's no way out of this without turning the small house into a war zone, but Barbara doesn't believe in no-win scenarios. A bit like Captain Kirk. A bit like Stanley. He'd say, there's always a way, and there is—give Kade up. Because the way she sees it, if she or Valdez shoot Kade now, the ones outside will open up on the house. Valdez has to see that too.

Barbara says, "You heard them, get outside."

Kade turns, keeps his hands out in front of him, with a half-smile on his lips. He passes Valdez, who sinks in the chair, the plastic mimicking his sighs.

Barbara gives commands, keeping her gun low, and tells Kade to step beside her. Then, she allows him room to maneuver. She places her gun against the back of his head and tells him that if he moves wrong, she'll blow his head off ... it wouldn't be murder. Then pushes the gun into his skull to show him what she means.

Not that she'd care one way or the other, the new situation requires new considerations. Before she wasn't willing to kill a man in cold blood, but now things have changed.

Barbara yells at Maria to get back inside the house, her voice knocking the woman out of her trance. There's an office to the side, away from Kade and the door. Barbara directs Maria there with her head. "Get down on the floor and put your hands over your head." Maria opens the screen door, steps into the house, and lies down on the floor. "Put your hands over your head." Barbara waits until she's sure Maria's down and doing what she's been told, and then looks behind her. Valdez still hasn't moved. Barbara can't focus on that now. Control. Confidence. That's what she needs.

With Kade in front of her, she looks down and sees the bulge of the gun in his waistband. Valdez was right. Barbara grabs the gun out of his waistband and throws it down and to the side. She shoves him, hard, in his back, pushing him toward the door. He takes a few scooting steps and stops at the screen door, looking back over his shoulder, trying to size her

up. She recognizes that look from the other night. She pushes him hard once more, and he's out the door, shuffling onto the porch.

No one moves as the screen door slams shut, bounces open again, and then shuts softly.

Barbara keeps her gun on the back of Kade's head then shifts to the men outside, moving from one to the other ending on the one with the shotgun. Barbara slams the wooden door shut behind Kade and locks it.

Once the door's shut, she allows herself a moment to breathe. From behind the door, she hears the men outside order Kade off the porch. Tell him to keep his hands up, don't do anything stupid, and get in the car. One saying, "you remember my fucking car, you asshole, the one you fucked up." Then there's the sound of car doors opening and closing and the roar of an engine.

Barbara walks back into the living room and checks out the window. The Honda drives off, taillights blinking on before taking a right turn around the end of the block.

Valdez holsters his weapon and the sound of the gun dropping in the bucket causes Barbara to turn. "What just happened? Who were they?"

CHAPTER 26:

KADE

GILLIAM, STANDING IN THE FRONT YARD, COM-plains about his car as he hands the shotgun to one of the others. Then he asks, "Who's in the house?"

Kade looks over his shoulder. "Two cops."

"What cops?"

"The one from the business card," Kade says. "And the black bitch that stopped me on the highway."

"The one whose car you stole?" Gilliam asks. "Why they at the house? Why are they in there?"

Gilliam doesn't ask about the one from the business card. Deep down, Kade knows they both expected Valdez to come after him just like he did. Gun pointed at him, daring him to make it righteous. Kade's a little surprised it didn't go down the way Valdez wanted it to go down. It doesn't matter now.

Kade shrugs. "Don't know. Probably to tell the kid's mom he was dead. Don't see why, because she already knew." He leaves out the part where he was sure she was going to stab him with a knife. "Billy wanted me to kill her."

"Would you have done it?" Gilliam asks.

Kade ignores the question and stares at him.

"Would you have done it had I pressed you to do it? You told me no."

Kade keeps staring.

Gilliam bites his lip, lets the question go, tells Kade to get in the car.

———

IN THE HONDA later, Gilliam drives with Kade in the passenger seat. Joaquin is in the seat behind him, holding a gun to the back of his head, making him nervous. One slip of a finger. An errant trigger pull and his head's gone. It makes him think of *Pulp Fiction*. He doesn't want his face to be a bloodstain on the window, not like Eddie.

Now, Gilliam twists in the driver's seat to look at Kade and then back at the road. "I hope this plan of yours works."

"Aaron came up with the plan," Kade says, trying to shake off the awareness of the gun pressed to the back of his head. "It will work."

Gilliam's hands grip the steering wheel, wrenching the leather, which makes creaking noises. He is not happy with how things were going, but what bothers Kade is the gun pressed to the back of his head. He tries to brush off the urge to turn in the seat and punch Joaquin, the two-bit muscle in the face, but he can't do that. So, he slaps the dashboard instead. It doesn't help. Every turn, every bump, every time his head moves, the barrel is there. *Pulp Fiction* flashing through his head. Seeing Samuel L. Jackson and John Travolta and that stain on the back window of their car, and then Eddie.

Kade says, "Mind moving that thing, wrong move, bad bump, and I'm no more."

Joaquin doesn't. He presses the gun harder to the back of Kade's head.

Kade needs to have patience—focus on what has to happen. That's what Aaron told him. He swallows the urge to turn around and beat Joaquin with the gun.

Gilliam drives on for a bit before he tells Joaquin to take the gun off Kade. "Lighten up a little bit, will ya?"

Joaquin slaps the side of Kade's head with the barrel as he takes the gun from Kade's head.

———

PATIENCE, THAT'S WHAT Aaron told him he had to have. Kade knows what he's doing, and it ain't easy for him. He's putting faith in his friend's idea. Something he's not used to doing. Something that's not him. It's easier than he imagined but harder too.

Easy, because Aaron came up with the idea back at the apartment where they spent the night. It happened after Kade told him about his meeting with Mikey. Aaron asked Kade what he thought he'd say to Billy.

Kade told him he hadn't thought about it. Aaron told Kade he had and laid out a plan. Kade liked it, but it wasn't him. He doesn't plan. Aaron asked him to trust him and said he is doing it for Kirsten.

Of course, he is. That part, Kade believed. Aaron would do anything for her, and that's why he's still alive.

Then, Aaron got on the phone with Gilliam, telling him he had an idea of how to take Billy out. Told him that they needed Kade to make it happen. From the way Aaron talked on the phone, Kade knows Gilliam isn't too hot for the idea of Kade taking care of Billy. But that's how things go. Aaron argued with Gilliam over it. He told Gilliam, "This is war. Sometimes you're trying to kill someone, and then sometimes that person's your friend, helping you kill someone else." Hearing him talk like that, Kade thought Aaron sounded like he had balls. "Yeah, but war can be confusing." Later when Kade asked what he was going on about, Aaron told him that's what people call The Fog of War.

But Kade doesn't know anything about any of that.

He's not Aaron. He's not smart like that. He doesn't plan. That's why this is hard too; he's got to trust in the plan. That's what Aaron told him as they left the apartment on the way to Billy's, "Trust in the plan."

But trusting is harder than it looks.

Aaron told Kade this would be the most dangerous part, getting back together in one space with Gilliam. Aaron seemed to think they could pull it off as long as Kade didn't lose his temper. Kade asked, "What about him losing his fucking temper?"

"It will work. Gilliam will like it."

Kade wasn't too sure how good of a plan it was ... or if Gilliam would like it. But he went along with it.

Aaron said, "Have patience. You have to be patient."

———

NOW, GILLIAM DOESN'T look too happy about having Kade in the car, and he's not sure he has patience.

"I'm not too sure this plan of his will work. I'll go along with it if I can take Billy off the board before things fucking kick off," Gilliam says, nodding to Kade. "It's fucking bold. I'll give that fucking shit stick that. Your fucking lapdog can't kill you. No, he fucks that up. Fucks that up badly, but he can devise a devious fucking way to kill another man. Go figure, how does someone as worthless as your childhood butt buddy do something like that?"

"It will work," Kade says. "Billy met with me, and he let me live. We know who's in the bar, and it's Aaron's plan. It will work."

"Think bitch boy knows we're coming?"

Kade's sure of it.

"So far this plan of yours hasn't gone like either one of you ass-munchers thought it would," Gilliam says. "The lapdog wasn't supposed to be left behind—he's supposed to be here. We're supposed to have two vehicles—front and back. That was the plan."

Kade knows what the plan was, but plans change. "We'll make do with what we have because you won't get another chance."

"Bitch boy Billy's too frightened of me to come at me straight on."

Kade's not sure of that, but that doesn't matter. "I saw who came to Billy's aid, and it was pretty much what we thought. Listen, things are fucked, but they aren't that fucked. We won't have another opportunity to get everyone in one place like this. Sure, someone could have left since I was there, but they're expecting me to come back. We know no one else will be coming over."

"To hear you say it, they're expecting you to have killed that woman. Are you able to go in there and lie about it, lie rightly? Or you just going to start blasting?"

"My ride drove off," Kade says. "I can tell him whatever I want. No one can say otherwise."

"What'd you offer bitch boy Billy?" Gilliam asks. "Had to be something worth something for him to let you walk out of there alive. I would have killed you. He should have killed you."

"Yeah, well that's his mistake."

Kade knows he's the wildcard, and Gilliam knows Kade wouldn't have been a part of Billy's plans, meaning it's a blind spot for Billy.

"I offered him you."

Gilliam snorts. "That's something." Then he's quiet for a moment, which is rare for Gilliam.

Kade's been with him long enough to know a little bit about the man. He can be loud and brash, and he's like Kade—doesn't think things through. But Gilliam's got a mind for numbers, and he's fucking ambitious. There's a shift in Gilliam, in his tone. He's not the normal crew leader; now he's the Gilliam that used to confide in Kade. Back when

Kade was his only muscle. Back when Kade used to look up to the man, considered him something like an older brother. But that was a long time ago. Somber sounding now, Gilliam says, "Santiago says he's supporting me, but most of the others went over to bitch boy Billy or won't take sides."

"So he said," Kade says.

It's like they're back to how things used to be, five years ago. Kade's young and dumb, trusting in Gilliam and Gilliam trusting in him. Then Kade recounts the meeting with Billy, retelling who was present and who wasn't. What Billy said and what Billy didn't say.

Gilliam grins. "The ones that didn't go over don't have the balls to pick a side."

"Yeah, well, pull this off and you won't have to worry about them."

"Just holding what I got," Gilliam says. "That's all I want."

Kade corrects him. "What you won."

Gilliam likes that. "Think the others will fall in line? The city?"

Kade says, "We'll have to make sure this is as bloody as it can be. We can't have anyone getting out alive."

"Kill everyone in there," Gilliam says. "I like that; now that's fucking scorched earth!" He punches the steering wheel.

"Except for Aaron," Kade says, reminding him.

Then it's gone. Gilliam isn't the Gilliam of the past. He isn't the man Kade's looked up to. He's the current Gilliam. The one ready to go to war with everyone and anyone—the one about to declare war on his people.

Green on Green.

There was a time when Kade wouldn't have thought that possible; it was a sin.

Gilliam nods. "Except for him." Like he hadn't expected Aaron to walk out of the bar.

The car's quiet as they drive back to Mikey's bar. At a red light near the bar waiting to turn into the shopping center, Kade turns in the seat. He looks back at River and his brother, the one Kade wants to beat with his gun. "You ready to do what needs doing?"

The brothers nod in sync as Gilliam pulls into the shopping center. Turning toward Gilliam, Kade says, "I'll need a gun."

Gilliam shakes his head and laughs. He's very much the current Gilliam, the one that wanted Kade dead two days ago. "You're staying in the car. I can't have you getting an idea in your head that your friends aren't your friends."

He means he doesn't want Kade shooting him in the back.

That's smart. He would.

Outside the bar, Gilliam pulls out his phone and dials a number. He says, "Mikey, listen..."

CHAPTER 27:

AARON

MARLOW TELLS BILLY WHAT HAPPENED. Billy's not happy to hear any of the man's story because he keeps rubbing his temples and says, "So let me get this straight. He's in the house, and you're in the street, and these two cops show up, and they go inside the house—and you *fucking* leave?"

"I left before they went in," Marlow says, nodding like a bobblehead, "but yeah that's what happened."

And here, Aaron's stuck in a neighboring booth watching the whole exchange. Like yesterday, with his thumb up his ass, which isn't a part of the plan.

Billy sighs. "And then you left? Like you're there, he's inside the house, and you fucking leave? You left?"

Marlow says, "Well, I didn't want to be parked outside the house when they decided to start arresting people or shooting. They're fucking cops. I got warrants. I don't need none of that trouble."

Billy takes a drink of his beer. "And before that, you're watching him talk to the woman through the front window, and they do what?"

"Drink tea," Marlow says. "They sit in the front, drinking tea; she came out of the kitchen holding a tray with cupcakes and everything."

"So, he didn't just kill her at the door?" Billy slams his beer back on the table. "Why didn't he do that?"

Marlow shrugs. "I don't know why he did it that way," he says. "I don't know why he does anything the way he does, but he did do that. You know, on the way out there, I'm telling him that's how I would do it. She opens the door, and I pull the gun on her and shoot her in the forehead.

Give her three eyes, like he gave her son. And he says, what in broad daylight, what if someone sees you? I asked him who would see me, and he said someone in the street and then asked me what would I do about the girl, the sister. I said I'd just go in there, look for her. He said so the cops can find you at the scene of the crime?"

Billy, back in the booth, rubs his temples like he's thinking hard about what he's hearing. "How'd he say he would do it?"

"He didn't," Marlow says. "He sat there questioning me and picking at me. Sat there with the gun in his lap, asking me questions. I got sick of it. So I say, okay, how about this? She invites me inside, and I go in to ask where the girl's at and wait for her to come down."

"How would you get inside?" Billy points at Marlow. "Like what would you say, and how do you think she would react, knowing you know she's got a girl. She don't know you. That'd freak her out."

"That's what he said," Marlow says. "He said that wouldn't work, either. First, he said she would wonder why I want the girl. And second, he asked me how I would respond when she tells me she ain't coming down."

"How would you respond?" Billy kicks his foot out the side of the booth, extending his leg. "What'd you say?"

Marlow thinks about the question for a minute. "I asked him what he would do, but he kept sitting there, doing nothing but poking at me. Then when we get there, he gets out of the truck and goes up to the house like he's visiting. Like a door-to-door salesman. I told him the neighborhood has no soliciting signs, so he just looks out of place. But he don't look out of place. He's got his hat in his hand, looking sad, you know? He's up there knocking and then steps back from the door, acting all polite and shit—putting on a freaking show."

"Then what happened?"

"The mom opens the door and stands there on the step like she can't believe he's there. I hear her invite him in, asked if he wanted some tea."

Billy asks, "Did he want tea?"

"How am I supposed to know that?" Marlow says. "All's I know is they go in, and he sits down in the front room, which gave me a great shot through the front window. Watched the whole thing. She goes into the kitchen. Then comes back out with the tray—"

"—and the cupcakes—"

"—and cupcakes, okay I don't know if they were cupcakes, but they were something on the tray. She sets the tray down, and then she talks to him. He didn't say much."

"Where was his gun?" Billy sips some more beer.

Marlow, using his hands to talk now, demonstrates an action. "On the way to the door, he shoved it in the back of his pants."

"She see it?"

"No, he never took it out. He just held that tea with two hands. How you going to kill someone if you got shit in both hands?"

Billy throws one arm across the back of the booth while using the other to take a drink of his beer. "Might as well've been his dick."

"But see, she did all the talking. I don't know what she's talking about, but I can see his face, and he's not happy to be hearing it."

"Then the cops show up?"

"Right," Marlow says. "These two cops show up in an old car."

"You recognize them?"

"No, the guy cop, he gets out and starts up the driveway. The girl cop, she stood by the car for a moment, rubbing her foot over the grass. I don't know what that was all about, but she got a good look at me as I drove away."

"I'm sure she did."

Aaron can't believe what he's hearing. So much for his plan. Cops weren't a part of it. He wonders what would have happened had Gilliam showed up first. He was able to text him before they took his phone. Kade was negotiating with Billy, and Billy said he wanted his *Good Faith*, like what the fuck is that?

"Anyone else going to show up?" Aaron asks.

Both men turn in the booth to look at him. "Who the hell would show up?" Marlow says. "Why the hell are you asking?"

Aaron says he doesn't know, just wondering, trying to backtrack.

Billy says, "Well keep your thoughts to yourself. You're a hostage, so act like it, and shut the fuck up, alright."

Marlow says, "No one else showed up that I know of."

Biting annoyance is in Billy's tone. "Because you left."

"Like I said—"

"—cops," Billy finishes the man's sentence. "So you said."

Aaron stops listening when the bar phone rings. Mikey, standing in the U-shaped bar, picks up the phone. He holds the phone to his ear, not talking. Just listening.

Aaron knows what's being said because he told Gilliam what needed to be said.

———

LAST NIGHT IN the empty apartment, Aaron was on the phone with Gilliam, explaining the idea to him. "Listen, we can't kill Billy."

Gilliam said, "What do you mean we can't kill him? He's the fucking reason all this is kicking off. He wants to go to motherfucking war."

"I'm not saying you can't kill everyone else," Aaron said, "but you can't kill him—that'd be too much."

"Too much for who?" Gilliam asked. "What you think I give a flying fuck what the City thinks?"

"*They* care about what they think."

"So, what are you saying? We walk in there and blow the fucking place apart?"

"That's exactly what I'm saying."

"What about Mikey, I don't want him coming after me. The best way to keep that from happening is to take him out."

Aaron thought about that and came up with an idea. He especially liked the idea after hearing about Mikey's meeting with Kade. Aaron told him, "Let Mikey go."

"Let him *go*?" Gilliam said. "I can't let him go. He's a better killer than Kade. He'll fucking hunt us down and kill us all. You ever see *The Departed*? He's like Marky Mark. He'll be waiting for me to walk into the apartment. Wearing a plastic tracksuit with booties and everything, fucking take me out. I can't let him go."

"Look, we bring Kade on to get us in the bar; he got us the meeting. The plan is we get in the bar, do whatever Billy wants, and then you come in; take everyone else out, right? Well, you don't kill Billy; you don't kill Mikey. You let Mikey walk out, and then, you take Billy hostage. You ransom him back to the City. Use Mikey to broker the peace. Because, look, Mikey's the middle man in all this. His only thing—call it a mission or directive or whatever else you fucking want to call it—his only thing is to keep our cousins out east happy. So let him make peace with the City. That will keep our cousins happy. Those fuckers in the City will be so freaking happy about you bringing Billy to them for judgment that they'll give you Tulsa."

"And then what—I'm in charge?"

"And then you're in charge," Aaron said. "Or something like that. Let the City take care of Billy's fate. He's overextended himself. You're just calling him on it."

"What if this don't work? What if Mikey goes to Billy? We can't have him tipping the bitch boy off. We can't have anyone getting out of there or getting ready for us to walk in—it'd be a fucking slaughter."

"You call Mikey," Aaron said. "You call him before you walk in the door. You lay it out. Don't let him talk. You tell him, look Mikey, we got no problem with you. What I need you to do is go out the back door for a bit. Tell him you're coming in the front door, guns blazing or some shit. Tell him, Billy's time is done. Tell him you'd like him to arrange a meeting with the City to keep the peace. You have to say it like that—use the words to keep the peace."

"What if he don't listen?"

Aaron had thought about that too. "Then he don't listen—and everyone dies."

———

NOW, MIKEY PLACES the phone down on the receiver and looks over at Aaron. He uses two hands to slick his hair back and then lets the hands fall down his face to his sides. He licks his lips—appears to be thinking. Then, he says something to Paul Anders about having to get something from the back. He slips out the back door and is gone. No one notices.

Billy and Marlow are still going on about Marlow driving off at the sight of cops. Billy making Marlow go over it again. Marlow starts with the part about the cops, and Billy tells him he got that part. "Why the fuck did you feel the need to leave?"

Marlow starts to answer when the front door flies open. Three men, wearing masks, carrying guns, burst in. The gunshots happen almost simultaneously.

His body slinks in the seat as he watches Paul Anders take a shotgun blast to the chest. He drops below the table of the booth. There's a bunch of shouting. Most of it coming from Gilliam. Cussing and cursing and

179

yelling, and even more blasting and shooting. A woman screams, and Aaron sees the back door fly open. That was Lou. Her partner, Renee makes for the back door, but she collapses at the door. Hand outstretched reaching for the door. Shot down.

Aaron doesn't see much else.

Not that he wants to see what's happening. Everything collapses into blood and guns, guns and blood.

Then the shooting stops.

Gilliam's voice: "You can come out from under there. It's done."

Aaron pulls himself from under the table and surveys the room, thinking they used a lot of bullets. He finds Gilliam standing next to him, covered in blood, and grinning like he just got laid. He's got his hand out to help him out from under the table.

Billy's alive, still in the booth, with Marlow dead, lying face down on the table in front of him, gunshot to the back of his head.

Billy finishes his beer and sets it down in Marlow's blood.

Billy says, "I guess this is why the others haven't shown up."

Gilliam smiles and says, "Guess that's why."

"You going to kill me too?"

"Wasn't planning on it," Gilliam says. "Not your time. Not yet."

Billy hums to himself and turns to Aaron. He starts to say something, but to Aaron, it sounds like a groan.

One of Gilliam's men shuffles forward, gripping his stomach with one hand while dragging a shotgun with the other. Aaron knows the man as Joaquin, meaning the other one standing next to Gilliam is his brother River.

Gilliam addresses Joaquin. "What's wrong with you?"

"Gutshot," he says, wincing through some unknown deep pain. Trying his best to stay upright, but his knees shake so bad even Aaron can see it.

All Gilliam says in response is "Shame." Then he pulls a semi-automatic pistol from the front of his waistband, levels it on the man, and shoots him before Joaquin can say anything. Joaquin collapses into a heap.

Aaron glances at River, who's left blinking, trying to understand what just happened.

Gilliam shifts his stance and puts the gun in River's ear. He pulls the trigger. Blood flies from River's other ear. His body falls to the floor. Gilliam drops the gun to his side, holds it there, and turns to Aaron. "The problem with brothers—kill one, have to kill them all."

CHAPTER 28:

VALDEZ

VALDEZ STANDS OUTSIDE EDDIE'S MOM'S HOUSE, fuming as he tells Barbara, "You should have let me do what needs to be done."

Barbara, who's still on the front step of the house, says, "I was not going to let you kill him."

Valdez points at her. "You don't have a say in the matter."

She tells him she does.

"You don't," he argues. "You might think you do, coming along with me on this, whatever this is... what...a journey, but you shouldn't have gotten in the way. I had him. That was the moment. There won't be another like it. I had him right there with my gun on the guy, but there you were, in the way, stopped me from doing something..."

Stupid? Not that he could have done it anyway. He figured that out. He's still too much of a cop; he can't shoot unless it's righteous, and that wasn't righteous.

Valdez turns to walk away, frustrated at himself and frustrated with her.

Barbara steps off the porch, trying to keep pace at his side. They move toward their car. "I do. This is an investigation. We don't go around murdering people. Even people who deserve it."

Valdez tries his best not to look her way. "You're saying had he pulled you wouldn't have said he didn't pull?"

"No, what I'm saying is, I'm not going to lie for you. My husband taught me better. OHP taught me better. You know better. He needs to be brought in. Not murdered in the street."

Valdez stops with his hands on his hips. "That was a house."

"Yeah, well that's not going to happen now."

Valdez turns. "No, it's not." He continues down the drive.

"Why do you think he was there?" she asks.

"I don't know, but he was there to kill Maria; that's what she told me on the porch. She said God told her he killed Eddie."

"God told her?"

Valdez reaches the car, opens his driver's side door, and explains over the top of the car. "Said God came to her in a dream, allowed her to watch the whole thing. She knew Eddie'd been shot in the head. She knew Kade did it. She was going to stab him with that big freaking kitchen knife." Valdez uses his hands, holding them apart, to show Barbara the length of the knife.

Barbara opens her door. "Not like that was a secret. Kade killing Eddie. I'm sure it wasn't hard to figure out. You figured it out."

Valdez stands there at the car door and stares back at the house. "No, it's not like it was hard to figure out." Quiet for a moment. "Eddie deserves justice."

"Killing Kade isn't justice," she says. "That's revenge."

"What's the difference?"

Barbara touches her left breast. "Us—we're the difference." Then she half-chuckles to herself. "There's a flag in my supervisor's office that is the thin blue line. Above the line, the thing says, 'Sometimes there's *justice*, and sometimes there's *just us*.' I stared at it while I got chastised for what Kade did to me. I brought it up and told them how wrong it is. There's no *just us*. We have to stand for *justice*. "

"Right," Valdez says. "That's bullshit." He gets in the car.

Barbara gets in the passenger seat. "No, that's not bullshit," she says while shutting the door. "There's no *just us*. There's *justice* and then there's *vengeance*, and we aren't that. We aren't vengeance or revenge."

Valdez's mind jumps to Charlotte as he jams the keys in the ignition and starts the car. "*We?*"

"Cops—you want to go do vengeance, you want revenge, leave your badge on the table. Trust me, this world doesn't need any more crooked cops." Barbara puts her seat belt on. "What you think is going to happen now? Think he'll come back, and—"

"—Remember how nice we were to him and not kill her?"

Barbara sighs. "Listen to me," she says, "You did the right thing. I know it doesn't feel like it, but you did."

She's right, and he hates it.

"Yeah."

He drives, but he doesn't know where he's driving.

Scratch that, he knows where he's driving. He's driving with a direction in mind, in uncomfortable silence, and he's okay with that because driving clears his head.

Barbara's in the passenger seat with her left leg up under her and her right arm resting on the window seal. Hand against her chin, staring out the window, thinking. Thinking so hard, Valdez swears he can almost hear her thoughts, but he ignores that and keeps driving.

Valdez is going to get the proof he needs to take Kade into custody. Maybe at that point, Kade will pull on him, and it will be righteous. Be justified. He gets what he wants. Or it won't be—doesn't matter now.

He's not going to tell her where they are going. He'll use this moment as a test, see where she's at on this journey … because that's what they're on, a journey. See what type of cop she is.

That's why Jamison brought her on to keep him from doing something stupid. Jamison must have thought ahead enough to know he needed to bring someone in that Valdez would listen to. Someone strong enough to stand up to him but knows when to keep quiet. She handled herself at the house. Kade would have pulled on him. Had he, there'd be a lot of problems and a lot of unanswered questions.

At least they got something from the house, and what they got was Kade admitting to sending a message to Valdez. *"I guess you got my message."*

They're on the turnpike, heading east when Valdez's phone rings; it's Jimmie. Valdez answers.

Jimmie says, "I'm calling just to check in because you know, wanted to make sure you didn't fucking forget about me."

"I didn't forget about you."

"Well, that's good to know because, you know, you were supposed to come see me this morning."

"Yeah, I got busy," Valdez says, looking at Barbara.

"Busy," Jimmie says. "I don't know what the fuck that means. I had to fucking shit my brains out, had a baby turtle in my shorts—"

"—I get what you mean."

"Left and then came back."

"You left?"

"What'd you want me to do, shit my pants? I like you, but I don't like you that much. Got here just in time to watch her pull up and go inside. After midnight, I watched your boy break a bunch of car windows; that was some funny shit. Then, he drove a golf cart into the front end of a car."

"You didn't stop them?"

"You told me to watch the girl. I watched the girl. She never came back out."

"We just ran into Kade," Valdez says. Barbara turns in her seat to listen to the conversation.

"Where at?"

"Eddie's mom's."

Jimmie whistles and says, "Bold."

"Tell me about it," Valdez says. "Let me guess, you're calling to tell me because you had to shit, the girl left when you were gone."

"She's back at the apartment now but yeah. Some girl dropped her off. I'm not sure who she was—looked familiar though."

"Same person that picked her up?"

"You heard the part where I said I wasn't here, right? I mean, I'm good at things, but if I could be in two places at once, I'd be in your mom and someplace else."

Valdez ignores the jab. "I heard it."

"Alright, just making sure."

"You check the camera?"

Jimmie laughs into the phone. "Yes, I checked the camera," he says. "What do you think I'm a fucking amateur at this shit? She left with the same girl not long after I left to go shit. Again, she looked familiar, but I can't place her. She showed up around ten in the morning, went inside, then they both left. Don't know where they went. I figured the best thing to do was come back here and catch a nap, knowing she's going to come back to the apartment. I mean Gilliam's kind of a Nazi about how the girls live their lives."

"Gilliam's kind of a Nazi in general."

"Yeah well, he's white."

"You're white."

"So are you, you Irish Bastard."

"That all you calling to tell me?"

Jimmie's quiet and then he says, "Yeah, I think. What do you want me to do now? Stay on the girl?"

"Yeah," Valdez says.

"You going to talk to her, or you just looking to play love connection for me?"

Valdez looks at the clock on the dashboard. "I'm going to talk to her, but if you need help in the love department, I mean hookers work well for the immediate. But you want something lasting, the only thing lasting from them are STDs."

"I already got a few of those."

"I know."

"Gave them to your mom too."

"I'm hanging up now." Valdez ends the call as Jimmie laughs into the phone.

CHAPTER 29:

BARBARA

BARBARA SAYS NOTHING AS THEY LEAVE THE HOUSE. Best to let him stew in his anger and frustration. Stanley told her that was the best thing for a man, especially for someone like him. He'd tell her, "Let me come to my conclusions—eventually, I'll admit you were right."

Which is what happens.

Valdez ends his call and drops the phone into the cup holder in the center console between them. After a moment of silence and a heavy sigh to go with his normal heavy breathing, he says, "You were right."

Barbara holds the silence long enough to make him wonder if she heard him or not. Then she says, "I know," while she removes her left leg from under her and dropping her foot to the floor.

Valdez turns his head. "You don't make this easy, do you?"

"No," Barbara says. "It wouldn't be fair if this were."

Valdez hums low. "You are right about what happened at the house."

"That the only thing I'm right about?" Barbara asks, turning in her seat, digging for more from him. "Anything else I was right about?"

"Yeah," he says.

"You not going to let it be that easy?"

"No."

"Didn't figure you would," Barbara says. "I know I was right."

Valdez talks without looking. "I don't want to admit it; it's hard to do, you know." He glances her way and then back at the road. "Admitting a woman's right, especially one I got no connection to."

"You got Jamison; he's your connection."

Head locked straight ahead. "I didn't have sex with Jamison."

"What makes you think I did?" Barbara says, feigns offense, bringing her hand to her lips to cover her mouth, using her best Southern Belle voice, which is just her playing Scarlett from *Gone With the Wind,* which was the only movie with a Southern Belle in it that she's ever watched. For all the great accolades the movie got—it's still a racist piece of trash. Except for Rhett Butler, he was sexy, in gorgeous technicolor.

"It's Jamison," Valdez says. "You were right about a lot of things. You were right to talk me down. I was going to kill that man. Maybe that would've solved some things. But then there'd be a whole lot of other things it wouldn't have solved. That was the right thing to do—that's hard to say to you, but then again, you're female." He exits the highway. "Charlotte always goes on about how you all are always right. Men should do as you say. Do as they're told, which I find is bullshit because otherwise how'd men come to dominate society. She tells me it is because women only let men think they're in charge. Ever seen a man not getting any—he's desperate."

"Sounds about right."

"You were right about the justice part. That's not easy to say either. But you were right, and I've seen something like—what you talked about—and I've never given it much thought. Yeah, the thin blue line is a thing; we hold back society from itself."

"Also means we're a step away from stepping over the line."

"Look, I said you were right; you don't have to keep at it."

Barbara pokes his shoulder. "I do. That's the point."

Valdez *humphs.*

"Stanley talked at length about good and bad; that is kind of a preacher thing," she says. "But what he said has always stuck with me. There's no good or bad. There's people and people are complicated. Born to do wrong in this world but had a Father that so loved Man he did right by Man."

Valdez says, "There's right and wrong."

Barbara nods. "There is."

"There's good and bad."

"There is."

"Evil too," he says. "I've known evil men. But killing Kade wouldn't have been evil—just right."

"You think Kade's evil?"

"I do," Valdez says. "He killed Eddie."

"Kade's not evil," Barbara says. "He's just living life the only way he knows how, looking out for himself. That's something Stanley always told me, 'Look at the people you work with. The youth aren't evil. Men can do evil things, but they aren't evil. There's always good within us.' I wasn't sure how much I went along with it until Stanley was gone. When I start to think about people being evil, my mind would start the tape. 'Trust in Jesus,' Stanley would say. 'Although, men are wicked, redemption is possible in Jesus.'"

Valdez doesn't like that because his face scrunches and he sniffs once then twice, taking a heavy breath.

Finally, he says, "Your husband had to be a holy man to live with you."

Barbara turns her chin up, putting some lightness in her voice. "How I know he went to heaven."

"You're not real popular with your coworkers are you?"

"No, but that's not something I care about. It's doing right by people that I care about. That's what police work is to me. Justice. Doing the right thing."

"Even though no one is watching."

"That's the textbook answer; that's not always the easiest thing to do. Trying to do the right thing, that's the easiest answer for what I'm doing."

"You're trying to do right by me, aren't you?"

"Jamison asked me to, so yeah, I guess I am," she says. "He cares about you."

"I know. It's annoying."

"Charlotte told me about that other guy, Frankie?" Barbara says. "She cares about you too."

"I figured," Valdez says, "but that wasn't for her to tell."

"You brought it up this morning, otherwise, I'd have kept it to myself."

Valdez slams on the brakes, stopping the car in the middle of the road, hard. Tire smoke blows past the front of the vehicle. A farm truck blows around them on the left, honking his horn and giving them the finger.

Valdez checks his mirrors and turns the car around. He pulls the car to the shoulder and puts it in park, and then he leans back in the driver's seat, dropping his hands to his thighs.

He's quiet and then says, "Charlotte met Eddie once. I insisted the boy come to dinner. He asked me why... this was happening just a few months after I got him out of jail, three months into our 'relationship,' what Jimmie calls it, and there I was waiting for him in my old red and

white Mustang, arm hanging out the window. Something I can't afford but can't afford to live without... Eddie argued with me, saying he thought this was a bad idea, echoing what Jimmie told me earlier. Jimmie asked me why I wanted the kid to meet Charlotte. I didn't know how to answer that. I just wanted the kid to meet her. I figured if he's going to trust me, then I have to show him my underbelly.

"Eddie didn't want to get in the car and asked me why. I told him 'Either come or don't come, but I want you to meet my wife.' I told him it was because I'm asking him to trust me, so I'm showing him some trust. He needed to trust me if this was going to work. Eddie told me he didn't trust me. 'That's why I need you to meet my wife,' I said. He asked, 'What's meeting your wife going to do?' I told him, 'I met your mother. I met your sister.' He told me he didn't see the point while trying his best to not be that scared kid I picked up in the jail. He asked, 'What's it going to do?'

"The dinner was at the restaurant, Mexican, because I thought Eddie might like to be among his people. A joke. Eddie didn't find it as funny as I did. He said, 'Just because I'm half-Mexican doesn't mean that I like to be reminded of it. It's like if I said let's go celebrate Saint Patrick's Day every day because you know you.' I told him, 'You're part me, part Irish, you think we're that different?' He said, 'Just because I'm brown, I don't need you being all racial and shit. That's Trump shit.' I asked him if he ever looks in the mirror. To which he said of course. I said, 'Then you're reminded of it regardless of what anyone else does. Don't take it personally, and you might just make it in this world.' I walked him over to Charlotte. She hugged him, which surprised the kid. He looked over at me confused, so I shoved the kid into the booth and told him, 'It's about trust.'"

"Is this where it happened?" Barbara asks.

Valdez points at the opposite shoulder. "Right over there's where the car was parked; I can still see the tire tracks."

"What do you think happened? I mean, after?"

Valdez bites his lip to think about it. Then puts the car in gear and turns around. Gets back to the Turnpike, but he doesn't go back in the direction she thinks he would. No, he goes northeast. She doesn't say anything about it because he's answering her question without talking.

At the next exit, Valdez gets off the turnpike, Crosses the bridge and then gets back on, going back toward town to the spot where Kade stole her patrol car.

"Where'd you pull them over at?" he asks.

Barbara tells him that it's a few miles down the road. She points him to the spot. He pulls over and parks again. Doesn't speak.

Then Valdez says, "Tell me where the chase ended."

Barbara tells Valdez to drive on for a bit and then to exit the highway, take a right onto Elm Place, and then go down to the light. "See the light, take a left, and go down to that road, Oak. He went in there, took a turn, and ended up over by that elementary school."

Valdez follows her directions, ending at the elementary school. He exits the car and asks, "Where'd you lose sight of him?"

She throws her hand behind her. "Back over there; he took those turns faster than I did."

"But you came upon your car here?"

Barbara can still see her patrol car's tire marks. "Yeah, right here, off in the grass."

"How long?"

"I don't know, eleven seconds."

"Not long then?"

Barbara shakes her head.

Valdez nods and says, "Shawna."

Barbara sees something flash across his eyes; he's hunting. Hot on the scent of something, but she doesn't know what it is. Valdez marches off toward the houses on the other side of the school.

CHAPTER 30:

KIRSTEN

KIRSTEN IS BACK AT THE APARTMENT AFTER leaving with Shawna, which was a mistake and a stupid risk but one she had to make. She'd been up all night and wasn't thinking right. That's what she tells herself. A bullshit reason, but it is the only reason she's going to admit.

Being here, back *home*, it's clear; Kirsten wants to do something. Something for Eddie. She wants to make a difference. She thought the only way she could do that was by going with Shawna to see that cop from Eddie's message. He might be able to help her, but he wasn't there, and that was a letdown.

The apartment is empty, go figure—the girls don't pay any more attention to Gilliam or what he wants any more than anyone else. Kirsten heard them talking and spreading rumors of war but avoiding Kirsten. No one respects Gilliam. Not like he believes they do. Even Kade says he's a two-bit criminal and one-bit pimp, meaning he's nothing and an even worse pimp.

The empty apartment leaves her alone and lets her wallow in her anger. Angry at the world, at herself, at Shawna, at Kade, Aaron, Gilliam, and anyone else that's done her pain. Angry at Eddie for dying.

She's alone. She's always been alone, but this feels different. She should have told Eddie when she had the chance. That was her intention during that last conversation, but that conversation didn't go the way she wanted. Now there's no fixing it.

He's dead.

Boys are stupid. Men even more so. Kirsten missed the opportunity, and he missed the important things. But girls know. They see.

At the kitchen table, Kirsten searches for a cigarette among the half dozen open, empty packs. She picks each one up, flips the cover, and finds them empty. She discards the empty ones over her shoulder until she finds the half-empty pack she used last night.

Clutching the pack, Kirsten plucks a cigarette from it and snatches the lighter off the table. She stands there, hands cupping the end of the cigarette, and lights the cigarette. The flame brightens her face and brings warmth to her fingers. She puffs a few times to get the cigarette going. Then she holds the cigarette at her side.

Smoke curls around her.

She waits.

Alone.

Fuck Eddie for doing this to her, for leaving her alone.

But she's not alone.

Kirsten examines the cigarette between her fingers and guesses she'll have to stop smoking.

The whole time they were gone, Shawna asked Kirsten questions about Kade. About what Kirsten thinks she's doing, talking to the cops. Shawna said, "What if Kade finds out we came over here?" "And how would he find out?" Kirsten asked. Shawna would tell her brother about the police station. That's what Shawna would do—she would tell Kade. That's what happens when people fall in love. They do stupid things.

Like Eddie.

Eddie's dead.

They do stupid things. Make mistakes. Say things they shouldn't. Hold back what they shouldn't. Then those mistakes compound, and there's no going back to before. And sometimes those mistakes are betrayals, and there's no coming back from those either. Like she betrayed Eddie by not telling him. If she had, he wouldn't have left. He would still be here. He wouldn't be dead.

Fuck him for dying.

Shawna will betray her. Her bitching made that clear. So, outside the station, in Shawna's car, Kirsten reached across Shawna's body. Jammed her right hand against Shawna's throat. Squeezed, turning the skin white around her fingers. Made Shawna look her in the eye. Kirsten told her, "He's not going to find out, understand." Shawna, wide-eyed and fearful, nodded her head, showing she understood. Kirsten let go and said, "This was stupid anyway. I don't know what I was thinking."

That was a lie; she did know what she was thinking.

The apartment door flies open—kicked open—interrupting her thoughts and bringing everything she's been waiting for and more.

Through the door comes Kade, smiling in a way she's never seen. Aaron's there too. Gilliam is last through the door, bleeding from his ear. He's screaming, "I'm going to fucking kill him," as Aaron's ushering a bound man to the couch, keeping his body between Gilliam and the bound man.

Kade's holding Gilliam back, getting blood on his white t-shirt. He tells Gilliam to calm down. "Think about what we got to do; we aren't done yet."

And the other person, someone she doesn't recognize, has his hands and face covered and bound in duct tape. Blood covers the duct tape. A river of blood down his neck and the front of his shirt. Down to his chest. His hands are bound in front, and his eyes are smiling like he's heard the biggest joke and he's the only one that finds it funny.

There's blood on Aaron too. Blood coming from Gilliam's ear.

And everyone's talking all at the same time.

"The fuck we aren't," Gilliam says, his hand going to his injured ear. "He fucking bit my ear off."

"And we gagged him for it," Kade says, trying to inject some calm into the situation.

Aaron tosses his head back over his shoulder. "We got Mikey to worry about."

The man plops down onto the couch cushions and holds up his hands, giving Gilliam the middle finger, which causes Gilliam to explode again. He rushes against Kade, who braces for the impact, but not well enough. Kade's stance gives, and the two of them fall back into Aaron, who falls onto the man on the couch. Kade and Gilliam crash to the floor. Everyone cusses at everyone else. Gilliam and Kade wrestle on the floor, making it difficult for Aaron to get up. The whole time, the bound man's eyes are laughing along as he uses his two hands to swat at Aaron.

"Fuck this plan," Gilliam says, sounding very much like Gilliam. Kade lets go of him, and Gilliam rolls to his side, takes a knee, pointing at each person. "Fuck you and fuck him and fuck that fuck on the couch. Fuck you all. This plan's fucked."

"Just because your ear," Kade starts to say, but Gilliam throws a punch. Strikes Kade on the chin and sends him to the side. Aaron's there, kicking Gilliam as hard as he can, sending Gilliam backpedaling to his ass.

Aaron says, "This will work, but you got to calm down."

Gilliam sits there with his hands beside him, and stares at Aaron. Kade laughs and picks himself up off the floor. On one knee, touching his jaw, moving it from side to side, he says, "He's finally got some balls."

The bound man tries to get up off the couch, but Aaron prevents him from getting up. Gilliam scoots back on the floor. "This was a mistake."

Kade says, "It's fine."

"This is not fine," Gilliam says, pointing at his ear. "He fucking spit it out the window. What are we going to do about that? We can't just go back and pick it up, sew it back on."

"He spit it at you in the car," Aaron says, "and it went out the window, so get over it. It's done."

"Big balls," Kade says, staring at Aaron, getting his feet under him. "Seems Eddie taught you a thing or two." Aaron gives Kade a hand. Kade grabs Aaron's arm. Aaron pulls Kade up.

Aaron looks proud, takes in Kade's praise.

"Fuck you two fucks," Gilliam says, pointing at them both.

Kade turns to look down at Gilliam. "Relax, everything's alright."

Gilliam says, "Alright—this isn't fucking alright, it's not okay, and it's fucking messed up. What are you saying? That you mean you both planned for that bitch boy to take my ear?"

Both Aaron and Kade shake their heads.

Aaron says, "No, but we knew there'd be some issues. You planned for some. We planned for some."

"This is a big fucking issue," Gilliam says, again pointing at his ear.

"That's a small issue," Kade says. "Like your dick."

Gilliam, straightening his back and smiling, says, "Your sister doesn't think so."

Kade takes a step forward, hands clenched, face a mask of rage. Kirsten steps in, clearing her throat. Kade stops, and everyone looks her way, including the bound man. "Anyone mind telling me what the hell's going on?"

Everyone tells her no, except the bound man, who through the gag says something that sounds like a yes.

"We've been busy," Aaron says.

"I noticed," she says, stubbing out the cigarette on the table. "Who is this?"

"Billy," Kade says.

Kirsten turns to her brother. "Billy Vaughn?"

Billy tips his head toward Kirsten. He's bowing. He looks pathetic but seeing the look under those eyes, there's nothing pathetic about Billy. He's well built, handsome, with dark hair, even if he's covered in shiny duct tape and blood. There's a fire in his eyes.

"That's right," Gilliam says, getting up to his feet. "Bitch boy Billy fucking Vaughn. Take a good look because, in a few hours, he's going to be nothing."

Back at her brother, Kirsten asks, "What's that mean?" But he waves her away. "Don't you do that, don't wave me off. What the fuck is he doing here?"

Kade tells her, "We needed a place to take him."

Aaron says, "Yeah, we... umm... what do we call what we did? Kidnap, coup?"

Gilliam says, "I took care of a problem."

"Where's Eddie?" she asks her brother, ignoring Gilliam.

"He's dead," Kade says without any emotion.

That makes what comes next easier for her. Easier for what she's going to have to do.

She's smoked three cigarettes, thinking about what she needs to do. Thinking about how those were her last cigarettes. Thinking about what comes next. She knows what she has to do now. She knew it this morning. She knew it last night. She knew it, but now she knows it. It's a part of her. A compulsion. It's the only thing she can do to make things right.

It's the right thing.

She knows that.

The right thing. Right for Eddie. Right for her. Right for everyone.

He's dead.

"Well, he can't stay here," Kirsten says, crossing her arms and tapping her foot.

CHAPTER 31:

JAMISON

JAMISON PULLS UP TO VALDEZ'S HOUSE. THE HOUSE is in a cul-de-sac, quiet, dark, and rundown with weeds growing in the cracks, a tarp-covered car in the driveway covered in dust and leaves, and a broken fence, rotted and fallen. Only one coach light works near the front porch and the front door is open. Lights are on inside.

Jamison kills the ignition and unbuckles. He reaches over to the passenger seat, picks up the report, and opens his car door, thinking of the phone call an hour ago.

Valdez had called him. "Meet me at the house."

Jamison asked, "What house? your house?"

Valdez told him he had some information. Jamison had some information, too. Valdez told him he looked forward to hearing it. "Remember where I live?"

Jamison spent the whole day trying to get the information. Now, everything they needed was in this folder in his hand, and it feels good, feels like he's a cop again.

Which is the point and his reason for doing all this. Jamison wanted to set things right. Fix his friendship, which might not happen, but he's trying.

Valdez was right in that interview.

Jamison had lost sight of it all. Working for Meredith Hudson had done that to him, made him blind. The price of climbing the ladder. Somewhere along the way, he stopped being Jamison.

But Valdez never stopped being Valdez.

At the door, Jamison knocks on the glass. Valdez appears and opens the door, inviting him in. Jamison enters the house, stepping into the foyer. There are pictures of Valdez and Charlotte, of their kids, the boy and the girl, now a man and woman. Kids with families all their own. Valdez shows Jamison to the kitchen, which is off to the left through the living room. Barbara's there at the kitchen table, drinking a beer. She jumps up when he enters and hugs him.

The hug is nice.

Barbara breaks the hug and asks Jamison if he wants anything.

Valdez says there are drinks in the fridge, but Jamison refuses. Then Valdez says, "Don't worry, we're just having one."

Jamison says, "Long day?"

Barbara tells him it was.

There's a smell of food cooking. The burner on the stove's on with a silver pot sitting on top. There are some buns on the counter. "What smells good?" he asks. "Chili?"

Valdez smiles. "Not Chili, Coney sauce," he says, "Had it shipped from Detroit."

"Detroit?" Jamison asks.

Barbara says, "He had it shipped in, for—"

"—my dad," Valdez finishes. "Got it for him for his birthday. Loved this place around the corner from our old house. That Irish Bastard."

"You got your dad chili?" Jamison says, setting the file down on the table and taking off his suit coat. "Why are you eating it now?"

Valdez says this is what he ordered for himself.

"Not chili—Coney sauce," Valdez corrects, moving to the stove to check the contents of the pot. "This place used to make the best Coneys around. You know, had one of those names that sounds like every other Coney place. Their Coney's aren't like every other place. My pops hasn't been back home for years, so I bought a shipment of chili and dogs and buns, all packaged in dry ice and sent here."

"Hope they didn't pack it in ice from Flint," Jamison says, knowing that's really where Valdez is from.

He laughs and says, "That's good." He moves from the stove, retrieving his beer from the counter and taking a drink.d Valdez looks different. His day with Barbara must have changed him a little bit. That's what Jamison had hoped for, but he didn't expect them to get along so well.

"What'd you find out?" Barbara asks, taking a drink of the beer as she settles into a chair, straddling it.

"Just jumping into it," Jamison says. He puts his hands on the back of a chair and then points to the file. "The ballistics are the same."

Valdez straightens up. "As the gun that killed Eddie?" he asks and then puts his beer bottle on the counter.

"The gun from the car, the ballistics are the same?" Barbara asks trying to clarify.

Nodding, Jamison says, "Everything matches. That's the murder weapon. The report's in there if you want to read it." Valdez moves from the counter, stepping around Jamison, and picks up the folder. He flips it open. "That was a good find ... and smart."

Jamison grips the back of the chair.

"There's an arrest warrant in here," Valdez says. "What's with the warrant?"

"I figured that's enough," Jamison says. "The ballistics, the relationship, I figured it all would be enough, right? Kade steals your car." Motioning to Barbara. "And then that gun's found there, and there's a bullet matching the ones in the gun to the one in your kid's head. I figured that was enough."

Looking at the folder, Valdez says, "Enough for the judge."

"Enough for the judge."

Valdez sets the folder down on the table and steps back. "You didn't have to do that."

"I know that," Jamison says.

Jamison knows he didn't have to do that. Getting the warrant is him saying he's all in. On this. On the investigation, on Valdez, on Eddie, and everything else connected to this.

"There's no going back," Jamison says, but he is unsure who voiced it, him or Valdez.

The outcome could ruin him if things go sideways.

Barbara clears her throat and looks from Valdez to Jamison. "We should tell him what we found."

Valdez shrugs and moves away from the file and table. "She wouldn't let me arrest Kade."

Jamison lifts a questioning eyebrow. "What do you mean, let you?"

"Found him at Eddie's mom's house," Barbara says, explaining. "And Val was going to kill him. Pulled his gun on him. "

"If he pulled that gun on me," Valdez says, "I wanted to be ready. He wouldn't pull on me. I tried to get him to, but she wouldn't let me put him down."

"*Jesus*, Dez," Jamison exclaims, turning to Barbara. "*Why* was he there?"

Barbara says, "He was going to kill the kid's mom."

"Really?" Jamison says. He can't believe it.

Nodding his head and smiling, Valdez adds, "Admitted trying to send me a message, which sounds like an incriminating statement to me."

Barbara smiles and takes another drink. "And then Valdez found the shell casing." She holds the bottle up to let what she said sink in with Jamison.

Jamison asks, "What do you mean you found the shell casing?"

Barbara motions to the paper sack on the table. "In there are Kade's pants, his jeans, in the pocket is the shell casing. We... eh... need permission to book it into property, but everything's legal so far."

"Where the hell did you come up with his pants?" Jamison asks. "And, you have permission. This is still a case, but... legal... why would it not be legal?"

Barbara tells him it's complicated and about the woman Valdez barged in on and took the pants from, where they found them.

Valdez sighs. "The pants are from the girl. He took them off, and she was supposed to burn them, but she didn't. We have his shirt too."

"You what?" Jamison asks. "What girl?"

"Shirt's got blood on it," Barbara says.

Jamison asks, "You have his clothes?"

"Yeah," Valdez says. He takes a drink. "He's screwed."

Barbara starts the story at the beginning. "We were driving around. We went to visit where the kid got killed, and then, I took Val to the last place I saw Kade."

Valdez interjects, "Shawna Reed's neighborhood. Her house backs up to that school."

"Ryan Horn's girl?" Jamison says. "The one he used to beat up on?"

"The same," Valdez says, grinning.

Barbara says, "We're standing there at the school, and Val gets this look like he just smelled blood or something. Tunes me out and turns everything off. Starts walking. Looked like a bloodhound. He made us walk around the block to get to this house." Barbara takes a drink and clears her throat. "He knocks on the door while I'm asking him, 'Whose house is this?' And all he tells me is, 'Shawna's.' I'm like, 'Who is Shawna?' He doesn't say anything, just stands there facing the door. Then this woman opens the door. She's got dark hair. Still pretty. Tank top, shorts. Looks like she's a recovering addict that's put on some weight, but not used to it. Her clothes are a bit too tight, but not because she's fat, just not right for her new body. Anyways, she opens the door, using half the door to block half her body. Sees us standing there and then her eyes focus on Valdez like she knows who he is. Then she asks, 'You the cop?'"

Smiling at Jamison, Valdez squints. He adds, "Small f-ing world—Frankie Green's girlfriend."

Jamison nods. "Ex-girlfriend, who left Frankie for Ryan, who last I knew was slinging dope out of some shitty ass bar."

Barbara nods and goes on with the story. "That's a good word for it. She looks at him like she can't believe it's a small freaking world. He just pushes past her and walks into the house. So without saying anything else, this woman just throws the door open for me and walks back in the house behind him."

"I saved her life," Valdez says. "That counts for something."

Looking at Barbara, Jamison sees she is confused by Valdez's statement. He explains. "Almost killed herself," he says, pointing at Valdez, "and he didn't obey orders. I told him not to. What does he do? He goes over there to talk to her. Good thing too because she'd just shot up a shit ton of heroin. He brought her back to life. That's why she let you in."

Barbara turns her attention from Jamison to Valdez. "You saved her life?"

"After Frankie died," Valdez says, rubbing the back of his head. "I hit her with Narcan."

"He saved her life," Jamison says.

"That's why she let us in," Barbara says, "because you saved her life? Why didn't you tell me that part? Here I thought you just barged your way in—that's some fourth amendment shit."

"I figured Kade ran to her house after dumping her car," Valdez says to Jamison, ignoring Barbara's comment.

"We're in the living room, and she asks us to sit down," Barbara says. "She's got like no furniture, but there's beer bottles everywhere. She's got that black tank top, doesn't fit, and she's not wearing a bra. Kept tugging at the straps like she's afraid they might fall. Looked nervous as heck talking to us. Valdez sat down and goes, 'I know you were with Kade.' And

this nervous-looking junkie doesn't even bat an eye. She says, 'He spent the night the other night.' Like it's nothing. Then the Shawna girl says, 'He ran from the cops.' Like she knew the whole story, but she didn't know the whole story because Valdez told her it was me he ran from. And she looked at me, shaking her head, and then went right back to talking to Val. She said, 'His clothes are in the back room.' Again, it's nothing. She didn't even try to put up a fight. She could have lied to us, but she didn't."

"She knew what happened," Valdez says. "She knows Kade killed someone. She knows he's in the wrong. Got it on recording."

Barbara tells Jamison, "So she takes us back to the back bedroom. His clothes are in a pile. Valdez grabs the pants, checks the pockets, and feels a shell casing. He reaches in and finagles the thing out to look at it without touching it."

"9mm," Valdez says, "the right size."

Barbara says, "I asked the girl if she had a paper sack. She nodded silently and disappeared. She came back with a sack. We put the clothes in there as best we could without touching them."

Valdez says, "It's evidence."

"I know it is *evidence*," Jamison says.

Barbara says, "Before we left, Val asked her if she had seen Kade lately, she said no. He asked if she'd seen his sister, and she shook her head. He had to ask her again. Then she said yeah. He asked her if they had tried to come to see him. She said they went to see a cop, didn't know if it was him, but yeah."

Valdez explains it to Jamison. "Coop called me, told me two girls had come to see me."

Jamison takes it all in. They did some good work. They have the clothes from the murder with blood on them. That blood's going to be Eddie's. "That's damn good work. That's…" then his voice trails off because they all know what comes next. "Do we know where Kade is?"

Valdez says, "I don't know where he is, but I might know someone that does."

CHAPTER 32:

KIRSTEN

THEY LEAVE THE APARTMENT, SAYING THEY WERE going to Gilliam's trailer because it's in the country. No one will hear any screaming or gunshots. Gilliam threatened to kneecap Billy. Kirsten told him he wasn't going to do it at the apartment. Said there were people everywhere. They would love nothing better than to call the cops on him, her, and the apartment.

So they leave.

Then she leaves; she couldn't stay there. Not after that. Not after seeing her brother, hearing him say what he said. Looking at her like it meant nothing, telling her Eddie was dead. Like Eddie meant nothing, and Eddie means everything, at least to her he does. He meant everything to her. He was her future.

Kirsten knows her brother and knows when he's putting on an act. Even when it's not a very good one. He wasn't even trying to convince her he didn't do what she feels he did.

At the McDonald's, in her booth, Kirsten listens to Eddie's voice on her phone. *"I've never lied to you about loving you. There's a lot I have lied about, but I never lied to you about myself. Except for this one thing..."* She breaks down into tears. Crying and thinking that one thing was him working for the cops, working for someone named Valdez.

He lied to her, but she wasn't any better. She'd kept the truth from him, too. Had she told him he might have stayed with her.

Kirsten should have told him but didn't, and now, there's no coming back from that.

He's dead.

There's movement beside her, but she's too teary-eyed to look up. She doesn't want someone seeing her red splotchy face. So, she keeps her head low and looks away.

The shadow lingers.

And somehow, Kirsten knows who it is, but doesn't know how she knows, but she knows it's him. Eddie said he would come for her.

She half-turns her body a little in the booth and picks her head up from her hands to see a large red-faced man staring back at her. He's rocking from side to side on his toes, sucking on his bottom lip like he's preparing to say something to sit down or something. That'd be the gentlemanly thing to do. But he doesn't say anything. He just sways back and forth. He looks like a cop.

Kirsten doesn't say anything either. She remains silent and forces the tension and stress out of her body.

The man takes her not saying anything as a sign, silent permission, to sit in the booth. Seated, he spreads his massive form out and throws his arms on the back of the booth. The majority of his bulk rests against the table. Relaxed. Like this is the first time he's sat down all day. And for a long time, he doesn't say anything. He stares at her. Stares at her with those big red cheeks. Irish, she thinks. Not what she would have guessed for someone with his name, but here he is, coming to her like Eddie said he would. He's staring at her, but not like Billy stared at her. No, he looks more like a father, concerned, like someone that's there to deliver bad news but doesn't know how to say it. Like he cares.

Then he asks, "How far along are you?"

Kirsten loses it and breaks down at the table in front of him. Then after she recovers, she asks through trembling sobs, "How do you know?"

"I know," he says. "I can see it."

Kirsten pulls herself back together, sniffling, and wipes her eyes with her fingertips. She blinks and pulls her blonde hair back out of her face, off her shoulders. She shuffles in the seat, trying to sit straighter. "But how?"

He speaks in a half-whisper. "It doesn't matter. What matters is did he know?"

She shakes her head.

The man asks, "What are you going to do, now?"

Kirsten shrugs and shakes her head again. "I thought I would have Eddie. I thought we could go away together. Leave all this behind, but that's not going to happen now."

"It's not going to happen now," he says, repeating her words. "So, it's time to figure out what happens next."

He holds his hands out over the table.

"Eddie had some money saved, asked me to look after it." The man pauses, waves his hand in front of his face. "That's not true. I took it from him. For safekeeping. He hated that. It was money he made working for me. But it's yours if you want it."

"Are you..." She doesn't get very far. She knows who he is, but she can't bear to say the words. Can't bear to ask him if he's the cop, if he's Valdez. How can she trust a man she's never met?

It doesn't matter; he supplies it for her. "The cop? I'm him."

"I should be surprised to see you, but I'm not," she says. It's a lie. "I tried to come see you today."

"I know."

"I couldn't wait for you to come back."

"That's okay," Valdez says, voice patient and calm. But this life has made her paranoid. She knows he's here for something. "I never made it back to the office, but I know you came by. I know it was you. I talked to Shawna."

"You did?"

"I did."

"How'd you know? What'd she tell you?"

"What she knows."

"Going there with Shawna was a mistake, but one I could explain away if I needed, but I guess I don't. Eddie said I could trust you. Shawna knows more than she lets on, but I don't know what she knows. She didn't tell me, and I didn't ask." A single tear falls down her face, and she brushes it away with her left hand. "I wanted to find out..." Kirsten licks the salt of her tears from her lips. "...I need... did Kade..." but the words won't come and it's frustrating.

Valdez is patient, and he doesn't interrupt her or try to offer her the words. His face says he couldn't provide her words because her words are her own. He's letting her come to this on her own.

"I wanted to know how he died, who did it."

"Do you?"

"I do," she says, unsure if she does but not knowing is terrible. More tears fall. This time, she doesn't attempt to wipe them away. She reaches down and snatches up her phone. Gripping the phone in her hand and searching for her voice, she asks, "Did my brother do it?"

The cop nods.

She knew, but now she knows.

Valdez asks, "How much do you want to know?"

Kirsten rocks back and forth in her seat, giving him a full-body nod, as the tears fall. She cries silently because she already knew the answer. She sniffles and tries to keep her face from erupting into a mess. She takes a moment to control herself, but it is like picking up the pieces of a shattered mirror. She tries the best she can. "I want to know it all."

Valdez starts to say, "That's..." but she holds up her hand, cutting him off. She wasn't done saying what she had to say.

Valdez nods in understanding.

Kirsten needs time and takes her time to say it. "...I need to know it all," she says. "I loved him. He... we were supposed to be together, but... Kade never liked that about him. Never liked that he loved me. He didn't think it was right."

"Because he was a kid?"

"Because he wasn't... how do I explain this to you? He wasn't full-blood. He was a half-breed, and that bothered Kade. Bothered Gilliam too. I don't... I can't live this life anymore. Not after." She motions to her belly. "I don't know what to do. Eddie is dead, but Eddie said I could trust you. Said you would come for me, and now you have."

Valdez reaches across the table and draws her hand to his. His fingers find hers and intertwine. He squeezes her hand with tenderness. "I can't do your thinking," he says, "but I can tell you what you want to know. But you have to ask, or else, I'd be killing a piece of you, and I can't do that."

Kirsten licks away the snot from her upper lip and brushes her blonde hair out of her face with both hands. She tucks her hair behind her ears and looks down, eyes focusing on the table. "I need to know. Did Kade do it?"

Valdez squeezes her hand. "Yes."

The words travel through her like lightning.

"Was he... did Eddie work for you?" she asks.

"No, he didn't work *for* me. He worked *with* me. I asked him to help me, and he agreed. He knew what he was getting into. I'm sorry he's gone."

"Me too."

"I would have told him not to be stupid."

"He was stubborn."

"He was a good man. He wasn't when we started. You made him that. He did all this for you."

"He wanted us to leave," Kirsten says. "I wasn't able to, not with a brother like mine. He wouldn't allow it. The Green won't allow it. I'm in this, and Eddie hated that. He wanted me out of this, but how do you leave? How do you leave with people like them? Like Gilliam, Kade, Aaron, or anyone else. They'd come after me. No matter where we would have gone, they'd come. Especially Kade, he'll never let me go."

"Your brother," Valdez says.

"Did Eddie talk about me?"

"All the time."

"What did he say?"

"That he loved you."

"He did love me," Kirsten says. "Eddie said that in his last phone message. Said I could trust you. Can I trust you? Do I trust you?" She pauses, realizing Valdez doesn't know what she's talking about. "He called me. Called me before... he called to say that I could trust you. He said you were a good person."

"I tried to teach him what was right."

"What happened to him shouldn't have happened. I mean, he shouldn't be dead."

"I can't argue with that," Valdez says. "Your brother thought otherwise."

"Kade can go fuck himself. I loved Eddie. He was going to be the father of my child. We were going to have a life together. I would have left for him. I would have tried."

"He would have been a good father," Valdez says. "He didn't have a good one. Sometimes that makes for the best ones."

Kirsten tilts her head to the side and raises an eyebrow. "You don't know what he would have been like."

"I spent a lot of time with him. I know what he would have done."

"You didn't know he was going to die."

Kirsten searches his face. Underneath the cop exterior, she sees the hurt, sees the tears are there, but so is the fire.

"No," he says. "I wish I had known."

"He knew. I think he knew. That's why he called me." She holds up the phone.

"I think you're right about that."

"Why?" she asks. "Why did my brother do it?"

"Because of me," Valdez says. "I think."

"There's got to be more to it," she says. "Kade knew what Eddie meant to me. There's got to be more of a reason."

Valdez shakes his head. "I don't think there was. There's a way of dealing with what Eddie did. And that's it. That's what Kade did. He dealt with it. What I'm interested in is how they found out."

Kirsten's mind returns to her last conversation with Eddie in the closet, searching his bag and calling his mom. "Before, Eddie was worried Gilliam found something in his things, something his mom put in his bag."

"A business card," Valdez says.

Kirsten looks down at the phone in her hand. With a few taps of the screen, she brings up the message and readies it on the screen. "Eddie said I could trust you."

She places the phone on the table. She pushes the phone across the top of the table. Valdez lets go of her hand and picks up the phone. He listens to the message. When it's done, he slides the phone back across the table, and for a long time, he doesn't say anything. Then finally, he puts both of his hands on the table, palms down, and straightens his back in the seat.

"There's only one way this ends."

"I know."

"I'm not going to ask you to betray him," Valdez says.

"I know."

"But I need to know. You have to make that decision. I can do this without you. I understand if you don't want to say."

"I know where he is," she says. "I know what you're asking without asking."

"For Eddie then."

Kirsten gulps and then, cradling her stomach, tells him where her brother went.

CHAPTER 33:
VALDEZ

VALDEZ LEAVES THE MCDONALD'S WITH THE GIRL inside. The girl's a mess. She loves Eddie, and he loved her. But Eddie kept part of himself from her, and now she's paying the price for his transgression and taking a step she can never take back. He walks out of the building toward his Mustang parked in the parking lot. Toward the three cops who are waiting for him.

Jamison has his back against the trunk of Valdez's vehicle, his hands in his pockets, still in his charcoal suit. Barbara is beside him, sitting on the trunk, kicking her feet back and forth, swinging her feet, heels bouncing against the taillight. And Jimmie is separate from them, standing as far away as he can on the passenger side of Valdez's Mustang with his chin resting on his hands, nearly asleep.

As Valdez approaches the car, Jamison steps away from the trunk of the Mustang. He opens his mouth as if he's going to ask a question but then stops. He knows better than to ask Valdez what he found out, so he remains quiet. But Valdez can see it there on his face; he wants to know what she said. And who can blame him, who wouldn't?

But it doesn't matter what Jamison says or doesn't say. Barbara does what Barbara does. She slides off the trunk of the car. "What'd she say? Do you know where we are going?"

Valdez shifts his attention away. "I need a cigarette."

He reaches in his pocket and retrieves a crumpled pack of cigarettes. The pack is gnarled beyond recognition. There's only one cigarette left, which seems about right for the day. He withdraws the lone cigarette from the pack, crushing the rest of the pack. He throws the crumbled pack to

211

the side and jams the end of the cigarette in his mouth. He reaches into his pocket, withdraws the lighter, and with hands around the cigarette, lights it. The smoke enters his lungs and allows him a moment to think.

Jamison paces back and forth, muttering something to himself.

Valdez glances at Jimmie, who stays put, half asleep, waiting. He'd been doing surveillance all day. It's boring, he's tired, but it paid off. Valdez didn't even bother telling Barbara or Jamison how he knew to come here for the girl.

Barbara steps closer, eyes up at him. "What did she tell you? Where are we going?"

From behind the flame and the smoke of the fresh cigarette, Valdez slips the lighter back in his pocket, deciding to leave out the part about the girl being pregnant. "She told me..." he starts but doesn't finish, choosing instead to finish his cigarette. He's had to sneak cigarettes throughout the day, and he hates sneaking them. So, he smokes his cigarette, thankful to not have to sneak them. He shuffles back and forth on his feet ... almost swaying.

Barbara grows frustrated with his lack of answers. She whips around, dismissing him, and walks away back toward the Mustang. She says something about the smoke bothering her.

Valdez glances at Jimmie and takes the cigarette out of his mouth, letting out a stream of smoke. "They're at Gilliam's."

Jimmie picks his head off his hands, returns the head jerk, and says, "I'll get the shotgun." He goes to the trunk.

Barbara whirls around and throws her hands up in the air. "Why didn't you just say that?"

"He's got a good reason for playing games with us," Jamison says.

"Now's the time to see what kind of cops you are," Valdez says.

"What do you mean?" Barbara asks. "You think this will be Kade in the living room all over again? You being the big bad cop you think you are? Acting like the rest of the country sees us?"

"This will be like Kade in the living room all over again, but the outcome's going to be different. You both need to know that." Valdez glances at Jamison. "Need to see it. This isn't like before. This is going to be different. There's only one way this ends."

Valdez stops to take a puff on the cigarette.

"It's in Wagoner County, the country," he says, blowing smoke from his nostrils, doing his best bull impression, "way out east."

Jamison stops his pacing and looks to Valdez then to Barbara. "Outside our jurisdiction."

Barbara considers the information and plucks the cigarette from Valdez's lips. He doesn't stop her. She takes a drag of the cigarette. "What's the plan?"

Valdez shrugs. "Depends."

"On what?" Jamison says, stepping closer so he doesn't have to yell. "On if we get the Sheriff out there? On if we can do this quietly? We can't do this quietly."

He turns to motion to Jimmie, who's already in the trunk of the Mustang, bending over at the hip, and digging around in the trunk.

"You both know how Gilliam is. We can't get the Sheriff involved because we shouldn't be in his fucking case in the first place. You know that. I know that. The Sheriff would shut this fucking goat rope down in two seconds. He won't let us go out there. Not like this. Not with you. Not after that fucking disaster of a meeting you had. You're too close to this. And think, if we pull this off, what are you going to tell the judge? You went there, got him out of the trailer, brought him across county lines, and all is right with the world?"

Jimmie's head pops up from the trunk. "Could work." Jimmie comes up with a shotgun, and he racks it. "It's not like we haven't done it before."

Jamison closes his eyes and squeezes his lips together. "*Jesus* Dez, you can't go across jurisdictional boundaries and hogtie someone and bring them back to town. This isn't the Wild West—that's not how things are done, not anymore."

"I thought you were all in," Valdez says with a smile. "That's what the arrest warrant tells me. Tells me it's either make or break for you. How far you willing to go on this? How far before you get mud on you? When's your name more important than doing the right thing?"

"I'm all in for legal shit," Jamison says as he puts a finger on Valdez's chest, presses against Valdez's shirt. "So far, this shit's been legal, but that's stepping over a line, and you know it."

Barbara sighs. "And you and I both know the Sheriff won't do what needs to be done. He'll try to make too big a deal about it, and Kade might get away."

"Not you too," Jamison says. "You're here to prevent shit like this from happening. You're supposed to stop him from doing this shit."

Barbara takes a hit from the cigarette before handing the cigarette back to Valdez. She lets the smoke out the corner of her mouth. "I'm also a State Trooper. I've got the jurisdiction, so I can go wherever I want."

CHAPTER 34:

JAMISON

THEY TAKE TWO CARS. JIMMIE DRIVES HIMSELF, alone, which is how he prefers it, and Barbara and Jamison go with Valdez. Barbara lets Jamison have the passenger seat as she takes the back seat. And most of the way out to the country, Jamison doesn't speak. Partly because he doesn't know what to say and partly because there's nothing to say.

Valdez told Jamison, before he got in the car, looking at Jamison over the top of the car, "You're wrong about this not being the Wild West. Don't delude yourself into thinking something different. This is Oklahoma: Land of the Red Man."

His meaning is this is Green Country.

This is the Wild West. This is the moment where Jamison either risks everything or bails. He's not bailing now. He's come too far.

The road's dark. They're on the turnpike, heading east, out into the darkness, out into the country, away from Tulsa. Away from Major Crimes, and away from who they were. Away from who they *are*.

They're different people now.

Jamison thinks about that as the street lights throw up small pools of light on the roadway. Then they reach the point when the lights fade into nothing and the highway collapses into darkness.

They're different people now heading out to do something that's against their code, but at the same time—this is righteous.

Jamison wrestles with the knowledge that someone at Major Crimes betrayed Eddie. In the interview, Valdez hinted at it. Well, he went beyond hinting. Before today, Jamison didn't think someone in Major Crimes could do something like this. Give up a kid just for what ... money?

Valdez didn't do it. He wouldn't let Eddie down.

So how far is Jamison willing to go? He's doing this for the right reasons, but it feels like, in a way, he betrayed Eddie by letting Frankie Green die. Something Valdez has never forgiven Jamison for. He's not forgiven himself for it either. One event set into motion others, cascading into turbulence with an unknown ending, like a stone dropped in a pond, sending ripples across the surface. Sure, the water will still and the surface will calm, but the pond will never be the same. And no one will ever see evidence of the change.

Sometimes it's just like that. A death, even one of someone you've never known, will change everything.

From the backseat, Barbara asks, "How far?"

Valdez tells her it isn't far and explains he and Jimmie know where Gilliam lives because of their surveillance. He tells them it wasn't easy to find because Gilliam didn't stay there much. But he did come there now and then. Said Gilliam doesn't ever drive straight there. He likes to change cars frequently like Joe Pesci in *Casino*. He uses a couple of parking garages in Tulsa.

Valdez knew all this just like he knew where Kirsten would be.

It surprised Jamison but only a little. At this point, it's clear Valdez and Jimmie have done a hell of a lot more on this case than either one of them had let on. They've crossed a line.

That was the point of Jamison and Meredith talking to Valdez about Eddie's death. He wasn't supposed to be running the kid. He wasn't authorized. But Cooper allowed it. Why would he? Which brings Jamison back to the interview. It doesn't seem like yesterday. It sickens him that Valdez accused him of forgetting what it was like to be a cop.

He is a cop.

So in a way, this is a way to prove to Valdez that he didn't forget Frankie Green and didn't forget that they used to be friends.

He didn't forget how to be a cop.

While driving, Valdez explains what Kade's sister told him. "There's at least three people at the trailer. Aaron Murphy with Kade Carradine and Peter Gilliam. Aaron's Kade's best friend. The driver of your stolen car. They grew up together, but Aaron isn't anything like Kade. And he's in love with Kirsten."

"She love him back?" Barbara inquires.

Valdez chuckles and says, "Nope."

"Gilliam with Kade and Aaron equals three," Jamison says. "We have four. Four to three. Those are okay odds."

Valdez turns in the seat, nodding, and agrees. "We'll have to park at least a half-mile out and walk in the rest of the way."

"I'm so glad you waited until we're on our way before saying something," Jamison says. "I would have changed before we came out here."

"What, you afraid of some dirt?" Valdez asks.

Barbara says, "He's wearing one of his better suits ... with his better shoes."

Valdez lifts his chin. "Better?"

"Favorite," Jamison says, correcting her and amazed she remembered. "I'm wearing my favorite pair of shoes."

Valdez looks down at the floorboards at Jamison's shoes in the dark and snorts. "You'll be fine. It's an easy walk through the field."

"That's fine." Jamison doesn't say much else. There's nothing to say.

There's only one way this ends.

Jamison's fingers touch the gun at his side and then the badge while thinking about choices, thinking about what choice he's made and the ones he will make. Will he choose the gun? Or the badge?

Then he thinks about the type of cop he's been and the type he is and the type he wants to be. And about how he got here and where he's going.

He thinks of his father.

At his father's retirement, Chief Crawford Collins, a legend in Tulsa, told Jamison, "It's not what you have on someone but how you write the report."

Jamison Sterling knows how to write a report, but he doesn't know how he's going to explain what's about to happen. He's never made an arrest that he didn't gain something from—that's the sort of cop he was, the sort he *is*.

Collins knew that. He said, "There's those that seek the truth and don't care about the uniform. And then some who just like to take their calls and look good in their blues."

Valdez told Jamison once that he falls in a third category. He liked to look good in his blues, somehow not doing any more work than he'd have to and take his calls.

And maybe Valdez is right—that's the worst kind of cop, only doing it for himself.

Not because he's lazy. His body and his looks show that he's an example of discipline. He knows what he wanted out of this gig, and it wasn't the satisfaction of catching bad guys—it was the recognition.

That's what he's cared about, but he doesn't remember where or when that became important. It's not what his father taught him. And that's not how Jamison started his career. He let the recognition take over.

After making sergeant, Jamison came into Major Crimes as the city's representative. Hudson asked him to be a part of her unit to investigate dirty cops. Before that, he was the PIO, Public Information Officer. Major Crimes gave Jamison the best of both worlds: he got to be a cop and look like a cop—investigating other cops and talking to the media. It suited him well. But, that's also how he forgot how to be a cop.

Valdez was right.

Falling in line behind Jimmie's car, Valdez pulls his Mustang to the side of the road. Valdez parks near a corpse of trees. Jimmie's door flies open, and he's out of the car before Valdez can kill the engine. All angles, sinew, and lean muscle, Jimmie walks between the two vehicles, staring at Jamison as he does, and carries his shotgun low at his side.

Barbara's out first as Valdez looks over at Jamison. "Are you here with us?"

Wordlessly, Jamison returns the look and gets out. He removes his sport coat and tie and throws them in the car—giving his answer.

Jimmie positions himself away from the group next to the trunk of the farthest tree. He stares off into the distance, eyes on a trailer parked in a field.

Stepping to the back of the Mustang, Valdez retrieves his vest from the trunk and straps it to his chest. "I could use a cigarette."

"You and me both," Jamison says. He slips a vest over his head and straps the sides down, making sure to not catch the folds of his shirt.

Barbara slips her vest on her shoulders too and grabs the rifle, an AR-15, from Valdez's trunk. She loads the magazine into the rifle and slips the single-point sling around her shoulder. She lets the sling hold the weight of the weapon low and pointed at the ground.

Then Valdez grabs two extra magazines from a backpack and hands them to Barbara. "You ready?"

Barbara nods.

Jamison's fingers swipe against his badge again, caressing the metal. He licks his lips and checks his gun in the holster, pulling it and dropping it several times. Then, he touches his pocket to make sure the warrant's there. A piece of paper won't mean much if things go south, but it gives him some comfort knowing it's there. It might help them if things don't go well—give them some legal standing. It's his last vestige of legitimacy.

He knows, coming out here they've stepped across a line.

The three of them join Jimmie at the tree, and in the distance, Jamison can make out the lights of the trailer. There's no moon, the night's dark, and the clouds are low. Sounds from the trailer reach them at the edge of the field, country music playing.

Valdez touches Jimmie on the shoulder and waves them forward. Shoulder to shoulder, the four of them start through the tall grass marching toward the trailer, the light in the middle of the field.

CHAPTER 35:

AARON

AARON LETS THE COUNTRY MUSIC WASH OVER HIM.
Red-dirt, Oklahoma-grown bullshit, Gilliam sitting across from
him, drinking a beer, still bleeding from his ear. He keeps fussing with it,
so he keeps opening the wound, causing the damn thing to keep bleeding.
Blood all down his neck and the front of his shirt. And still, he won't stop
touching his ear.

The trailer's small. A little silver bullet thing, barely big enough for
the three of them. Like the place Michael Madsen had in *Kill Bill*, except
no fucking snakes. Beer bottles and beer cans littering the floor and the
tables. And there's a little TV with the old-style antenna sticking up from
the top of it, tinfoil touching them. A digital box underneath. There's
tinfoil on the tables with some burnt spoons and needles. Knives everywhere. Just as Gilliam's got guns in every room. He calls this place his
"Fortress of Solitude."

Aaron sits across from Gilliam in a black beanbag chair like they're
teenagers ... beer in his hand too. He sips it, thinking about what
comes next.

The next part should be the easiest of this whole plan. Kade goes and
talks to Mikey. Mikey sets up the meeting with the City, but what he
didn't figure out is what they are going to do with Gilliam.

Aaron listens as Gilliam bellyaches about his ear and gloats about
Billy Vaughn, who is trussed up in a hearty amount of duct tape, sitting
near Aaron, in the littered debris of beer cans and bottles. Billy stretches
his shoulders, rolling them back and forth. And he stares at him like he's
trying to read Aaron's thoughts.

Aaron tries to think quieter so that he can't hear them. But he's smart enough to know that's not what Billy's doing. Billy's reading Aaron's face because he's not doing a good job of keeping it neutral—everything's right there.

Kade's been gone for hours, and he didn't explain what he is going to do with Gilliam.

"Kade should be back by now," Aaron says.

"Where the fuck is he?" Gilliam asks, bringing his hand from his ear for the umpteenth time. "I mean, he left like four fucking hours ago. You'd think he would have been back by now."

Shifting his eyes back to Gilliam, Aaron sips his beer. "He went to meet Mikey, but you didn't do it as clean as it needed to be done. We left Mikey with some problems to clean up. I'm sure Mikey had to answer some questions about the bar."

Gilliam fumes. "How dare that jumped-up dick stick call me, on my fucking phone, and ask me to talk to that fucking two-bit jackoff. Who does he think he is?"

"Michael Collins," Aaron says because he can't resist supplying an answer to the rhetorical question.

Gilliam's eyes glare at him as he sips the beer, finishing the bottle. He drops it to the floor with the six others. He pulls another from a small ice chest near his recliner. "Where did you fucking get your balls?"

"Excuse me?"

"Your balls, your testicles, where the fuck did they come from?" Gilliam asks. "You used to be such a good puppy. You followed orders. Kept your tail between your legs. Nose and eyes down. Let any bitch coming around sniff your ass. But now, you think you got some teeth. Well, let me tell you, I got some fucking teeth." Gilliam snaps his teeth. "I should fucking show you what those teeth can earn you." He motions to the revolver in his waistband. "I should fucking take you out back and treat you like Old Yeller. Put it right to your head, in your fucking mouth, pull the trigger. Show you what your fucking snapping's going to get you."

"You do that, and Kade'd be all over you," Aaron says.

Gilliam breaks into a sneering smile. "There's that puppy, hiding behind the skirts of his fucking butt buddy," Gilliam says. "I'm glad you're a good loyal dog to someone. You weren't fucking loyal to me. Couldn't even kill a man. You're a worthless piece of shit. If you can't do that, you're worthless. You know that. You know what? I don't want to get up, why don't you just open that little hatch under your fucking chair and stand in it." He withdraws the revolver from his waistband, pointing it at Aaron. "And I'll just put you down here, easy peasy, and then that way I don't have to fucking get up and waste this buzz I got going on."

"I'm not hiding behind Kade," Aaron says. "I'm trying to keep all of us alive. It was my plan, the preemptive strike."

"Yeah, well some great fucking plan. I got my fucking ear bit off by that fucktard over there. Did you plan that? I bet you fucking did, you sniveling canine afterbirth piece of shit."

Aaron shakes his head in protest. "How was I supposed to know that Billy Vaughn would turn fucking feral."

Again, he glances down, and his eyes meet Billy's smiling eyes.

Gilliam puts the revolver down in his lap.

"We shouldn't have left that apartment," he says. "We should have stayed there. At least then I could have gone and fucked something. Could have had my ear looked at. Sure, that bitch you're all soft on might think this is gross. She said as much, said it grossed her out, but scars are manly, no? Badge of honor. I went to war, and I fucking won." He pounds his chest with a closed fist. He looks like he's saluting Hitler. "I deserve to celebrate. Not sit here with the likes of you. I'd have fucked her nicely. She likes my cock, you know. She likes it better than that Mexican half-breed she pulled around on the leash. She likes it a lot."

His hand reaches down the front of his jeans, grabbing his crotch.

"She likes to have it jump out at her, squirt her in the eye," Gilliam says. "Fuck that piece of shit wet back. He was only with us because of his daddy. We should have stayed there, and I could have gone and fucked your little girlfriend. Let you watch. Make you watch. Let you see what you can't have. Won't have. Won't even try for. How pathetic are you? How'd you like that? Maybe, I beat her to an inch of her life and make her take you anyways. Course I'd have to beat you too to get you to do it. You're nothing better than a fucking dog, so you might as well go hump something you hold so dear. I could kill that. Just like I could tear her up. That'd been nice. We should have stayed there. It'd been more fun."

Gilliam pauses to smile at his thoughts. Then he sticks his tongue out at Aaron and holds his beer in front of his face. Extending two fingers to act like he's licking pussy—Kirsten's pussy. Giving Aaron a graphic demonstration, making it as disgusting and perverse as he can.

Aaron can't stand it and finds himself standing before he even knows he'd gotten up. Finds himself holding one of the Rio brothers' guns. Gun extended in his hand, pointed right at Gilliam, who's still licking his fingers. Still being perverse. Gilliam sees the gun and Aaron holding it. Retracts his tongue into his mouth before taking a sip of the beer.

"You think you got it in you?"

Aaron says nothing.

"You don't fucking have it in you," Gilliam says with a half-smile on his lips. "You know that. I know that. If you had it in you, we wouldn't be in this fucking mess. You're like that kid from *Old Yeller*, too chicken shit to kill his dog. Well, I'm not a fucking mutt like you. So, you know what? You can't fucking kill me. You know what? You're not that kid. The thing about that chicken shit was he could do it. He did it. You can't. Just as limp and impotent as your dick. Are you going to do it, boy? You think you got it in you to pull that trigger. Do it."

Aaron's senses condense until the only thing he sees is Gilliam sitting in the chair.

Gilliam shakes the recliner as he yells, daring Aaron to pull the trigger, "DO IT! Do it you fucking piece of dogshit. Pull that fucking trigger, you fucking pussy. Show me that you got some balls. Show me that you're not that fucking scared little kid that loves my bitch so much. Show me you're a fucking man."

Aaron wants to pull the trigger. Wants to. His finger hovers over it. Even presses against it. His heart hammering in his chest in the way he wants to hammer the trigger.

But he can't.

He can't kill. He doesn't have it in him, and Aaron knows it. Just as Gilliam knows it.

"DO IT!" Gilliam yells, grabbing both armrests, shaking the recliner. "Do it! Pull the fucking trigger because if you don't, I'm going to fucking kill you."

Aaron doesn't pull the trigger as his world comes back, expanding until he sees the rest of the trailer and hears other sounds besides his breathing. Like the drip of a faucet and the fan of the window unit. The gun's heavy in his hand.

Aaron glances at Billy, who's still just staring, rocking back and forth, struggling against the tape. Eyes and mouth smiling under the tape. Billy would do it. Billy would kill Gilliam and everyone else. Kade thinks Billy put Eddie in Gilliam's group just to take Gilliam down. Aaron wasn't sure that was true. But now, looking into Billy's cold eyes, he can see the man's ruthless enough to do it ... to remove Gilliam from the game.

Gilliam relaxes into the recliner. He sips his beer. "I knew you couldn't fucking do it."

Aaron lowers the gun.

"You couldn't fucking do it just like you couldn't kill Kade. It's not in you. You're the fucking mutt in all this. No wonder that girl liked the half-breed wet back better than she liked you. I bet he has a bigger cock than you—excuse me *had*."

Aaron collapses into the bean bag chair, defeated. He lets the gun fall to the floor beside him.

He can't kill.

Billy looks at him, and then his eyes flicker to the gun on the floor.

"Why don't you be a good fucking puppy and go fetch me some more beer," Gilliam says. He uses the beer bottle in his hand to point toward the bedroom. "It's over there next to the bed."

Aaron hauls himself out of the beanbag chair, goes to the bedroom, and near the doorway to the bedroom, he takes a moment to glance out the window just as four figures emerge from the darkness, carrying weapons. One raises a rifle at the window just as surprised to see Aaron as Aaron is to see the figure.

Aaron drops below the window as one of the figures yells out.

"KADE," the voice says. "I KNOW YOU'RE IN THERE. COME ON OUT."

Gilliam throws his beer bottle against the back wall. "KADE'S NOT HERE," he yells. His eyes ask Aaron who's out there.

Aaron shrugs. "They got guns."

"Well, I got a gun." Gilliam holds up the revolver. "More all over, pick one; get on a window."

But Aaron doesn't move.

"What's wrong with you, boy? I told you to grow a pair and pick up a goddamn gun and get to where you can see something. Hard to shoot at something if you can't see nothing."

Billy's head swivels from Gilliam to Aaron.

The voice outside says, "Then you won't mind us coming in to have a look around."

Gilliam shouts, "YOU AIN'T COMING IN HERE," shaking in the recliner, "IF YOU DO, YOU BETTER BE LOOKING FOR A BULLET. BECAUSE THAT'S ALL YOU'LL FIND HERE. IT'S WHAT I'LL FUCKING GIVE YOU."

He struggles to get out of the recliner. Once on his feet, it's obvious to Aaron that Gilliam's shitfaced, way beyond drunk. He stumbles some, having to use the wall to right himself.

"We don't want violence," the voice responds.

"YEAH, WELL YOU GONE AND FOUND SOME," Gilliam yells back. He extends his hand toward the window closest to him and pulls the trigger of the revolver.

Although he might've been aiming for the round window, all he does is put a hole in the wall. Aaron drops to his stomach, and Billy throws himself sideways.

Gilliam asks Aaron, "What are they doing?"

Gathering courage, Aaron crawls to his knees. Then he's on his feet, crouching again. Sneaking a glance out the window, he sees one figure now. A big hulking guy with a handgun down at his side.

"You're surrounded, and we got a warrant."

"YOU AIN'T GOT SHIT, AND YOU AIN'T COMING IN HERE," Gilliam yells. This time he aims the revolver a bit better, shooting out the window in the door. "ANY CLOSER AND I'LL START SHOOTIN' AT YOU."

Aaron drops from the window, moves to the back of the trailer, and glances out another window. There are figures here too. A woman with a rifle points it at the trailer. And if he didn't know any better, he'd think it was the woman from the car stop a couple of nights back.

Stumbling and fumbling with the ice chest, Gilliam picks up the last beer from the chest. He breaks most of the stem of the bottle trying to get the bottle cap off one-handed using the wall. He drinks what is left. The beer spills down the front of his shirt and over his bleeding hand, which matches the ear.

The next bit happens fast. Billy Vaughn's there, on his knees with his hands in front, hands loose, tape hanging from his wrist, holding the gun Aaron left on the floor. He removes the tape from around his mouth with his other hand. He's smiling. Gilliam drunkenly turns from the window to Billy, but before he can do anything, Billy shoots Gilliam once. The bullet hits Gilliam in the stomach. The blast is deafening. The

sound echoes in the trailer. Before Billy can pull the trigger a second time, Gilliam levels his revolver and empties the remaining cylinders into Billy, who now is also pulling the trigger of his gun, emptying the magazine. The barrage of gunfire sounds like the climax of a fireworks show and fills the small trailer with booming blasts and quick muzzle flashes. It lasts seconds.

When it's done, all Aaron can hear is ringing in his ears. He blinks his eyes. He sees Gilliam's dead, lying dead in the recliner. Billy lies on his side, still breathing, but not for long.

Only one thought crosses Aaron's mind, run.

He leaps forward, landing on his stomach, and pushes the bean bag chair to the side groping for the hatch Gilliam mentioned. He opens it and slithers over the edge, landing on the ground in a heap of dust. The hatch snaps shut above him, shutting out the light and leaving him in darkness. The ringing fades, and the sound of his breathing returns. And then the sounds of the night begin their symphony anew, heralding the full return of his hearing.

From under the trailer, he sees four pairs of feet move toward the front of the trailer, toward the door. Arm and arm, he crawls forward, throwing one elbow in front of the other, using his knees and toes to propel himself on the ground underneath the trailer.

The first pair of feet ascends the steps to the trailer. And then a second, finally a third. He hears a curse and a thud as they break the lock on the door. He hears the whine of the door's hinges as he rolls his body out from under the trailer. He can almost hear their disbelief as they stare at the death scene.

Out from under the trailer, Aaron crouches, keeping his back to the trailer as he moves under the windows until he's sure he can't wait any longer. Chancing discovery, he runs through the field and into the night.

CHAPTER 36:

BARBARA

T HE FIRST THING BARBARA SEES IS THE BLOOD. IT'S all over one of the bodies. Old blood, dried blood, new blood. Broken beer bottle in this one's hand, revolver in the other, ear a mess, sitting in the recliner. She recognizes the earless man as Gilliam from Eddie's mother's house. Beyond him, a second body, still breathing. He's lying on his side, tape still wrapped around his wrists, and in his hand is a gun.

"That's Billy fucking Vaughn..." Jamison says and looks like he's about to say more, but Valdez cuts him off, telling him he knows who it is. Then Valdez cusses and kicks the side of the trailer out of frustration. Kade's not here, and the trailer's empty.

Valdez says, "It's over. Let's leave them like this. Let someone else find them."

Jamison skulks out, leaving Barbara frozen in the doorway, telling them he has to make a call.

"You were supposed to leave your phone in the car," Valdez says.

"Well, I didn't," Jamison says, descending the steps. He retrieves his phone from his pocket.

"You stupid son-of-a-bitch," Valdez says. "You should have left your phone in the car."

Jamison checks the phone. "There's a voicemail," he says. "It's the hospital..."

Valdez loses his balance and starts to collapse on the steps of the trailer. Barbara rushes to his side, grabbing at his arm to help him.

———

229

LATER DEPUTIES WALK all over, crime scene techs take photographs and news helicopters buzz overhead.

Outside the trailer, Barbara leans against a deputy's push bars and tries the "I'm a State Trooper" stick with the sheriff to explain why they're there. Tell him what they were doing.

All he tells her is, "You're suspended. You shouldn't be here." Shutting her up. Then he says he knew about her, had already called her bosses, and she'll be lucky he doesn't take it further than that.

So, she doesn't help them any.

But then the sheriff rubs the bridge of his nose and says, "At least you had a fucking warrant."

They could have done what Valdez suggested. Leave. But Jamison wouldn't have it. There wasn't any question for him. Jamison said he'd gone as far as he was willing to go, and he knew the only way to come back was to own up to what happened.

Thinking about it now, what concerns Barbara is how much she agrees with Valdez and how much that scares her. She knows why Jamison did what he did. Why he made the call. She just doesn't agree it needed doing. And that's what scares her the most. Scares her because that isn't her.

Something's changed.

Something in her.

Like the breaking of scar tissue. It's uncomfortable, painful, scary, but for the better. Is it better?

Jamison reverted to his old self: went into damage control mode. Turning on the charm. Controlling his emotions. Commanding the situation. It's clear if she's changed, so too has he. Only, he changed back—because he went as far as he was willing to go. And it was too far.

That's what Jamison says to her when they have a quiet moment, standing off to the side of the trailer, behind some deputy's empty patrol car, lights still flashing, as he paces in front of her. "We went too far."

"That's bullshit," Barbara says. She wants to tell him they hadn't gone far enough. They should have kicked in the front door of the trailer, but even thinking it, it scares her. She knows who she sounds like. It's not her, and he calls her on it.

"That's not you," Jamison says. "You don't sound like this. You're all about doing things the right way, but right now you sound like him." He motions to Valdez, who's standing next to Jimmie smoking a bummed

cigarette, staring at the trailer. "You sound like him. You were with him for one day! We shouldn't be here."

"But we are here," she says, her way of saying he needs to deal with it. "And you are here right alongside us."

"We are," he says. "I am, and I can control this. The sheriff thinks we can get ahead of this. I don't like it any more than he does, but we can swing it. Say we were going to surround the trailer and then call his guys in for jurisdiction. He doesn't like it any more than Meredith will. But it's something and will sound plausible enough to those fuckers circling overhead."

Barbara peers into Jamison's eyes. "Is that all you care about? How you look? You don't get it." She uses his words against him. "You don't get what I see in you. You could be so much more. You're one of the most amazing men I've ever met. Stanley withstanding. But you're all about how you look. All about the glory, the recognition—you don't want to rock the boat. You don't want people thinking badly of you. You want people to love you. You want to look like a cop, dress in that uniform, but you don't have what it takes. You care more about how something looks, the optics, than about what's right."

Jamison slaps his leg and points over her shoulder. "You sound just like him."

"Maybe that means it's true."

"Or that you've lost perspective. You're suspended, and I made a mistake. I shouldn't have asked for your help. I've only hurt you. You shouldn't be here. Yeah, you had permission, but I don't know if I can protect you on this."

"I chose to be here," Barbara says. "You know that, or you should. You brought me in. So, screw my bosses if they don't think so. I know unless I redeem myself, I'm out—and the only way my half-ass backward cowboy-playing supervisor would even consider anything as worthy of redemption is something like this. Bring in the bad guy myself. Like we've stepped back a hundred years. Otherwise, I know I'm done, and they know I'm done; they're just waiting for things to blow over so they can dismiss me quietly."

Jamison, sounding like he didn't listen to her at all, says, "I want to protect you."

"I don't need you to protect me," Barbara says.

Jamison doesn't say anything. He stands there, head down, chin tucked, mouth tight, holding back his words.

"Do you know what the Green Mafia is?" Jamison asks her.

"Of course," she says, thinking of Kade's tattoos.

Jamison frowns. "Valdez was working on bringing them down." Jamison rests against the trunk of the car. "This crew is Tulsa's Green Mafia. Billy's connected to Gilliam—the dead guy in the recliner—that's why Valdez was running Eddie. He was trying to get Eddie in with Gilliam to get to Gilliam's boss—the other dead guy—to get to his boss. Valdez wanted to take the whole organization down. When he... when I interviewed him after Eddie's death. That's what he told me. Eddie was the key to everything, and Valdez had gotten close to blowing this thing open."

"What?"

"The dead guy on the floor, Billy Vaughn—William Vaughn, the part-time leader of Tulsa's chapter of the Green Mafia while the main guy's in prison. He's a big deal. With him gone... Billy Vaughn is the reason I made the call because this fish jumped out of our hands."

"What are you talking about?"

Jamison lost her somewhere along the way. He's smart. She's always known that. "Mikey Collins," he says, touching his temples with one hand. "Never mind. Mikey's not what you say completely Green in the same sense those fuckers in the trailer are. He's more like Boston Green."

"What are you saying?" she asks, still not understanding.

"We're fucked," he says. "That's what I'm saying. We're fucked. That's why I had to make the call. We just stumbled into a shit hole. This thing could be a federal case. Fuck who killed Eddie; that doesn't matter now."

"I don't get it."

Jamison throws a thumb at the body bag coming out of the trailer. "That dead fucker kept the Green of this city in check with the help of his Boston friends—Mikey Collins and associates. We stepped into a deep shit hole. We went too far. Valdez fucked us. Fucked me."

"No he didn't," Barbara says, shaking her head, still not sure she understands Jamison's theory. "We might get in trouble for being here, but we didn't cause any of this."

"Valdez did by running Eddie."

"And he paid the price. Eddie's dead."

Jamison says, "None of that matters now."

Then the Sheriff calls him over, so he leaves her standing there.

Jamison's wrong about one thing. Valdez didn't fuck them. At least not her. He gave her back something she lost when she lost Stanley. Good memories and her confidence. She never processed her grief fully. Valdez and Charlotte allowed her to take the next step in the healing process. Jamison gave that to her too.

Barbara is exhausted, but she still has a promise to fulfill—her promise to Charlotte.

That's why Jamison brought her in. Whether he admits it to Valdez or not, neither of them will let Valdez face this alone. He wanted Valdez to know he still has friends. Even new ones. Valdez is facing the same thing she faced, except she did it alone.

He's not alone, and he won't face it alone.

CHAPTER 37:
VALDEZ

VALDEZ HEARS HER COMING DOWN THE HALLWAY
before she appears in the doorway of Charlotte's room. The click-clack of her boots on the tile gives her away. He tracks her steps down the hall from the elevator. He knows who it is, and he's not surprised she came. The click-clack gets closer to the doorway. Barbara, still wearing the same clothes from the trailer, stands at the doorway.

Valdez is in the recliner with a full view of the doorway to the hall. Charlotte is still in the bed—the machines doing all the work. He looks at his watch to check the time. He's been here a few hours. "What are you doing here?"

"I couldn't let you be alone," she says.

Valdez snorts and motions to the other chair to his right, inviting her in. Barbara steps in and puts a card and a single flower on the table next to Charlotte's bed, which will be the first of many more to come, he's sure.

Seated, Barbara smooths out her jeans. She keeps the jacket on. "The room's a bit cold."

They sit like that for some time.

Valdez motions to Charlotte. "We fought a lot," he says. "We had problems, a lot of them if I have to be honest. Up and down, like any marriage, but it was our marriage. I'm a stubborn Irish bastard."

Barbara nods. "You are."

"I see that you're thinking of your husband—something I've picked up on after spending the day with you. It doesn't bother me that you're here. You should be. Had it been anyone else, it would bother me."

"No other place I'd rather be."

235

"No one else is here," Valdez says. "Jimmie was, but he could barely stay on his feet. You see him fall asleep getting his ass chewed? He says he's retiring soon, but I don't know what he's going to do. Jerk off or something. I told him to go home, get some sleep, he'd done good work. I hope he won't get fucked over with me."

"I wonder if anyone else will come by."

"I can tell you who is not here. Jamison's not here; he's busy trying to salvage his career."

"He's not wrong, you know?"

Valdez dismisses her with a wave of his hand. "I knew better than to trust him. I thought he had changed, had come around. Pulled his head from his ass. I should have known better."

"Don't worry about that," Barbara says. "Right now's for Charlotte."

There's a long pregnant silence.

Then Valdez says, "I fucked it up once or twice, talking about my marriage. Did some things I shouldn't have. But that came from arrogance, not hatred or disrespect. Even though what I did was disrespectful." He pauses. "Those things happened during our one-year break; she called it a separation."

He waves his hand in front of his face as if wiping it away.

"At the end of it... after we got back together. When I looked at her, I could see she wanted to know what had happened to me during that time. I knew better than to tell her everything. I told her some things, but some things I left out."

"Did she ever ask?" Barbara asks.

Valdez nods. "All the damn time. She wanted to know. She was a zealot about it. That was rough, but we got through it. We always got through it. We always got through our problems. But Charlotte's just as stubborn as I am. I thought we had the rest of our life... we met in high school. Hell, we were too young to get married, but hey, we loved each other. To be honest, I was too immature to get married, but what the heck did my eighteen-year-old self know?

"Nothing, I knew nothing. I don't know shit even now, but Charlotte, she's the smarter one. It's because of her we got through it. We had two kids. Two wonderful children. Raised them. The two of us, kids ourselves, somehow able to bring life into this world and didn't fuck it up. Had debt. Got through that. Survived this job. Got through all of it. We even recovered after 'the *separation*.'" He uses air quotes when emphasizing "the separation." "But God knows I thought we were getting a divorce then. She wanted it, but hey, what do I know? This... this is different. I don't know if we're going to get through this..." his words drift off, and they sit silently for a long time.

"Did you call her family?" Barbara asks.

"No," Valdez says, "not yet. Kids yes. But her folks, no not yet. The doctors put her in a coma. Trying to help her heal. They'll bring her out of it if it comes to... there's time if it comes to that. I needed to be here though. I left her. I left to run off and do my own thing. I thought I had an understanding with death. Thought he'd let me get..." He breathes. "... justice for Eddie, but I guess that wasn't in the cards. I'll call them when the sun comes up. There's choices to be made."

She says nothing.

Valdez watches her in the half-darkness of the room. Her eyes stay locked on Charlotte.

Valdez breaks the silence. "Doctors said there's an infection. I don't know. They seem hopeful, but what do they know."

Barbara shakes her head. "It was hard when Stanley got to the end." Then she's quiet.

In the window behind him, the sun breaks over the horizon. The light worms its way through the blinds, crawling across the room, throwing horizontal bands of light.

"I'm not from here, you know," he says after some time. "I grew up in Flint Michigan. My father grew up someplace else but ended up working there. I don't know; there's something about him being in the mob, but what do I know. Tony Cappello is what they called him, which means Tony the Hat. But that was before I was born. He went west and started a new life in Michigan. I don't even know what our real name is. My mother never talked about my dad or what he had done. I don't even know how he got out, you know, if it were the mob? They didn't talk about it. The only things I know come from old associates of his that floated in and out and around. You know how it is; he must have left in somewhat good standing to only have two attempts on his life. One guy said he threw a guy off the roof just to see him go splat," Valdez claps his hands. "My pops overheard him telling me that story and got pissed. But I don't know anything about him beyond Flint.

"That Coney we had was leftover extra I ordered for his birthday. There are blogs and shit written about Coney sauce from Flint. Some say

it has its religion. When we moved down here, I didn't know anything or no one. I went to a school where I was white and that meant I was in the minority, different. I fought. I played ball and then I met Charlotte. She was a cheerleader, believe it or not, and she had all that cheerleader personality to go with it. She's from a family you don't fuck with, not in these parts. But I knew right then, when I saw her, she was something. Asked her to a dance. It wasn't prom, I don't remember what type of dance. Isn't it funny that your memory does that to you. You forget little details but remember the big picture? You know what she said? Why not, 'like you don't seem so bad.' I love that about her. I love that she doesn't take shit from anyone.

"She's the best of me, you know? She's everything about me that's good. Everything about me that matters. I don't like this. I feel like learning to be a detective all over again. Learn to do nothing. Like how I started, but this is ten thousand times worse. I'm just a man, useless, powerless. Just sitting back, observing, doing nothing. I can't do nothing, and it fucking sucks."

After all that, all Barbara says is "It does," because there's nothing else to say about it.

Valdez shifts in the seat.

"Why did Jamison bring you in?" he asks. "Like I get why he did what he did, I think. After tonight, I'm not too sure. I thought he'd changed, but I guess he changed back. I guess we do that, but why did he bring you... you of all people?"

Barbara stifles a small smile. "So you won't face this alone."

"Guess that makes sense. We used to be close, he and I."

Barbara motions to Charlotte. "The other night, she asked me to do it too—be here with you," she says. "Said things weren't going good, and she didn't want you doing this alone. She loves you so much. Said she feels like, with her dying, she won't be able to be here with you to comfort you, like a wife should, you know? She said you need it. Despite all that you are, that gruff exterior, you need compassion and love. Called you the most loving man she's ever met. She said otherwise you'll push everyone away. Said you've already done some of that, started pushing people away, and she can't have you doing this next bit alone. She asked me to sit with you. She knew she didn't have any right asking me because we just met, but she knew to ask and knew that I would."

Valdez listens to what she has to say, processing her words.

Barbara reaches toward his recliner and his hand. "I think Jamison did what he did at the trailer because he thought he was doing the right thing."

"But in doing that, the right thing, he did the wrong thing. He should have left some things out," Valdez says. "We could have walked away."

"That's what you would've done."

"That's what I would have done. We didn't because we did what Jamison wanted."

"You know, after spending a day with you, I feel that way." Barbara's voice isn't as warm as it was just a moment ago. "That's not me."

"I thought Jamison had changed," Valdez says, "he hasn't changed. You can sit there, telling me you changed, but I'm not sure he's changed. I'm not sure I changed. Do you think we can change?"

"Be different people?" Barbara asks. "Stanley used to say we change every day. He said we wake up different people than the person that went to bed. Said, 'What greater gift was there from God than to have a new day to put correct yesterday's mistakes.' That's how he knew God existed. That's what he told me on our first date when he was in Seminary. He always thought that was the greatest gift God gave us beyond giving us life and his Son. He called it God's third gift. He had whole sermons on it."

"But do you think we can change?"

"I do," Barbara says with confidence. "I have to. Stanley thought so. So, I have to think so. I have to think that life is about more than this. That what we do today influences tomorrow, and there's a reason for that. If I accept that, then I have to spend every day trying to be better than yesterday. Otherwise, what's the point?"

"Is that how you got over..." Valdez doesn't finish the question.

"His death?" she suggests, nodding, "You know, yeah, that's some of it. I'm not over it. I won't ever be over it. Someone dies, they take a piece of you with them. There's a hole that won't ever be filled, but that doesn't mean they're gone."

Barbara reaches over and touches his heart and then his right temple.

"They're always here and here," she says, "always with us. We have to work a little harder to see them. Imagine them there, feel them, but they're there. You know just as well as I do that when you die your body's just that, meat. You see it. That person's gone, but for their loved ones, that just means that person, now, at least a part, still lives on within them." She touches her left breast. "Stanley's always here with me. He influences everything I do. I'll never forget him. I love him."

"I love Charlotte."

"You do, and that's a good thing. Hold on to that. Me saying that won't mean much now. Even less after she passes ... if she passes. When you're in the dark, remember this. Charlotte will be there to pull you up and out of that darkness. Stanley's always there for me. That's how I got over him leaving."

CHAPTER 38:

KADE

K ADE PULLS UP TO A ROAD NEARLY THREE MILES from Gilliam's trailer. Aaron throws himself in the passenger seat, breathing hard, sweating. He's covered in dirt, leaves, and grass all over his body like he's been hiking through the woods. Scratches on his face and arms. Aaron shuts the door, and once settled, he says, "That was fucking scary."

Kade starts driving.

Roles reversed. Except they aren't.

Kade asks, "What happened?"

Aaron melts into the seat and glances over at Kade before looking over his shoulder. "They shot each other," he says. "Then the cops were there. Everywhere. I don't know where they fucking came from, the cops, but they came looking for you. Started yelling. Gilliam started yelling. Everyone yelling and then..." Aaron stops talking.

Kade drives, staring straight ahead. "Relax, just tell me what happened."

Aaron tries to relax. "Gilliam started calling me a dog," he says starting slow. "Then somehow, Billy got a hold of a gun." Kade notices he leaves out where that gun came from. "Then Billy shot Gilliam, and Gilliam shot Billy. It was crazy, man."

Kade says nothing.

Aaron asks, "How'd your meeting go with Mikey?"

"It didn't, and that's alright with me."

"There wasn't a meeting with Mikey?"

Kade's okay with whatever happens because, at the end of the day, he's only out for himself and Aaron should know this. Kade knows it, and it is not like he's hidden it. So, what's going to happen next, he's going to substitute Aaron for Gilliam. Because Kade's original plan, his only one, the one not shared but formed during that drunken night in the empty apartment, was to pick Gilliam up from the trailer, take him someplace, and put a bullet in his head. Just like Eddie. Just like Billy did with Frankie. Just like everyone else he's taken care of.

"He canceled," Kade says. "Mikey called me after I left the trailer and said something about his bar. Said he was pissed off about the cops showing up, said it's bad for business."

"What did he say exactly?"

"Said Gilliam fucked up, let one of them escape."

"Lou," Aaron mumbles as if he already knew that.

"Lou?" Kade says, "No one mentioned her to me. That wasn't the plan. Why didn't you say anything?"

Aaron doesn't answer him. "What'd he say on the phone?"

Kade lets it go. "Mikey said some neighboring business called the cops when Lou went running down the back alley. She collapsed right in front of some Vietnamese nail-polishing bitch who was out there smoking a fucking joint. They called the cops. Cops showed up before Mikey could get back to the bar to take care of the issue. Said he's been talking to police this whole time, just got free. Honestly, I think he was asking me to come meet him so he could take me out. He seemed ... angry... you know?"

Aaron asks, "What's the plan now?"

"How the fuck should I know; this was your plan," Kade tells him.

But he knows the plan. The plan's always been the plan. All he has to do is be himself.

Aaron uses his hands to speak. "Yeah, okay, things changed," he says. "Plans have changed, and I don't know what to do next. I didn't think this far ahead. The City's going to come after us." The way he says it sounds like he's begging Kade to come up with a plan.

Thing is, Kade has, but he tells him, "I don't like thinking too far ahead for this very reason."

"I know that," Aaron says. "You didn't think any of this through."

"Sure I did," Kade says. "Did it before showing up at Kirsten's to talk to you. Did it before I left Shawna's. Did it the moment I hung up with you when it became clear I couldn't even trust my best friend.

"There are things that I'm good at, and there are things that I am not good at." Kade turns the wheel; Aaron stays focused on him. "Like I'm not good at long-lasting relationships."

"That's true," Aaron says.

Kade turns to him and touches his chest. "Like you're my only friend, you know that?" He points at Aaron. "I got to thinking about that after talking to Mikey. Shawna's not my friend. Yeah, I fuck her now and then, but you know, she's not my friend. I don't have any other friends. I have Kirsten, but she's different, she's my sister—more than that— she's my twin."

"Yeah," Aaron tells him.

"You know, she's always liked you," Kade tells him, dangling the thread for distraction and time. "But she's never wanted to fuck you, not like you do her."

Aaron starts to protest but Kade keeps on.

"And you know, besides, we look alike; it'd be like fucking me. You want to fuck me?"

Aaron shakes his head.

"I didn't think so, but I just had to make sure because I can't have my only friend fucking me; that'd just make things weird. But then... you did it, didn't you? You fucked me?"

Again, Aaron turns his head sharply to protest, but Kade slams his hand down on the steering wheel.

"You were my friend. That means something. Or it should have meant something," Kade says. "You've done a lot of things for me. We've moved a lot of drugs. Ran a lot of jobs. Fucking earned for Gilliam, for Billy, for Tulsa, and the City because you know what we are, we're fucking Green. Except that might mean more to me than it does to you. Now, you might not understand what that means to me, but being Green's like being a family. And you know Gilliam betrayed me; he showed me he wasn't part of my family. That hurt. But there's only a few guarantees in this life; ultimately the only true one is we all end up in the same place."

Kade pulls the car to the side of the road. The tires crunch on gravel. Aaron's not Eddie ... but he might as well be.

Aaron speaks to the glass, like he knows what's about to happen. "I'm Green."

Kade tugs on Aaron's shoulder to get him to look him in the face. "Me too, but you don't have to worry about that anymore. You know who I am, and you know who I look out for."

"Kirsten," Aaron half-whispers, blurting it out like that's going to save him any. "You're right, okay. I do love her, but I know it wouldn't have worked. I wanted to make sure she was safe. I'm sorry—"

"You know the difference between you and me?" Kade asks, thinking if Aaron sits here, eye to eye, shows some true balls then maybe he won't do what he's about to do, but if Aaron does what he does, then it is how it is.

Kade unlocks the doors, and Aaron lunges for the door, struggling with the handle, legs, and arms bumping against the dash, the seat and the door, but Kade's already on him, grabbing his arm, pulling him from the door as his eyes find the gun in Kade's hand, surprised to see it appear from nowhere. Kade drives the gun forward against Aaron's forehead. Kade's hand holds Aaron's chin still as he presses the gun against the skin, leaving a deep red and white impression.

"You're not me," Kade says and pulls the trigger.

CHAPTER 39:
KIRSTEN

SHAWNA WAKES KIRSTEN, SHAKING HER ARM, saying, "You need to get up."

Kirsten's lying on the couch in a room off the living room wrapped in a quilted blanket. She opens her eyes and sits up on the couch, using her elbows to support her weight. Shawna takes a step back, giving her both time and room. "What time is it?"

"Still early, but you need to get up."

Kirsten blinks a few times. Shawna's dressed and ready for the day, but something's not right here. "What's going on?"

Shawna looks like she doesn't want to answer, but then she whispers, "Kade's here."

A jolt of fear runs down Kirsten's back. "He's here?"

"In the kitchen," Shawna says. "He wants to talk to you."

"Why's he here?"

"Because you're here."

Kirsten asks Shawna to borrow some clothes. Shawna brings her a pile of things that could either be clean or dirty—Kirsten's not sure. She changes into the clothes, taking her time because the baby's starting to show. Shawna's things don't fit right. She takes her time getting dressed because, fuck her brother, he can wait.

Shawna sits on the couch watching her with her hands in her lap. She doesn't say anything.

Slipping a shirt over her head, Kirsten notices the red mark on Shawna's cheek. That tells her Kade's been here a while, and whatever Shawna knew or didn't know, Kade now knows.

The pants are the hardest thing to slip into, so Kirsten asks Shawna if she has anything bigger. Shawna leaves the room for a minute and returns with a pair of jeans that might fit. Barely. Shawna tells her she just bought those because her old clothes don't fit anymore. Says it's a benefit from getting off heroin."

Kirsten figures it's her way of saying she's gotten fat.

"Dying kind of does that to you, but it's only a matter of time..." Shawna starts to say. She doesn't finish the sentence.

Kirsten glances out the window. Aaron's truck is parked outside, so she takes her time putting on make-up, using the light from the window and the mirror on the closet door, and it might as well be war paint because she knew Kade would come for her.

Shawna tires of waiting and turns on the television, flipping through the channels on the TV, and lands on one of the local news station's "extra" channels that replay earlier broadcasts on loop until there's a new one. This broadcasts from earlier this morning, and the words, "two found dead in a trailer," echo through the room. Kirsten's heart jumps into her throat.

Shawna clicks to a different channel.

Kirsten says, "Go back."

Shawna clicks back.

The male morning anchor says, "Police found two men dead in a trailer in Wagoner County this morning after an attempted warrant service, according to Wagoner County Sheriff..."

"Oh God," Kirsten says as her hands go to her face.

The female anchor says, "It appears the two men had shot each other. The reasons are unknown, according to the sheriff's office." The TV transitions to the Sheriff talking.

"Aaron's truck's out there, but Aaron's not here, is he?" Kirsten shuts her eyes to avoid Shawna's answer.

Kirsten finds Kade in the kitchen.

"Took you long enough," Kade says as she enters the kitchen. He's sitting at the kitchen table, with a glass full of whiskey next to him and a half-empty bottle next to that, his hand wrapped around the glass. Wearing a fresh white shirt—she can tell because of the creases from the folds. His eyes are red and bloodshot. He doesn't look like he's slept in days.

Kirsten steps into the kitchen and to her assigned seat, opposite him, the only one still at the table. He's moved the others off to one of the

walls by the back door. Her brother's not here. Whoever this is, this is someone different. This isn't her brother—he's gone. He died with Eddie.

Kade drinks the whiskey. He closes his eyes for a moment. She knows he does this when he doesn't know what it is he wants to say. "I know what you did," he says. "Shawna said you guys went to the cops yesterday."

Kirsten expected this. "What else did Shawna say?"

Kade raises an eyebrow. "You saying you didn't go to the cops?"

Kirsten crosses her arms and slumps against the back of the chair. "No, I'm asking what else she told you."

"Said you wanted to talk to one of them," he says.

"Ever since our father left, you've been different, darker, more withdrawn," Kirsten says. "It's not that I had any love for him, not after what he put me through, but I survived. But with you gone, when you went to juvie for me, when you got out, you weren't ever really you again. My brother was gone. Not that I was myself either. Scars are like that; they stay with you. That's why they're scars. You don't know what it's been like. You don't know me. You and I... we aren't anything anymore. We're nothing. You live your life. I live mine. You think you're protecting me, but you're not."

"You don't know what I've done for you."

"I know exactly what you've done," she says.

Kade slides down some in his chair. He takes a drink of whiskey.

"I went to the cops," she says. "You want to know why? Well, fuck you! I don't want to tell you. You don't deserve to know. But I'm going to tell you because there's a part of you that is still the boy I grew up with; you're still my brother. So fuck you. Yes, I tried to talk to the cops. I wanted to know what happened, what happened to Eddie. He's fucking dead, but you know that."

Kirsten pauses to take a few heavy breaths. She didn't expect him to let her say so much uncontested.

Kade doesn't say anything. He takes another drink. Keeps his eyes on her.

"But you can't do that, can you?" she says. "You can't say shit because I know what you did."

"Oh yeah," he says. "What did I do?"

"You killed Eddie."

Silence.

Kade knocks the whiskey glass against the table. "How'd they know to come to the trailer?"

"How do you think?" Kirsten sinks back into the chair and folds a leg over the other, wishing she had a cigarette.

"You told that cop. That's the only way they would have known. I want to know why."

"You fucking piece of shit," Kirsten says, spitting her words. "How dare you ask me why I fucking told the cops where you were. You know exactly why I fucking told them. You killed Eddie. You're not my brother. My brother wouldn't have done that to me. So fuck you," she adds, throwing her head back. "If I talked to the cops about where you would be, then I did, but that's because you killed the father of my child. So, you can go fucking crawl off and die for all I fucking care."

Kade says nothing. He finishes his glass in one long gulp, sucking down the liquid. He puts the glass on the table, scoots his chair back from the table, and stands. For a long moment, he stands there looking down at her, nodding his head back and forth, thinking of what he wants to say, or to see if she'll back down any.

She doesn't, so he doesn't say anything.

Kade steps around her and leaves the kitchen.

Kirsten stares at the digital clock on the wall, trying to control her heartbeat and keep from bursting into tears. She stays like that for a long time, listening to Kade walk through the house. There's a pause. Then the front door. And then the sound of Aaron's truck. And then nothing.

After a while, Shawna appears in the doorway to the kitchen. "You don't know what he's like."

Kirsten doesn't say anything. No sense in arguing.

Shawna defends herself. "I told him we went to the police station. He hit me. I told him we didn't talk to any cops because the one you wanted to see was at the hospital. That's what that one cop said, right? He said he was with his wife at the hospital. Made a big deal about it."

Kirsten uncrosses her arms and relaxes. Kade's gone. "Can you give me a ride?"

Shawna retrieves the glass from the table and puts it in the sink. "Sure, where do you want to go?"

"I need to go see someone," Kirsten says. "Not a cop. This is something I should have done for a while."

Shawna nods. "I'll get my keys."

CHAPTER 40:

VALDEZ

VALDEZ'S EYES OPEN TO DISCOVER MEREDITH
Hudson—the last person he expected to see—standing at the foot
of Charlotte's bed. She's staring at Charlotte, stroking her braided blonde
hair, wearing her pantsuit. "What are you doing here?"

"I wanted to come to talk to you," Meredith says.

Valdez doesn't remember falling asleep. Barbara's gone. He doesn't
remember that happening either.

"About what?" He sits up a little more.

"Can I sit?"

Valdez snorts and motions to the chair next to him.

She sits. "I wanted to come to talk to you about last night. Tell you
Jamison did a lot for you. He pulled out all the favors, you know?"

"He could have just left it alone, but he didn't do that."

"No, he didn't," Meredith says, "but he did the right thing, and that's
what's most important."

Valdez rolls his eyes. "Did he ask you to come here?"

"No," she says, "I told him to go home."

"But you've seen him?"

"Of course, I've seen him. You two ran an off-the-books investigation
with a suspended State Trooper. What do you think we've been doing
all day?"

Her look doesn't invite him to answer so he doesn't.

Meredith says, "I wanted to talk to you about Jamison because he
really went to bat for you. If it hadn't been for all the good work you and
that trooper did, you'd be facing a suspension or worse right now."

"That's because Jamison felt the need to do the right thing; I get to keep my job. Yay. My wife's dying, and that fucker could have kept his mouth shut."

"He could have, but then where would you be?" she asks. Her eyes flicker to Charlotte.

Charlotte in bed, on the machines, saw this coming and tried to talk to him about it. He wouldn't listen. Asked Barbara to be with him because she couldn't bear to have him go through this alone. Charlotte his wife, his love. His Charlotte.

"I'd still be here," Valdez says. "I'm not going to pat Jamison on the back for doing the right thing, fuck him. He knew what he was doing. We did a lot of work on this, and yeah, we got the ball moved a lot on Eddie's death. But I know you, and I know what you're going to do. So yeah, I get to keep my job, lose my wife, and Eddie's killer gets away because I messed up—makes me all warm inside."

"Would you listen to yourself?" Meredith says. "You sound like a child. Grow up. You did good work."

Meredith stands and pats the creases in her pants.

"Is that what you came to say?" Valdez asks.

"No, that's not why I came. It's a reason. One I think was a mistake. I came to tell you Jamison did the right thing, but he felt terrible about it. You did good work and for that, we can find Kade and bring him in, but maybe I shouldn't have come."

Meredith steps away, but Valdez reaches out for her arm to stop her. "I'm sorry for being an asshole."

"I'll tack it up to you being distraught about your wife." Meredith pauses. "Cooper's how they found out about Eddie."

"Tom Cooper?"

"Cooper worked with Billy Vaughn. We... and by that I mean Jamison, think there was some sort of internal struggle happening within the Green Mafia in Tulsa. Maybe even bigger than that. We found a bunch of dead Vaughn guys at Michael Collins's bar, and we found two dead Peter Gilliam guys, the Rio brothers.

"We think that Gilliam kidnapped Billy Vaughn, and somehow he got free and there was a shootout. Explains what you found in the trailer. I don't know. I don't know if we'll ever find out, but Michael Collins disappeared after talking to the cops about the dead people in his bar. Didn't reappear until he took a shot at Cooper outside Major Crimes. The bullet

skipped off Coop's skull. Lives and breathes as we speak. Downstairs if you need to know. He said it was Collins. Said a lot of things. Cooper let it drop to Gilliam, at Billy's word, you were running Eddie against Gilliam as a way to discredit Gilliam."

"His mom put my business card in his bag to remind him to be a good kid," Valdez says. "Gilliam found it. Kade put it on the window as a message."

"Are you going to tell his mom she got her kid killed?"

Valdez shakes his head and then asks, "You going after Collins?"

"In this town?" Meredith says. "No. He's Crawford's boy and working for some heavies out east. It'd be career suicide, not to mention the mortal kind too."

"What's going to happen to Coop?"

"He's going to enjoy that gunshot to the head and the healing process. Then rehab, but he'll be doing it in retirement, and not on our insurance. He said he got his real estate license and will do just fine. Personally, I think he's only a piece of a larger problem, other dirty cops, but what do I know. He's a symptom of the disease and not the disease."

"He'll get what he has coming," Valdez says before Meredith can accuse him of threatening to hurt Cooper, "or he won't."

Meredith glances at Charlotte. "I'm sorry, by the way. I hope she gets better."

"Yeah, me too."

———

AFTER MEREDITH HUDSON leaves, Valdez decides to stretch his legs and smoke. He goes down to the alley with the dumpsters to have a cigarette and think about what she said. At the dumpsters, he won't be bothered. It's a good place to go and think. He'll be close in case something happens. The nurse promised she'd call him no matter what. Before leaving the room, he held Charlotte's hand and kissed her on the forehead. Promised he would be right back.

Behind the dumpster, he looks out at the road that wraps around the hospital. He pulls the new pack from his pocket.

He should quit smoking.

Charlotte's been on him for years about it. She says he drinks too much and smokes too much, and if he has to be honest with himself, he'd admit that's true.

He sticks the cigarette in his mouth. Jamison could have done things differently. But if Valdez still has a job, then he can overlook some things. He wasn't fair to Jamison. The only person who acted like a cop over the last three days was Jamison, but he can't help but get in his way. That charm's going to be the death of him.

Jamison's theory is good. There are some holes, like any theory, but Valdez's been doing this long enough to know he won't know everything.

He never does.

Sometimes he knows nothing. Barbara had that part right.

With the lighter at the end of the cigarette, Valdez wonders if Barbara's going to come out of this okay. If she doesn't, she was kind of screwed from the beginning, letting Kade steal her car.

Where did Kade go? Why wasn't he at the trailer?

Smoke falls out of Valdez's mouth as he shuffles side to side on the balls of his feet. He finishes the cigarette and tosses it, then pulls another from the pack.

The early evening glow blazes across the undersides of the puffy white clouds. Beautiful. Hopeful. His eyes fall back to the road, and he catches a glimpse of a white male crossing in front of him. Blond hair, tattoos, wearing a white t-shirt with blue jeans.

Valdez puffs on the cigarette a moment longer. Why'd that guy look familiar?

And then he knows.

Kade.

"Oh no, Charlotte!"

CHAPTER 41:

JAMISON

JAMISON ENTERS THE HOSPITAL WITH FLOWERS AND a card, feeling like Valdez *was* right. Jamison's not a cop anymore.

After spending the day with Meredith, trying to un-fuck the situation and trying to salvage the investigation, he went home to get some sleep. He undressed and crawled into his bed and tried to go to sleep, but he couldn't. His mind kept thinking about the day. About the investigation. Then the night, walking to that trailer, he felt like a cop. That's what he's been missing. Walking through that field, he felt like a man again. Felt like he was doing the right thing. But then everything went to shit, and it left him picking up the pieces, trying to save everyone's ass.

Fuck them.

Sure, he's got a pretty good idea of what happened. All the pieces. He did the work. Meredith liked his theory, but it meant nothing because he couldn't sleep. He kept thinking of Barbara, thinking of Valdez, what it must be like for him to be in the place he is, and think of Eddie.

Jamison called Barbara and asked her how Valdez was doing.

"He's dealing with it." Then she explained she had just gotten home herself and needed to get some sleep. Said she wanted to take a shower, feel like a human again, and then told him, "I know you did the right thing."

"I feel like shit," Jamison admitted.

"I was wondering after all this is done, and I sleep for ten days, if you'd like to go get more of that pie you remember so fondly."

"Like a date?"

"Yeah."

At the nurses' desk, one of the nurses turns to him. She was speaking to a man that looks vaguely familiar, who impatiently waits for her to take care of Jamison. She says Valdez went downstairs, probably to smoke. Charlotte's doing better. She seems to be responding to the drugs, and the coma's helping her body fight the infection. But it's too early to tell. Prepare for the worst. The nurse says, "She might pull out of it, and when she does, she'll love those flowers," motioning to the roses he's carrying.

Jamison nods. "White roses are Charlotte's favorites."

He enters the room. Charlotte looks so small in the bed. Her skin's pale, and she's lying there with the machines doing all the work, making a soft humming noise.

Her husband's going to be so much harder to deal with if she's gone.

Jamison came to explain to Valdez why he did it and say he was sorry for doing it. That's not him. That's not how he does things. That's not what his charm's for, apologies. But he's here, dressed in the clothes he wore yesterday, with his gun and badge on his hip just like Valdez. They're on the same team, and they were friends once upon a time. They can be friends again.

Jamison places the flowers on the table at the foot of the bed. A card is already on the table. He picks up the card; it's from Barbara. That's good. She's a good woman, probably better than he deserves. He places Barbara's card back on the table and puts his next to hers, a typical Get Well Soon card.

In the hall, a nurse yells, but Jamison doesn't understand what she says. When he turns, the man who had been standing at the nurse's station is now in the doorway, a gun down at his side, surprised. His eyes flick to Charlotte and back to Jamison.

Kade.

Jamison doesn't think; he reacts, muscle memory. Throws back the folds of his sport coat with his off-hand and drives his gun hand down to his weapon in the holster.

Like he's trained a thousand times—one smooth motion.

Jamison draws, leveling the gun at the guy.

CHAPTER 42:

VALDEZ

VALDEZ BREATHES HARD, CHEEKS RED, AND CURSES the doors of the elevator as they open too slow for him. He squeezes through the still opening doors and spots the scared nurse at the desk, a phone to her ear, dialing.

Valdez pulls his gun from his holster and steps away from the elevator.

The nurse points down the hallway toward Charlotte's room.

On the threshold of Charlotte's door, Kade stands with a gun. He steps into the room.

Then a gunshot.

Valdez sprints.

Then a second gunshot.

Valdez runs faster, reaches the door, and looks in the room to find Jamison, at the foot of Charlotte's bed, wearing the same clothes from last night, gun out and pointed down. At his feet, Kade, on the floor, bleeding. Jamison's frozen, eyes locked on the gun in Kade's hand.

Valdez shakes out of his disbelief, kicks the gun away from Kade's hand. He's still breathing, but Valdez isn't sure for how long and doesn't want to take any chances.

"You shot him."

Jamison blinks a few times. "I did," his gone suggesting he doesn't believe what's happened.

"I was supposed to shoot him," Valdez says.

"You were." Jamison stares at his gun.

"You shot him twice."

"I did."

Valdez holsters his gun and steps over Kade to enter the room. He removes Jamison's gun from his hand and tosses it on the bed. He hugs him. "You shot him."

Jamison accepts the hug, stiff and uncomfortable. "Should we get him some help?"

Valdez glances over his shoulder at Kade who's still on the floor holding his wounds. "We're in a hospital."

Valdez retrieves the doctor's stool from the side of Charlotte's bed and rolls it over to Kade. Kade's fingers grope at the wounds. Dark red blooms from underneath the edges of his fingers, and a pool develops on the white tile underneath him. His eyes shift from the fluorescents on the ceiling to Valdez as he sits on the stool.

Looking down at him, Valdez sighs. He never imagined an ending like this.

"You killed Eddie."

Kade nods, but the words don't come. His mouth opens and shuts, like a fish. He coughs. Blood on his lips now. Coughs again. More blood. He blinks a few times. He doesn't understand what's happening.

"You were his friend, and he died alone."

The dying man's eyes are open now, wide with fear.

Valdez, atop the stool, plants his feet on the floor next to Kade. "You won't die alone; I'll be right here watching."

BOOK CLUB QUESTIONS:

1. Originally, *The Dead Make No Mark* was titled Green Country. What does Green Country stand for in this novel?

2. The title *The Dead Make No Mark* refers to the concept everyone wants to make a mark in this world. This book has dead people. How did they leave a mark? In what ways did they influence events?

3. What is this novel about? What themes run through the narrative?

4. How have you seen people process grief and loss?

5. How is the loss of a friend or change in status a life-altering event?

6. Many of the characters in this novel are based on actual people in the author's life. What do you think this brings to the narrative?

7. *The Dead Make No Mark* is the 4th novel in the Tulsa Underworld Series. It is a standalone. But how does this novel fit into the narrative fabric of the series? What other themes and ideas in the opening trilogy find their way into this narrative?

8. Do you prefer a series or a standalone novel? Based on your answer, why?

9. How would a single or limited POV narrative have changed this story? How does the multi-view tapestry allow for story development?

10. *The Dead Make Mo Mark* explores policing and race. How well do you think the book tackled these issues? How sensitive do you think it was to other people's experiences and voices?

11. The author's decision to include a multiracial cast was deliberate. In what ways do you think this story could have been presented in any other way?

12. Often, the negative aspects of our heroes are ignored. How does *The Dead Make No Mark* highlight the negative aspects of its characters and use those aspects to allow the reader to empathize with the characters?

13. Which character(s) do you wish to see return? Why?

BIO:

MARK ATLEY IS THE AUTHOR OF THE *OLYMPIAN*, *American Standard, Too Late To Say Goodbye*, and *A Bright Young Man*, as well as a handful of short fiction. Mark works as a detective for a suburb of Tulsa, OK, and has dedicated his life to solving crime. Check out markatley.com for more information or follow him on Twitter: @ mark_atley.

**Discover more at
4HorsemenPublications.com**

10% off using HORSEMEN10

www.ingramcontent.com/pod-product-compliance
Ingram Content Group UK Ltd.
Pitfield, Milton Keynes, MK11 3LW, UK
UKHW040759171224
452439UK00018B/173/J